Professors
at Play

Professors at Play

ESSAYS
by Robert Wexelblatt

RUTGERS UNIVERSITY PRESS

New Brunswick, New Jersey

PS 3573 .E968 P7 1991

Wexelblatt, Robert.

Professors at play

Library of Congress Cataloging-in-Publication Data

Wexelblatt, Robert.
Professors at play : essays / by Robert Wexelblatt.
    p.   cm.
Includes bibliographical references.
ISBN 0-8135-1718-4 (cloth)   ISBN 0-8135-1719-2 (pbk.)
I. Title.
PS3573.E968P7   1991   90-28863
814'.54—dc20   CIP

British Cataloging-in-Publication information available

The following essays appeared first in *The Midwest Quarterly:*
"The Mad Scientist," Vol. 22, no. 3 (Spring 1981), 269–278;
"On the Law of Supply and Demand," Vol. 23, no. 3 (Spring 1982), 317–326;
"Not Being Earnest: A Lecture," Vol. 25, no. 1 (Fall 1983), 108–122;
"Between Recurrence and Invention," Vol. 27, no. 2 (Winter 1986), 181–193;
"*Ex Nihilo*, or For Openers," Vol. 30, no. 2 (Winter 1989), 137–150;
"Six Meditations On Letters," Vol. 32, no. 3 (Spring 1991), 264–281.

The following essays appeared first in *San José Studies:*
"Kleist, Kierkegaard, Kafka, and Marriage," Vol. 9, no. 1 (Winter 1983), 7–15;
"The Proverbs of Klaren Verheim," Vol. 10, no. 1 (Winter 1984), 97–104;
"We and Kafka," Vol. 12, no. 1 (Winter 1986), 20–31;
"Professors at Play," Vol. 15, no. 2 (Spring 1989), 3–18.

"Complaining Before and After 1984" first appeared in *The Iowa Review*, Vol. 16, no. 2 (Spring/Summer 1986), 68–87.

"The Unintelligible Hero" first appeared in *The Denver Quarterly*, Vol. 14, no. 3 (Fall 1979), 49–65.

"On Faculty" first appeared in *The Daily Free Press*, September 7, 1988.

Howard Nemerov's "Absent-Minded Professor" is reprinted by permission of the poet. The poem is published in *New and Selected Poems* (Chicago: The University of Chicago Press, 1960), 56.

Contents

Preface

I write fiction when I am up to it, poetry when I can't help it, letters when I must, essays the rest of the time. The pieces collected in this book were composed because of a wish to share something, out of fullness of heart, for pleasure, for relief, sometimes for an audience. None was produced merely to hold on to my job as a professor. In a sense, *Professors at Play* has been written by a professor at play.

These seventeen pieces can be gathered into three loose bundles. The tenor of the first eight is announced in the title essay. All have to do playfully with academic matters. Two of them are in fact not essays but lectures, more academic than which it is hard to get. A persevering reader will find the next half-dozen somewhat less playful and more professorial. These are literary essays of a sort unlikely to be confused with the admirable scholarship whose erudition, like cheese, may be valued by the pound. In their informal fashion, they are about questions or writers that have absorbed or obsessed me. The concluding pieces are unclassifiable, which I consider sufficient classification.

An essay is more journey than map. The word *essay* only means attempt; an essay is an effort at understanding and communication. But there is no reason why these trips and trials should not seek to deliver the same goods Horace prescribed for poetry. My hope is to have succeeded here and there in providing the sympathetic reader with a little profit, a little delight.

Robert Wexelblatt
February 1991

*P*rofessors
at Play

Pretext, Text, Context

Professors profess professing. Professing is the pretext, established by an institutional and traditional context. Colleges and universities have professors of this and that field of inquiry. They are supposed to profess their special subjects. From the first day of class the professor stands at the front of the room and professes. He or she may also lounge, sit, walk about, even place chairs in a circle and invite everybody to introduce themselves by their nicknames—no matter. Regardless of posture or personality, the professor still strikes the contextual pose and sounds the expected note. The students remember it not only from the previous May but also from a number of Septembers, all the way back to when professors were simply called teachers. This is my name and office number. These are my office hours. Here is the syllabus. These are the required texts for the course. Answer when I call the roll. And now, as to our goals. . . .

To profess literally means to own up to something—guilt, innocence, the Apostles' Creed. The word *professor* is now a title only vestigially recalling a transitive verb, like, say, *sergeant*. And just as there are several grades of sergeants in our army so, in our institutions of higher education, there are varieties of professors: assistants, associates, fulls, and emeriti. Undergraduates do not, as a rule, understand this hierarchy. Undergraduates understand the pretext and text, not the context, and rank is part of the context. Professors are keenly aware of context, but, fortunately, not while they are actually professing. Indeed, most professors concentrate on the text and forget about both the pretext (professing) and the context (institutional rank, the agricultural surplus that makes their work possible, civilization). To put it another way, when talking to students professors generally do their duty and become caught up in secondary signs, neglecting the primary ones. Students never miss primary signs, though. For example, in the act of lecturing a professor of biology will think more about how to convey the intricacies of how RNA transmits genetic messages than about whether he or she is conveying wonder at 9 A.M. Nor is this professor likely to speculate on whether the students are in the hall jumping through a hoop in the hope of becoming wealthy medical specialists in another decade.

After all, professors don't like to think of themselves as obstacles or even as physical objects. Still, there are crucial and regular moments when both pretext and context not only impinge upon but fill up the professorial consciousness. For instance, there is the regular reading of student evaluations, which seldom have to do with texts but have much to say about the manner of the professor's professing—that is, about the pretext. And there are the sessions devoted to what is called curriculum development. Here a professor may well become aware that to profess one text is to give it institutional value while denying equivalent worth to some other. In the syllabus, text reveals context, if anyone is looking.

• • •

Even to me this is a funny way to talk about teaching, but at least it gets one thinking. To think about professing is, in the above terms, to think about three things, though not necessarily all of them at once. Of course, thinking makes the transparent opaque. That is the trouble, especially with theoretical cogitation. Yogi Berra once yelled over to an officious Casey Stengel that he couldn't think and hit at the same time. Personally, I have no very clear idea of what I am actually doing in a classroom while I am doing it. It never seems to me quite to follow my game plan. Moreover, the sheer irony of professing often overwhelms me and my plan. This is a practical irony, resting on the discontinuities among my uncertainty about the pretext (how and why I am "professing"), the text itself (will drawing a cartoon on the blackboard help these sleepyheads to comprehend part one of *Notes from Underground?*), and the intermittent absurdity of the context (I am the professor here? I have authority? I am merely part of a bizarre medieval system for sorting out the young?). I have noticed that I make a lot of jokes about being a professor while I am in the act of professing. I have observed that these jokes both intrigue and disconcert my students. All the same, even as I mock the context it continues to govern the text; in short, I am aware that my mockery of professing is a form of professing—on some days, the only form. Example? Let's say my text for the day is Rousseau's and I ask the students a series of questions: Why do I get to stand up here and

move around and doodle on the blackboard, while you have to sit
down and keep still? Why is philosophy called a "discipline"? Why
not a bondage too? What do you suppose is the socio-economic purpose of my grading you every couple of weeks? If I am the professor
here, why am I asking all the questions?

Two Kinds of Professorial Discourse

In our system there are two general categories of professorial discourse, both determined by context: the lecture (in a big room with
a lot of students) and the discussion section (in a smaller room with
not so many students). In dramatic terms, I would say the lecture is
tragic, while the discussion section is comic. Indeed, in the ironic
and reflexive mode mentioned above, I have more than once used
lectures and discussions to explain the contrast between tragedy and
comedy and have done so with my tongue only semi-in-my-cheek.
In tragedies, as in lectures, we are confronted whether we like it
or not with exalted loneliness, an individual drenched in dignity,
vehemently preoccupied with abstract principles or ideas, eliciting
pity, terror, and boredom from an audience sitting in something like
the atmosphere of a religious service in a churchlike amphitheater,
all seats facing the stage on which this tragic actor declaims while the
fatal disease of professing runs its course for, more or less, fifty
minutes. A genuine discussion section, on the other hand, resembles
comedy in being horizontal rather than vertical, extroverted rather
than introverted, informal rather than formal, interrogatory rather
than declarative, accommodating rather than rigid, social rather than
solitary, commonplace rather than exalted, and generally happier in
mood if not in its ending. There is more ethos than pathos in a class
discussion; with lectures it is usually the other way around.

It is not to be wondered at that some professors prefer one of
these modes of discourse over the other. But calling them "ways of
teaching" rather obscures their nature as discourse; that is, as ways
of professing. The difficulty with speaking about teaching theoretically
is that it makes no sense to consider teaching without learning,
though professors do so all the time. Professors think nothing of

speaking about "teaching freshmen" or "teaching *Hamlet*" or "teaching political science." It is as if one should speak of *feeding* without giving any consideration to *eating*. You cannot feed somebody if they don't eat; no more can you teach anyone if they fail to learn. Of course it is absurd to speak of teaching *Hamlet* or political science, as neither is capable of learning. The same may be said for any number of freshmen. Therefore, it is perhaps safer just to say that lectures and discussion sections involve professors in different kinds of discourse, rather than kinds of teaching. One can exert oneself ingeniously and mightily in either context, just as one can employ the most savory recipes in cooking, but there is no guarantee anyone will learn or eat. They may lack the aptitude or the appetite. Professors are seldom judged by how much, let alone how well, their students learn. This is in itself a tacit acknowledgement that they may have little power over learning, and therefore over teaching as well. Professors can be, and are, judged on their discourse. Nevertheless, this is rather odd, as if one should deny that the proof of the pudding is in the eating. A great lecturer is an Oedipus, an Othello; a great section leader is a Socrates. To me, one of the overlooked aspects of the Socratic irony is that a man whose method was intrinsically comic should have had a fate that was so much more tragic than that of even the finest of university lecturers. Even in the *Apology* Socrates is cracking jokes. Plato loved him for his discourse, not for his having failed to teach a sufficient number of his judges. Socrates' pedagogical lesson is exactly the same as his ethical one: the end cannot justify the means.

Teachers, Learners, and Søren Kierkegaard

In his *Concluding Unscientific Postscript*, Kierkegaard (who was never outwardly a professor but inwardly was many things) writes most beautifully about teaching. I take his book out and look at what he wrote now and then as a good Christian might a memento mori. His is an eccentric statement—especially in its vocabulary—and yet at the same time I think it embodies both a general caution and a general inspiration. As I doubt Kierkegaard's remarks are widely known, I will cite the passage at length and then turn it over a bit.

The communication of results is an unnatural form of intercourse between man and man, in so far as every man is a spiritual being, for whom the truth consists in nothing else than the self-activity of personal appropriation, which the communication of a result tends to prevent. Let a teacher in relation to the essential truth (for otherwise a direct relationship between teacher and pupil is quite in order) have, as we say, much inwardness of feeling, and be willing to publish his doctrines day in and day out; if he assumes the existence of a direct relationship between the learner and himself, his inwardness is not inwardness, but a direct outpouring of feeling; the respect for the learner which recognizes that he is himself the inwardness of truth, is precisely the teacher's inwardness. Let a learner be enthusiastic, and publish his teacher's praises abroad in the strongest expressions, thus, as we say, giving evidence of his inwardness; this inwardness is not inwardness, but an immediate devotedness; the devout and silent accord, in which the learner by himself assimilates what he has learned, keeping the teacher at a distance because he turns his attention within himself, this is precisely inwardness.

This long passage has only three sentences. The topic of the first is how not to profess. Delivering facts and conclusions (Caesar divided Gaul into three parts; Hamlet is smarter than Horatio) is not a natural way for humans to talk to one another; that is, if you lecture people on subways and sermonize at dinner parties you will appear stilted and pompous. Kierkegaard implies that people communicate results—give orders, deliver facts—only when addressing others as less than fully human, less than ends-in-themselves, less than "spiritual beings." Moreover, he feels the only really useable and essential truths are subjective ones. Objective truths—i.e., "results"—certainly exist (2 × 2 does = 4), but these are not essential because they lack spiritual appeal and personal force for learners with enough soul in them to become first- rather than third-persons. Not only is the fact-filled lecture an unnatural form of discourse for Kierkegaard, he even believes it interferes with learning subjective, essential truths. In the transaction that is teaching, Kierkegaard emphasizes learning over professing. For him, a truth is learned when somebody "appropriates" it, makes it his or her own. He goes even further than this, specifying that the student is unlikely to make a "result" his or her own. Kierkegaard also treats subjective, essential learning in another way, suggesting that the truth itself is better understood as the process of appropriation than as a text. In other words, the learner's truth is the process of making a truth his or her own; it is not just a note in a notebook; it is not a text but a devouring of a text.

The topic of the second sentence is a contrast: the good professor versus the good teacher. The good professor differs from the good teacher not in mastery of material, depth of personal feeling for it, eloquence, erudition, willingness to profess long and hard, or the quality of the appropriated truths he or she possesses. No, the difference lies in the relationship of each to the learner. Incidentally, the translator's use of the word *learner* here is good; he understands that students can study and not learn, exactly as professors can profess and not teach. Anyway, the good professor fails to teach successfully because he lacks what Kierkegaard calls the "inwardness" of the good teacher. The error lies in "assuming . . . a direct relationship" with the learner. This direct relationship is a kind of arrogant possessiveness, an eagerness to see the class as a sort of collective extension of one's own professing. Such an assumption can lead to very fine lectures and superb student evaluations, no doubt one can appear absorbing, transporting, fascinating, entertaining, truly passionate in one's performances, and intimately concerned for one's students. The professor engages in "a direct outpouring of feeling." Students often enjoy such discourses, and why not? They like rock concerts as well. But the good teacher, who is never a force-feeder, understands that the proper relation between teacher and learner is *indirect*. Only in this indirect relationship is there space for respect, as a good parent will always leave some room between himself and his child and not smother her, particularly with his love of being her parent. For Kierkegaard, no learning of essential, subjective truth can occur in the absence of this respectful distance in which the learner can learn, can "appropriate." An unappropriated truth is either not learned or is not essential. Notice that, in his parenthesis, Kierkegaard says that if the truth in question is not essential (a set of historical dates, say, or the chemical symbols of the inert gases), then a direct relationship between teacher and learner is just fine. No space is needed then; the student requires no room to carry out the difficult act of appropriation.

The topic of the third and last sentence is real learning. Here Kierkegaard focuses, like learning itself, not on the professor but the learner. The teacher has not taught and the cook has not fed until the learner and eater have digested the lesson and the meal inwardly and for themselves. Kierkegaard understands that a student's devotion to his teacher is not learning, that discipleship is merely a form of puppy love and does not necessarily reflect well on either the devotee or the object of devotion. As he has already stated, genuine learning requires a distance between learner and teacher. In this space there is still room for a kind of devotion, but a devotion accorded the lesson itself which can be appropriated—accepted, nodded at—only if the learner digests it on his own. Kierkegaard calls this process of digestion the true "inwardness," implying that to be a mere disciple, let alone a teacher's pet, is outwardness, a confused sort of devotion for the messenger that ignores assimilation of the message.

I like Kierkegaard's sentences not so much because they seem to me true. Perhaps they are not true; maybe they do not even add up to an accurate account of good teaching or successful learning; perhaps they are bad descriptive psychology. "The communication of results," after all, is what the discourses of professing mostly are. I confess I do not like the Teutonic pompousness of these statements, though I am hardly inclined to hold this against them; nor do I care for the theological undertone of the phrase "the essential truth." No, as I indicated earlier, I admire Kierkegaard's statement as a cautionary and an inspiration; that is, it reminds me of what to avoid and what to strive for where professing is concerned.

While at work or play in a classroom one should avoid the mere retailing of finales, never treat students as pseudopods of one's own brain. One should avoid also: the encouragement of misplaced love; the presumption that students cannot understand the text (the lesson) but can understand the pretext (the professor professing); the annihilation of decent intervals. Conversely, one should always try to recall that, despite its collective appearance, the class is only a legal fiction; and that the aim of a good cook is to provide an edible, nourishing, and digestible meal, one that people will actually eat, not just to display his or her culinary virtuosity. Learning is more interesting than note-taking, just as eating is more exciting than reviewing a menu. Appropriation by a student may not be under the control of the teacher, but the teacher, as Kierkegaard says, can do much to encourage or prevent this activity. Serve, then clear out.

Eros and Professing

I remember the hectic romanticism of my sixth-grade classroom. No Provençal court or Viennese café could outstrip the intensity or baroque complication of the purely experimental and inconsequential flirtations among us incipiently pubescent youngsters. Not one of us understood what was gripping us; nor did our teacher. Mrs. W. was in her final year of service before retiring, a touch senile already, much given to dozing off while we did math problems. She finished out her career, I am convinced, innocent of the most essential fact about her classes, about the green and palpitating souls of her eleven-year-olds.

This eroticism had nothing to do with the classroom as a place of formal education, though much with it as a social locus, site of drama, emotional and hormonal hothouse.

It was not until I became a college student that I first noticed something erotic about teaching itself. This observation was both inadvertent and unwelcome, something I wished to put aside, like a desultory and displeasing metaphor. From my point of view as a student, it was preferable to think of the classroom as a rather abstract place, not so much an ivory tower as a cubicle immune to the very ideas being discussed. Ideas were to be taken seriously but not, so to speak, incarnated. Indeed, incarnation seemed to me to undercut an idea's seriousness. Therefore, I was suitably shocked by the rumors of certain professors pursuing students. I was alarmed when a rather unstable underclasswoman broke down during an especially animated discussion of sexuality and hair in *Hedda Gabler*, confessing to us all that her stepfather had raped her while shouting to her about her lovely tresses. But these were accidents, and the more serious notion of a *formally* erotic element built into the transaction of teaching and learning—a, so to speak, impersonal and structural eroticism—was not an idea I wished to entertain. As a student, I kept my eye on the text and not the pretext or the context. If I noticed that a certain professor seemed unusually insinuating in his or her pedagogy, I dismissed it as stylistic eccentricity.

When I first began teaching I naturally became more conscious of the faintly erotic element in what I was doing. The idea was still disturbing to me and I promptly repressed my awareness, as if to acknowledge it would in itself be unethical. Like many new instructors, I began teaching by delivering the sort of discourses one puts forward in graduate seminars. Graduate school is all text and no pretext, rather like a military training that consists wholly of battle history and advanced strategy without the least mention of combat. One professed the text. The pretext was talked about fuzzily, one presumed, in schools of education. Of course, as a twenty-three-year-old instructor I was flattered when a young woman barely three years my junior developed a crush on me—or I would have been, had I allowed myself to acknowledge the crush at the time. To me the problem was inadmissible. The issue was abstract and could thus be easily disposed of by a clear moral principle. Mine went something like this: A teacher is in a power relationship with his students. Moreover, his attitude is, in some crucial respects, like that of a psychiatrist toward his patients; in both cases what Freud called a *transference* can occur. In any event, though, it would be both unconscionable and fatal to succumb to any such temptation—an abuse of power, a confusion of affections, a defeat for the process of learning itself. I feel much the same way now, albeit absolute principles and quick judgments get a bit dented on the way to middle age. Human realities are always more complex than principles; life always squirts out from under the cookie cutter of theory. There are many good and lasting marriages between teachers and their former students. Abelard and Heloise might have had just such a marriage.

Nevertheless, the whole issue of meaningful emotional attachments, let alone actual sexual relations, is tangential to the question of the structural eroticism of professing. Now that I have been a professor for a good many years (so many that now my pupils are less than half my age), I can think more clearly about the matter, without so impenetrable a veil of moral rigidity, albeit I remain uncomfortable with the topic.

• • •

The first plain declaration of the erotic element in teaching I ever heard was the most extreme. I heard it while I was a graduate student in the sixties. The declaration was not intended by the man who declared it to be a revelation of the erotic in professing at all, but rather a political statement. As the then-radical professor who enunciated this idea also chanced to be a poet, he spoke in violent metaphors. The making of metaphors is a notoriously risky business: signifiers float free of intent. The speech identified traditional university teaching with rape. The old are ravishing the young. The Establishment is violating innocence. Warmongering authority is forcing itself on the tenderly pacific children of nature. There was a sort of rancid Rousseauism in the declaration, as I recall; it was pretty trendy, but, withal, a heady rhetorical display. It was the sixties. The metaphor stuck with me longer than the politics, though. To *profess* is to *rape*. This suggested that all of the gratification belonged to the professor and, of course, I had noted that this was all too often the truth in a lecture hall. It implied that students were by nature passive, resistant, and essentially powerless objects, putty in unclean professorial hands. The torrent of words, definitions, and tests constituted rapine. The metaphor was not original. I remembered Eugène Ionesco's second play, the one-act drama *The Lesson*, a work of the early fifties, which I have since offered with irony to students of my own. But, derivative or not, the speech was meant to be an assault on the whole educational *context*: the Vietnam War, Capitalism, Western civilization, the College Board, the Trustees. To me it was a revelation of the *pretext*, the nasty secret of professing. It rapidly crossed my mind that the self-righteous professor propounding these appealing ideas was perhaps a bit of a mind-rapist himself, but such a suspicion was unseasonable.

The sixties wore out and I dismissed the metaphor as one of the excesses of the time. About five years later, though, I was talking with a colleague late one afternoon about some students we shared. Of one unusually talented female my male colleague said excitedly, "I want to rape her mind!" He fairly shouted it, I recall, exultantly. He did not intend anything immoral by it, I am sure; he simply meant he wanted her to learn all he could teach her—at once. Nevertheless, I was startled that he wound up with the same metaphor. His face was not contorted into a sexual or political leer, but he certainly meant what he said.

Feminism has raised our consciousness of this troubling aspect of the educational context, and feminists are, I think, attracted to the same violent metaphor. In many areas of feminist discourse rape is inevitably the ruling metaphor. The conventional division between male and female principles (power, domination, impatient talk, and rationality *versus* nurture, accommodation, patient and affective silence, etc.) suggests that simply the *situation* of male teacher and female student is, due to our patriarchal culture and traditional pedagogy, fraught with sexual risk, quite apart from the moral motives of the parties. The extremism of the language ought to serve as a reminder of the genuine risks, of course, but also it should be a goad to professorial irony. Irony about the very situation of male-professor and female-student can be a saving grace, a reliever of the festering tensions through their airing, a simultaneous acknowledgement and rejection. I do not believe there are many ironic rapists. The appeal of the forbidden is lessened by plucking the apple and telling a joke about it. The appeal, though, is undeniable, even for those of high principle. I know one man, for example, a more than averagely decent one, who, after the dissolution of his marriage, stayed for two weeks with a former student. It was ambiguously at her invitation or his suggestion. There are, of course, students who wish to collect teachers. When he told me about this episode months later, he was a little shamefaced, but he concluded by smiling and confiding in a disturbingly *entre-nous* tone: "I *had* to do it. Just once. You know?"

Rape is too extreme a term to describe the tamer penetrations of professing by eros. But, as the more commonplace forms of the erotic in pedagogy are less stunning, so they are also less obvious—precisely because they are so commonplace. Consider, for example, how much of professing is a form of *courtship*. The professor is polite; for his or her intentions are "honorable." The professor attempts to win the students' affections by means of gifts (a paper extension or interesting anecdotes, say), inviting them to pleasant and flattering events (a coffee hour, a concert, a movie). The courtship may well take more directly pedagogical shapes: a complaisant manner in the classroom, the use of first names, showing excessive regard for jejune interpretations, making an ingratiating selection of texts, a subtle running-down of competitors—other disciplines, other professors. Then consider how three months' worth of professing might resemble an *affair*. Here the professor gives to his or her pedagogy a spicy hint of the illicit, a tantalizing lawlessness. The door is smilingly shut before class so *they* won't hear; discussion of shockingly intimate matters is conducted behind the backs of parents and authorities. An atmosphere of boundless enchantment and group-bound secrecy is fostered in "our class," which meets as if for a tryst. The relationship between professor and students is exclusive, enlivened by private references and in jokes; it has its own history. The professor disrobes and invites the class to drop its inhibitions as well. This is close to professing as *seduction*, a more general strategy of erotic manipulation. Here the professor approaches his shyly uninterested students as Don Giovanni does Zerlina. His baritone's sophistication, wit, and effervescence are deployed to make him or her irresistible. Not to worry, though; he is only winning the innocent over to the cause of knowledge. He is a professor; the "seducer" is merely a mask and, should the therapy succeed, he will not abandon his Zerlinas, at least not before the end of the semester.

Having said all this, only one embarrassing question remains. Is there a professorial equivalent of the orgasm? Of course. It is the moment of revelation, of "seeing it," of *anagnorisis*. In the best classes, as in the finest Greek tragedies, this is the apex of the emotional rollercoaster, the moment for the sake of which theaters and classrooms are built. When it occurs to everybody at the same time, the pleasure and the discharge of energy are considerable. Erotically speaking, the professor aims, not at masturbation, but at intercourse. Pedagogically speaking, however, the good professor will extricate him or herself in time, dropping all such impositions and sublimating the erotic into something more Platonic, into Kierkegaard's "devout and silent accord" which distances the professor in order that the student may "turn his attention within himself." It's not always easy to do. The distance opened by playful irony helps.

Professors at Play: Five Examples

Commenting on student writing is a mode of professing. As discourse, these remarks tend to resemble either the lecture or the discussion. Professors who favor the lecture will generally limit themselves to recording a grade and a set of summary remarks, often quite curt ones, sometimes a virtual lecturette. For example: "Your analysis of Kleist's use of social contract theory takes insufficient account of Rousseau's work, which he would certainly have known; however, the paper is well organized and generally well written. Do please watch out for comma splices and memorize the difference between *its* and *it's!* B + ." Professors who are most at home with the discussion format will "correct" papers more conversationally; that is, they will treat the student's essay as though it were spoken and will scribble little Socratic questions, ripostes, and bravos in margins and between lines as if these too could be heard. For example: "What did the British want out of the Opium War?" "But Epictetus *did* care passionately about *duty*, didn't he?" "Good insight!" This type of grader finds it hard to read anything without a pen in hand; this is the inveterate grader. Usually these assiduous professors will also offer a summary statement which, unlike their students, they will esteem more important than the grade.

There is, in fact, an endemic misunderstanding between professors and students about paper grading. Students seldom read a professor's comments as they were intended, if indeed they bother to read them at all. It is a reflection of this misunderstanding that a professor will define *constructive criticism* as a careful effort to indicate what students have done wrong, while students seem to define it simply as praise. Few professors and fewer students inquire into the connection between this ritual and actual learning. Looking back over my own experience, I can recall few instances where I learned much of anything from a professor's commentary or grade; and, though I may have learned much from the process of writing the paper itself, the process was essentially one-way. A memorable exception will be exemplary because it was so uncommonly instructive. I learned a lasting lesson and learned it efficiently, too: through only one humiliating sentence.

I had written a long paper on Aldous Huxley and Evelyn Waugh, about thirty tortuous pages of closely worked comparison and contrast, composed in a crabbed style that bordered on the Teutonic. The professor didn't bother telling me anything at all about Huxley or Waugh. However, above the grade on page thirty he wrote the following: "Although your prose occasionally reflects too exactly the (also occasionally) finicky mind and its tendencies (toward the parenthetical) this is nonetheless an excellent (because perceptive) essay." In a contradictory and incomprehensible gesture of kindness, he then added: "You write well. A." Normally, of course, I would have concentrated on this glowing postscript. In this case, though, the grade and the praise seemed to me mere afterthoughts. The sentence which had so playfully and accurately parodied my ludicrous undergraduate prose, on the other hand, caught me like a tuna on a gaff. I have remembered it for twenty years, and I still monitor myself for the parenthetical. Never since have I striven to write a sentence that would resemble one of Kant's. My face is still red, so to speak, as if I had been teased by a playful uncle.

· · ·

A couple successful classes of mine were actually desperate recourses to play. They were cases of improvisation, faute de mieux, certainly not examples of innovative pedagogical planning. But then premeditation is cold water thrown on the spirit of play, even in a lecture hall. In both cases I found myself at sixty thousand feet with no oil pressure.

The first emergency arose because of *The Importance of Being Earnest*. It was my own fault. The problem was not that I had assigned Oscar Wilde's perfectly insignificant comedy, but that I had scheduled a lecture on it. Not until the day before, when I sat down to compose my notes, did I realize how I had set myself up. How do you

lecture on such a play without sounding like an idiot or attempting an
unequal battle of wits? I tried out various approaches: telling Wilde's
life story; explaining the nature of high comedy, verbal wit, Walter
Pater, *l'art pour l'art* aestheticism, Wilde's views on superficiality,
dramaturgy and dance . . . all leaden, all missing the point. The hour
grew late. As I tried out each angle I began to hear Wilde's contemp-
tuous laughter, and it was infectious. Finally I laughed too. I laughed
as Wilde. It was then that the absurd but irresistible idea took hold
of me. I did not lecture the next day *on* Wilde but *as* Wilde. In a
sense, we impersonated each other. He had to wear my clothing, but
I got to use his ideas. He was much more amusing, witty, paradoxical, and insightful about his play than I could have been. Moreover,
he generously commented on other readings in the course—offering
a sharp appraisal of Ibsen, for instance, and of Aristophanes—and
amplified the general theories I had been developing of tragedy and
comedy.

Apropos: there is a story about Charlie Chaplin. It seems he was
entertaining guests at a Hollywood party by performing imperson-
ations of various celebrities. People shouted out their requests. Harry
Lauder? Woodrow Wilson? Nothing to it. A man called out the name
of Enrico Caruso. At once Chaplin sang a Puccini aria and did so
with stunning beauty. Afterwards a young woman approached him.
"Mr. Chaplin," she said, "I'd no idea you had such a magnificent
voice." "I don't," he replied. "I was just imitating Caruso."

The second class was slightly different, requiring a different sort
of discourse. The students—a group of first-semester freshmen—had
read Joyce's story "Araby" during their second week as college students. We were to spend a discussion section on it. I might have
lectured but could not face doing so. I anticipated their sullen, rather
frightened passivity. They were not yet sufficiently confident with
themselves or each other, let alone James Joyce, to respond well even
to simple Socratic questioning. At best I could expect the usual answer Socrates elicited: "Yes, certainly." I did not know what to do
and left it to the inspiration of the moment.

I entered on the hour and looked at the class. "Today," I said to
them, "I want you to pretend I am James Joyce. You can speak to
me about what you thought of my story 'Araby.' You may ask me

questions about it. If you like, you can accuse me of things or ask questions about my life—it's all fair game."

It was risky. The students might have remained as tight-mouthed as they had been the week before. But it worked. They all had questions—good ones too, far-ranging and thoughtful. The class resembled a presidential press conference. "How old is the narrator?" "Why did you put so much stuff about religion into your story?" "Was Dublin really so drab when you were a kid?" "Why does the boy live with his aunt and uncle?" "What's *The Abbot* about?" "How come you ended the story at night?" I had a livelier time being interviewed as non-professor Joyce than I could have had as Professor W., the one who gives the grades.

• • •

A certain professor of physics found himself more than a little disappointed with the students in his introductory course. They were doing poorly on examinations, appeared bewildered in class, were unresponsive to his leading questions. He might have become resentful, vindictive, or indifferent. Many professors do.

One late October afternoon the students arrived to find the desks in their physics class rearranged. In place of the customary three straight rows was one great circle with a single desk set squarely in the middle. On this desk, propped upright, stood a copy of their heavy physics textbook. Their professor, lounging by the window, silently invited them to be seated.

Once the perplexed pupils were installed, the professor walked to the desk at the center of the room. "This is your textbook. Possibly some of you may recognize it," he said. There were a few snickers. He continued, "For the next fifty minutes you can say whatever you like to this book. If it's up to it, the book may reply."

The students giggled openly now. The incongruous spirit of play provokes laughter—nervous or delighted. They giggled and then fell silent; however, this was a patient professor of physics. Eventually a young woman raised her hand uncertainly. The professor nodded to her dismissively—no need for a raised hand—and pointed at the book. The student lowered her eyes and looked with genuine resentment at the fat, double-columned text. "I hate you," she said evenly

and not without courage. "Yeah, so do I," echoed from another
point on the circle. "Me too."

"Why do you hate me?" asked the professor, speaking for the
book.

"Why?" asked the brave young woman who had first spoken.
"Why do *you* think?"

"Well, maybe it's because you don't understand me," suggested
the physics book.

After that, the remarkable class was off and running.

• • •

Pimps and Whores. That's what he privately called it—like Chutes
and Ladders. Officially, the game had a more respectable title: "Early
Capitalism."

My friend, a professor of social science, felt that his department's
series of lectures on the manorial system, feudalism, mercantilism,
capitalism, the rise of the bourgeoisie and the creation of the urban
proletariat was a bit dry. In his opinion, the students couldn't grasp
the workings of economic forces and laws in history and remained
ignorant of how these same forces and laws affected human beings,
affected themselves. So much of professing seems to be either expressing cynicism in a context of false idealism or idealism in a context of low-down cynicism. Pimps and Whores. It is difficult to decide
whether my friend was doing the one or the other with his little
didactic game.

The students played for two hours: about thirty of them in one
room. The professor showed up with a bundle of Monopoly money
and thirty three-by-five cards. The cards were marked with roles and,
true to history, were handed out arbitrarily: lord, merchant, freeman,
craftsman, landless peasant. There were, of course, mostly landless
peasants. The cash was allotted commensurately: lords and mer-
chants had most of it, freemen and guild-members a bit, detached
peasants zip.

The object of the game was simple. Whoever wound up with the
most money at the end of the two hours was the winner. Whoever
had nothing lost big.

Pimps and whores and chutes and ladders. Before long some were selling and some being sold; some went up the ladder, others down the chute. Unions were formed and dissolved; agreements made and betrayed; strikes declared and broken; revolution threatened and repressed. Bondage was reinvented and chosen over starvation. Wages went down and up and down again. Supply rose to meet demand; demand was cut to lower prices. Marginal utility came into play, particularly in the ferocious labor market. Bad money drove out good.

My friend the professor did not play. He observed calmly, as a professor should, while chaos threatened and greed flourished and desperation bloomed. He assured me that in his next class he would not have to say much either; the students would explain economics to *him*.

• • •

Version One:

> The explanation of poetry by examination of its sources is not the method of all contemporary criticism by any means; but it is a method which responds to the desire of a good many readers that poetry should be explained to them in terms of something else: the chief part of the letters I receive from persons unknown to me, concerning my own poems, consists of requests for a kind of explanation that I cannot possibly give.

Version Two:

> For a number of years now, I have been accustomed to receiving urgent epistles from persons wholly unknown to myself in which requests are made for information on the "background" of certain of my own poems. Now this bespeaks a widespread desire on the part of people that poetry should be explicable in terms other than its own. Criticism that presumes to regard origins as explanations is not the whole story of the recent study of literature, but it is one which surely makes many people reprehensibly happy.

One of these passages is by T. S. Eliot and the other isn't.

I was a first-year instructor of first-year composition. My students were submitting to this required course with the kind of condescending resignation the Chinese probably turned on the Mongols. In common with most college freshmen, they were quite certain they knew all about writing by now. I had no particular wish to deny this. On the contrary, I said that if they knew all about basic writing, we could move right along to more abstruse, subtle, and intriguing matters. I decided that we'd look into the refinements of style and promptly gave them such texts as a speech from a Christopher Marlowe play, a passage from a Waugh novel, a hunk of the Talmud, and George Orwell's "Politics and the English Language." No change. They offered little in our discussions, sitting before me with a sort of languid haughtiness. After all, I had failed to criticize their papers with what they deemed sufficient constructiveness. Besides, I was only a graduate student. Their unearned arrogance ended by annoying me and so I decided on a playful little challenge.

It was a simple idea and might easily have backfired. I took bits of good writing from a variety of sources, quickly composed inferior parodies, mimeographed the lot and gave it to the students, telling them what I had done. Their job was merely to tell good from bad, authentic from ersatz. No tricks.

At our next meeting, we took a formal vote on each pairing. To my surprise, in every case a majority chose the phoney over the genuine. In short, the result was both better and worse than I had hoped for.

The class, chastened, began working to better effect, while I, marginally more earnest, a wee bit more respected, a touch less playful, pondered my future in this last pair of texts, the better of which is by Howard Nemerov:

Version One:

THE ABSENT-MINDED PROFESSOR

This silly figure, the stalest of jokes
That ever we made from scholastic folks,
Has vanished forever from the public's mind;
And now, on any Fall day, you can find

His sharper successor, hard at work still,
As dead orange leaves bump his window-sill.
For the puttering pedants of earlier days
He grieves not a whit, and it would amaze
Him no doubt to suffer intrusion
From those fuddled old men who preached confusion.

Version Two:

ABSENT-MINDED PROFESSOR

This lonely figure of not much fun
Strayed out of folklore fifteen years ago
Forever. Now on an autumn afternoon,
While the leaves drift past the office window,
His bright replacement, present-minded, stays
At the desk correcting papers, nor ever grieves
For the silly scholar of the bad old days,
Who'd burn the papers and correct the leaves.

Complaining Before and After 1984

We all know complaining when we hear it. All the same, I think it proper and in the spirit of philosophy to begin with a little bit of definition; at least it will give me something to be inconsistent about later on.

In the vast and not completely charted realm of dissatisfaction, complaining is the intimate opposite of wishing. Intimate opposites, incidentally, are things like men and women: from the back you can sometimes mistake the one for the other. A wish means, at base: "I do not want to be as I am, to be what I am. And I shall relieve myself of this distasteful reality through delightful if wholly unrealizable fantasy." So, to wish is to deny what is real. Complaining, on the other hand, is apparently the very worst kind of acceptance of reality. Fundamentally, to complain is to say: "I am stuck where I am, as I am, and with the bad things that are happening to me. But I will seek a perverse and malicious relief in whining about it. Out loud." So, because one rejects and the other accepts reality, wishing and complaining are opposites; yet they are intimates because both agree that reality is decidedly unsatisfactory.

You might say that complaining is grown-up wishing or that wishing is what complaining regresses into. I mean this quite literally. An unhappy and imaginative fourth-grader is apt to do a good deal of wishing, but if he grows up to be a miserable certified public accountant, he will probably do a lot of complaining. Conversely, a large number of complaints wind up in wishes, though these are customarily negative and rather joyless ones. You may have noticed that after a good long bout of whining, people will express all sorts of merely vacant or rhetorical wishes, such as, "I wish I hadn't, didn't, needn't, wouldn't, or weren't." We can all furnish our own predicates.

Complaining is also, of course, the most popular competitive sport in the kingdom of the dissatisfied. Materialists will one-up each other with vacations and sports cars, intellectuals with book titles and obscure allusions, social climbers with dropped names and invitations— but the dissatisfied characteristically do it with complaints, as in "You think *you* had it bad? That's nothing. Just look at *my* scar!" In such a competition, the formulation of a really unanswerable complaint is as satisfying as spiking the ball in the end zone.

Now, stoicism is invariably impressive and an uncomplaining temperament is always highly reputable. I might as well at once admit the obvious: that complaining has a poor reputation, though most of us do a great deal of it. Complaining is in this respect not unlike sneezing in public: I expect we have all been guilty of both sneezing and whining—in fact, there are times when even the most self-controlled of us simply cannot help doing so—but this does not prevent us from feeling little sympathy for those who do either in our vicinity. Complaining—there is no getting away from it—is an undignified topic. Dignified things, like ambassadors and grandfather clocks, always appear incapable of complaining, and the most dignified people at their most dignified moments are utterly beyond it: Marcus Brutus accepting defeat at Philippi, Spiro Agnew pleading no defense, Charlton Heston expiring on Mount Pisgah, and so forth. Why, then, look into such an unpromising matter?

First, I have spent an inordinate amount of time in schools, especially universities. While I cannot speak about such institutions as the Coast Guard or the World Bank, I have always been struck by the intensity and persistence of complaining at virtually every level of education. I spent a couple years at Brandeis University, for instance, and my experiences there led me to suggest that the University's lengthy, hopeful, and surgical motto ("Truth even unto its innermost parts") really ought to be amended simply to "It's not fair," as I heard the latter phrase so much more often than the former. In Latin it wouldn't sound so bad, actually: "*Non aequus est,*" perhaps blazoned on a shield with unbalanced scales.

Students complain as a matter of course; it is a mode of discourse natural to the condition of their transitional and perpetually graded lives: they are too old for childish wishing and too young for taciturn resignation. But professors are likewise very accomplished at complaining, and at every rank. There are, for instance, those who complain that they do not have tenure and those who, no doubt feeling trapped by security, complain that they do; those who complain that their students are as passive as oil paintings and those who complain that their pupils continually interrupt lectures with annoying questions. Hard though it may be to believe, even administrators have been known to moan on occasion—and in public. "If any man wishes to become humbled and mortified, let him become President of Harvard College," whined the eleventh president of Harvard College. For all I know about it, griping may be an ineluctable accompaniment to the educational process, like the figured bass in a concerto grosso. In any case, though, an examination of complaining does not seem out of order to me, since I work in a place that enjoys so much of it.

In fact, this idea of looking closely at complaining is only indirectly mine; it was actually given to me by a thirty-two-year-old woman named Virginia. She was and continues to be a character in a long story I wrote one summer. Not just a character, but the narrator.

Narrators can get hold of all sorts of strange ideas. They are wilful and notoriously difficult to control. Perhaps this is because they think they are authors. Anyway, at one point Virginia became attached to the idea of complaining and wouldn't let go. In the story, she is opening up an art gallery, her own business, and is in a perpetual tizzy about all the people she must cope with: her artists, her children, her stolidly uncomplaining husband, her carpenter, her accountant, etc. She is a spunky entrepreneur, but nervously calls herself a "cowardly suburban Mother Courage." Like most modern narrators, of either gender, Ginny is pretty self-conscious, and the anguish of going into business makes her fully aware for the first time that complaining had always been one of her particular pleasures and greatest talents. Much to my surprise, though she did not at first strike me as having a philosophical bone in her imaginary body, Ginny insisted on pursuing this insight further. I begged her just to get on with the story, but she insisted: "it would be letting myself off far too easily to make light of my complaining. What I want is to do just the opposite; I want to make *heavy* of it, like those philosophers I was compelled to read during my sophomore year."

I am unsure just where Virginia spent her sophomore year, but since philosophers say the same things everywhere it scarcely matters. Anyway, here is some of what she had to say:

> The whines of dogs and shudders of horses notwithstanding, I have come to believe that complaining is one of the truly distinctive human activities. At the very least, it's one that we have perfected. That is to say, we are complaining featherless bipeds. Just about our

whole culture is a sort of complaining or, to put it a little more philosophically, complaining is our culture's efficient cause. The Bible fairly bursts with complaints (beginning with that business about the Garden of Eden and reaching a climax with Job); *Prometheus Bound*, the most primitive of Greek tragedies, is virtually nothing but whining; the sculpture of the Golden Age is an implied complaint (assuming Phidias himself was no mesomorph); music complains very gloriously, very lugubriously, depending on the major or minor; the history of politics is certainly founded on complaining; poetry is, at base, the quintessence of lyrical bellyaching. And so on.

Like my kids, my artists are great complainers one and all . . . even when they have nothing to complain of except being themselves. And this is the real clue to the whole issue. The purest kind of complaining is never about anything external. That is only how it gets itself expressed: the teachers, the critics, the weather, the family, the car, or the economy must bear the brunt of all the interior displeasures. Voluptuous complaining, jagged complaining, lustrous complaining—through these we inflict our irritation at being ourselves on those who are not ourselves. "Sorry to complain so much," people will say with shocking hypocrisy. The apology itself is a complaint.

In complaint as in art, every generation must produce its own stuff. In fact, we can judge a generation on the quality of its complaining as well as on the objects it picks to complain about. One generation complains that it can't make up its mind between Protestantism and Catholicism, another that you can't buy a good five-cent cigar, a third that social justice is irritatingly elusive. And, of course, they all complain about the last generation and the next one, in that order.

Even the Stoics, as I dimly recall them, complained . . . ; they complained quite shamelessly about the complaining of the non-Stoics.

As for happy people, they complain with surprising frequency because, being happy most of the time, it is simply impossible for them to bear in silence those rainy afternoons, those sleepless midnights when they are—no matter how happy by nature—a little less than happy. Woe to the companion of the unhappy happy person!

Men like to pretend that complaining is distinctively feminine; they have even reduced a myriad of the ills of our tangled innards to so many so-called "women's complaints." But, in my experience, men are the greater complainers. Not in quantity perhaps, but in quality, just as women do most of the world's cooking while the least overworked, most famous, and best-paid chefs are men.

Here I might say that I think Virginia's somewhat expansive idea of complaining is fundamentally an aesthetic one, and in this respect I quite agree with her. Some complaints, aesthetically speaking, really are better than others.

While the psychologists' concept of a "hierarchy of needs" has always seemed to me something of a misplaced metaphor, a "hierarchy of complaints" strikes me as just right. A hierarchy was originally a government of priests, which is what the Greek word literally means. Then Dionysius the Areopagite, who apparently knew everything worth knowing about the organizational chart of Paradise, used the term to designate the three ranks of angels, each rank having three orders for the sake of symmetry. But nowadays all that has been retained in common parlance of "hierarchy's" noble etymology is the Sesame Street notion that some things are above other things.

This is just where I object to the psychologists' hierarchy of needs: that is, the notion that when you've had enough peanut butter and jelly you want to meet Mick Jagger and then, perhaps, read a little Harold Robbins. The third need is not necessarily higher than the second, let alone the first. In fact, some people may achieve their very highest point, their apogee of needful expression, at the level of biology. For example, a man may be the most exquisite Lucullian gourmet and yet be satisfied to listen to a recording of "Hey, Jude" by the 1001 Strings while polishing off his sacher torte and smoking his Maria Mancini.

On the other hand, a hierarchy in the aesthetics of complaining seems to me very apt. Some complaints are truly nobler than others, more elevated and refined. The same person who will tell a whining child in a station wagon to shut up and stop complaining about the length of the journey may pay the very strictest attention to a performance of Mahler's *Kindertotenlieder*. Of course, we will not admit that it is the sheer elegance of imaginary complaint that attracts us to Gustav Mahler's music; we are more likely to say it is his passionate self-expression. Well, the whining child is expressing himself no less passionately when he moans for the twentieth time, ''Are we *there* yet?''

Yes, you will say, but the child is only repeating the *same* irritating complaint. True, but then the poet Friedrich Rückert wrote well over two hundred elegies on the death of his children, from which Mahler drew five for his songs.

You will now object that Rückert was lamenting a most serious and irreplaceable loss, while the child in the station wagon is merely complaining about a trivial matter. Trivial to whom, I will have to ask in return. To us? But which of us really grieves for Mahler's musical empathy with Rückert's terrible loss? More likely we will think of some loss of our own or even a literary one. No, on the criterion of sheer sincerity, genuine, spontaneous feeling, we should have to place the child's automotive complaining higher than either Rückert's poems or Mahler's songs. After all, the child's whining is wholehearted and unmediated by any secondary considerations, whereas Rückert forced himself to lament in rhyming couplets and Mahler in precisely weighed harmonies. If all the same we place Mahler's gorgeous grieving above the child's annoying whining, we might as well confess that it is because the one is beautiful and moving and the other ugly and exasperating.

We also cannot make the criterion of our hierarchy the degree of seriousness of the matter being complained about. It was William Hazlitt who pointed out that tragedy and comedy are both complaints about the difference between the way things are and the way they ought to be. In tragedy the matter of complaint is serious, while in comedy it tends to be trivial. No doubt this is why, as forms, tragedy has generally enjoyed greater prestige than comedy. However, as soon as we look at particular cases—say, a solemn heroic tragedy by Thomas Otway and a Romantic comedy by Shakespeare—we must confess that there is a higher quality of complaining to be found in the comedy than the tragedy. This is simply because Shakespeare's art is greater than Otway's—not merely his language, which by itself can make good literature, but not great literature. Actually, it is Shakespeare's profound artist's grasp of the human capacity to *do* things—things like complaining. Virginia would no doubt be quick to observe that Shakespeare's most famous play of all is largely *devoted* to complaining.

Virginia's idea about the huge element of complaining in Western culture is not wholly frivolous. In fact, it reminded me of two anecdotes I should like to offer here as exampla, as two types not only of the artist or thinker, but likewise as illustrations of two sorts of complaining, or even as two opposed orientations toward all those things about which life offers us the endless opportunity to complain. We might call them the ancient-heroic versus the modern-pathetic.

The first story concerns Alexander the Great. The tale is that when Alexander's conquest-weary and homesick veterans were near a decision to mutiny, having been on the march for over three years, he set himself high on a platform where the entire army would be able to see him, stripped off his robes and showed them that he bore on his own body the mark of every known weapon. He said not a word, nothing. The army pushed on towards the Gates of India, persuaded, I have always supposed, less by the pain Alexander had personally suffered than that, in disclosing his wounds, Alexander showed them a triumph more impressive than the sack of Persepolis. Like the Homeric heroes on whom he consciously modeled himself, Alexander was capable of complaining with enormous dignity—so much, in fact, that one might hardly notice it was complaining at all. In literature, such complaining is properly called tragedy, which *is* a sort of complaining through not complaining.

The second story concerns the German Renaissance artist Albrecht Dürer; it accounts for one of his more striking self-portraits. According to this anecdote, Dürer once fell ill during a journey. Distrusting the medical science of the rude village in which he found himself, the artist posted a circumstantial account of his symptoms to his personal physician back home in Nuremberg. To illustrate this description, he included along with his letter a small drawing: a full-length self-portrait in which the artist represented himself naked and pointing to the side of his abdomen. The caption reads, approximately, ''This is where it hurts.''

As I think about the form and style of modern complaining, I cannot help but feel that there is little that resembles the self-possessed, tragically dignified Alexander up on his platform and much that is like Dürer drawing out his complaint in a provincial sickroom for an absent Doctor. One might almost think that, among the many glossy new anthologies offered for sale each spring, at least one ought to be entitled, after Dürer, *This Is Where It Hurts: An Introduction to Modern Literature.* The heroic and tragic complaint, like Alexander's, expresses the universal in the particular; the old Macedonian campaigners could identify themselves with their leader. To take another example, Achilles' personal complaint is still that of Achilles—a hero and demi-god—yet his heel is as mortal as our own poor flesh is. When in the *Iliad* he replies to a Trojan's appeal for mercy, Achilles speaks of himself, but explains that there is no mercy for any of us. His speech to Lycaon mirrors the stern pathos of Alexander's silent appeal to his troops:

> See what a man I am also, both strong and comely to look
>   on,
> Great was the father who bred me, a goddess the mother
>   who bore me;
> Yet over me stand death and overmastering fortune.
> To me a dawn shall come, or a noontide hour, or an
>   evening,
> When some man shall deprive me of life in the heat of
>   battle,
> Casting at me with a spear or an arrow shot from a
>   bowstring.

It is as if Achilles understood the paradox that his invulnerability would be meaningless without his vulnerability. This is the sort of nobility taught us by the Greeks, the nobility Friedrich Nietzsche shrilly complained the nineteenth century had destroyed with its endless moralizing and psychologizing, lowering the quality of complaining even as it vastly increased the quantity.

Fate is character. Anyway, this is what I was taught in high school. A nice dramatic-psychological idea illustrated as usual by the standard high-school reading of *Oedipus Rex.* And yet how much truer to the Greek tragic spirit I found Oedipus' own denial of my teacher's

axiom when I later came across him complaining forcefully about it
at the end of his life in *Oedipus at Colonus:*

> Was I the sinner?
> Repaying wrong for wrong—that was no sin,
> Even were it wittingly done, as it was not.
> I did not know the way I went. They knew:
> They, who devised this trap for me, they knew.

Oedipus learns that his freedom can only be expressed in a context
of necessity. This is a bitter, tragic wisdom, but a wonderfully enno-
bling one, too. In fact, when he finally accepts it, Oedipus becomes
sacred, like the precincts of Moira, the terrain of Fate itself. But still,
he complains. He blames *them.* If this demonstrates nothing else, it
at least proves that at the end Oedipus is still man, still human, still
the answer to the Sphinx's riddle. Man complains on four, then two,
then three legs.

   This ancient sublimation of the human spirit of complaining in
epic or tragedy is bound to appear to us now like an expensive and
even deceitful portrait. I mean the kind in which the photographer
has contrived to make his wealthy client look almost hilariously better
than in actuality, the sort of flattering photo the client wouldn't mind
seeing in the newspaper or hanging on his children's walls. Nowadays, though, most complaining—even that offered by our public
figures—is far more like the snapshots left over from last summer's
torrid heat wave. After all, Alexander, Achilles, and Oedipus were
heroes and kings. Facing life as they did, from the top, they all respected themselves.

   It was Dostoyevsky, inventor of the modern anti-hero, who asked
rhetorically whether an educated, self-aware man of the modern
world can really respect himself at all. Others have probed here and
there, but no one, I believe, has poked his finger further into the soft
psychology of modern, up-to-date complaining than Dostoyevsky
did. It is a psychology I have never felt secure enough to call abnormal.

   Notes from Underground is a short novel in which, to adopt a phrase
from Woody Allen, Fyodor Dostoyevsky first succeeded in raising

"whining to a high art." He does so not through heroic self-possession or tragic wisdom, but through raw, suppurating, and ignoble self-consciousness. In chapter four of part one of the *Notes*, the anonymous narrator examines the spiteful pleasures of self-conscious complaint. The difference from the classic style is most striking. Listen to him improvise on his theme, like John Coltrane really letting go:

> I ask you, gentlemen, listen sometimes to the moans of an educated man of the nineteenth century suffering from toothache, on the second or third day of the attack, when he is beginning to moan, not as he moaned on the first day; that is, not simply because he has toothache, not just as any coarse peasant, but as a man affected by progress and European civilization. . . . His moans become nasty, disgustingly malignant, and go on for whole days and nights. And of course he knows himself that he is doing himself no sort of good with his moans; he knows better than any one that he is only lacerating and harassing himself and others for nothing; he knows that even the audience before whom he is making his efforts and his whole family, listen to him with loathing, do not put a kopek's worth of faith in him, and inwardly understand that he might moan differently, more simply, without trills and flourishes, and that he is only amusing himself like that from ill-humor, from malignancy . . .

Imagine! Trills and flourishes, and all to say: here is where it hurts, to inflict this knowledge on others, on his "whole family." This is not expressing the universal in the particular, but just the opposite. That is, maybe everyone else gets toothaches, but just listen to what *my* toothache is doing to *me*. Egoistic complaining of this sort is malicious indeed. It is a sort of sin.

Franz Kafka, in one of his penetrating late aphorisms, elevates the concept of complaining as sin to the highest conceivable level:

> The original sin, the ancient wrong committed by man, consists in the complaint, which man makes and never ceases making, that a wrong has been done to him, that the original sin was once committed upon him.

Dissatisfaction, not with a toothache—that is merely a symbol—
but with reality, with the conditions originally laid down for our
existence—each man and woman with his or her own existence and
all men and women collectively with existence in general—this becomes for Kafka the first sin, our fall from grace. (Could the *un*fallen
complain?) Yet such complaining is also the serpent that leads us to
bite the apple of knowledge: both complaining and biting are aggres-
sive, oral acts.

Having once set out on this path of knowledge running east from
Eden, our complaints have, moreover, dictated the program of our
astonishing discoveries. Gravity, inertia, illness, aging—such conditions we have tried to overcome through our inventiveness: with
our airplanes, drugs, and tummy-tucks. One might easily suppose
Dostoyevsky's Petersburg intellectual would fare better in the days
of dental bonding and novacaine. But if the sin is really the original one, then this complaining must be both universal and perpetual, ineradicable even by scientific progress or Californian self-help
healers.

Woody Allen's self-deprecating persona is at its best a burlesque
of Dostoyevsky's narrator. In effect, between the former's St. Petersburg and the latter's Manhattan there is no difference except a hundred years of human inventiveness and modern literature, which
breeds the ironic and unavoidable knowledge of what is intractable
to even a century of science and literature:

> Science has failed us. True, it has conquered many diseases, broken
> the genetic code and even placed a man on the moon, and yet when
> a man of eighty is left in a room with two eighteen-year-old cock-
> tail waitresses nothing happens. Because the real problems never
> change.

What can we do about these real problems that never change? We
can accept them in silence; we can complain about them as beautifully
and even gaily as possible, but there is something else we can also
do: we can protest. We can protest because we must, because who
knows whether the real problems that never change may turn out to

be really changeable after all? We can also protest in order to remind others that the real problems are really problems. We can assert our personal protests in the strongest terms. We have a long tradition of it. For example, in one of Søren Kierkegaard's books an irritable young man writes of our whole vast business concern of a universe as follows:

> How did I obtain an interest in this big enterprise they call reality? Is it not a voluntary concern? And if I am to be compelled to take part in it, where is the director? I should like to make a remark to him. Is there no director? Whither shall I turn with my complaint? Existence is surely a debate—may I beg that my view be taken into consideration?

Well, this is how intellectuals complain, and one should never underestimate the complaints of the intellectuals. Karl Marx, for instance, was for a long time troubled by a skin disorder and was not reluctant to complain about it. He is said to have remarked, while composing *Das Kapital*, "The capitalists will have cause to regret my carbuncles!"

Before we get carried away with the moral worthiness of complaining as protest, however, it should be admitted that complaining is also a thing many people do long before everything else has failed. This is plainly irritating, and here is an example. I have often to review the evaluations students make of my colleagues, the marketing reports on their pedagogy, so to speak. Not long ago I read a complaint recorded by a dissatisfied undergraduate: "Professor X. is far too demanding of and unsympathetic toward his students. It is useless to talk to him about the material when you haven't read any of it." It may be noted that complaining sometimes creates respect for that about which the complaint is lodged—especially when the complaint is manifestly premature.

Complaining can also be a sort of parasitic mood. Certain kinds of behavior are like viruses: they inject themselves into an organism and establish conditions in which they are able to reproduce like mad, the poor host be damned. I believe some people are afflicted with their complaining in this viral way. In such cases, complaining would be as uncontrollable by the complainer as a fever is by its victim. At best, such a person might be able to channel his or her complaints; eliminating them is out of the question. One sees this sort of thing most clearly in young children, with whom a bad mood is always on the surface and with whom complaints multiply themselves indiscriminately: first they hate the meat loaf, then the milk, their clothes, bedtime, and their siblings. But at least children do not mask complaints as something else. In adults, this chronic viral complaining can take on many odd, protective colorations: for instance, pounding out the "Revolutionary Etude" or devoting long essays to the subject of complaining. Such grown-up activities are known as displacements or sublimations, suggesting that they are at least okay with psychologists. Give your whining an air of high culture, put it down in octava rima or daub it in bold acrylics and people won't be so annoyed with you. On the contrary, a few of them may invite you to dinner.

But meanwhile, the viral devil of complaining—the passive dissatisfaction, the profound dis-ease—goes on eating away at the organism that now calls itself artistic and arrogates to itself as many privileges as that dignified claim will win. In this way, complaining can even become quite necessary to the artist—not surprisingly, as he will, not without some justice, begin to call it his inspiration. Nor is this process of sublimated complaining limited to poets or musicians.

Some lawyers are very good at it: talented ones soon become masters of reflexive courtroom objection and the very best are capable of inventing entirely new kinds of civil litigation. The difference between mere whining litigiousness and a genuine thirst for justice may be absolute; however, as this distinction is a wholly interior one, it is very difficult from the outside to tell which is which. This must be why our courts are congenitally clogged with complaints. Indeed, the large if not excessive number of lawyers employed in the United States suggests that formal complaining is, for Americans, not only a way of doing business but virtually a national pastime. After all, as I recall, one of the major sources of the American national consciousness was a series of famous complaints about British economic and defense policy in the eighteenth century. The American Revolution was, in many ways, a revolution made by lawyers. This proves nothing against the sources of American patriotism, Heaven knows, but it does reveal that the spirit of complaint can lead to highly consequential and liberating actions. An irritation can suggest a new train of thought, new thoughts can beget protests, and protests may lead to insurrections. This was clearly understood in the old feudal days when, if somebody complained about the king, he could be brought up on a charge of lèse majesté and dealt with as a traitor.

My point here is that free thought is unimaginable without complaining, though complaining is no more a sign of independent thinking than tuberculosis is of literary genius. It's just that, historically, the two have often been found together.

So, to complain has a legal meaning as well as a psychological one. To lay a complaint before a court is to assert that an injustice exists and to seek its redress. In this sense, George Orwell's cautionary novel *Nineteen Eighty-Four* is a very complicated complaint, meticulous and imaginative, an extrapolation from an unacceptable present to an entirely repulsive future. The connection between the present and future is not only real, it is sometimes quite personal. Orwell gave the number of the room in which he labored during the war to the dreaded torture chamber where Winston Smith confronts the rat. But, of course, the novel is hardly personal; it is a protest, a legal complaint seeking an injunction, a restraining order, asking nothing less than justice and sanity for the world at large.

In fact, Orwell's whole career was that of a profoundly protestant writer. He was a man who complained constantly not that an injustice had been done to him, but rather than human decency was being multifariously outraged in his time.

When I first read *Nineteen Eighty-Four* as a boy, the fact about it that most impressed me was that Winston Smith, the novel's protagonist, was born in the same year as myself. Now we are both forty. I am, of course, infinitely better off than Winston Smith. So far as I am aware, I do not even share his varicose ulcer, the wound of his oppressed individuality; that is, the physiological manifestation of many repressed complaints and stifled protests. But I cannot wholly escape the idea that Orwell's book was meant in some special way for my own generation, for all of us once whining and protesting, but lately more accommodating, baby-boomers.

I have therefore endeavored to remain mindful of his complaints and warnings about such things as the betrayals of which intellectuals are fully and perpetually capable, that utopian schemes generally tend toward controlled insanity, that indoctrination is ever ready to substitute itself for education (noting especially that in Orwell's Oceania only those who have no intellect are granted intellectual liberty), that the abolition of privacy spells the annihilation of the individual, and that a science dominated by government is likely to be reduced to examining only two questions: how to read the minds of human beings and how to kill large numbers of them without warning.

But none of these protests—serious and ever-timely as they are—constitutes Orwell's *special* complaint, the uniquely Orwellian gripe. Others have seen these things too, but absolutely no one has seen more clearly or complained more eloquently about the pernicious political and moral effects of the perversion of language. No one argues so lucidly that the degeneration of language is, in fact, equally a cause and an effect of cultural and political corruption. For example, Orwell observed that the weakening of language encourages us to accept words without examining their relation to objective reality. Our thought is impoverished and the truth obscured by clangorous slogans and reiterated nonsense. Orwell's historical sources for such political concerns are obvious enough: there are Stalin's grand dictates on the collectivization of Soviet agriculture, Mussolini up on his balcony fulminating about the grandeur of Imperial Rome, or Hitler screeching about the future of the Fatherland.

For my generation, however, these dictatorial linguistic grotesqueries were at first only of historical interest. At most, they appeared to us trivialized in the comparatively crude advertising of the 1950s. However, in the mid-1960s, just as we came of age, the debasement of political discourse about which Orwell complained suddenly appeared before us in all its ignoble obfuscatory panoply and has yet to go away.

There was something called the Pacification Program in Vietnam, for example. To pacify means to make peaceful, as when a screaming baby is given a rubber nipple to suck on. "War is Peace," says Oceania's Inner Party. Why not reverse it? Pacification was, of course, war. People were removed from villages of questionable loyalty to crowded camps, the villages burned, along with crops and domestic animals. As a Roman once said of a similar program: "They make a desolation and call it peace."

There was something called the Phoenix Program, which seemed to entail the systematic assassination of civilians suspected of communist sympathies and not the rebirth of some fabled fire bird in Arizona.

Notice also that these things were called "programs." Programs sound rather good in themselves. A program suggests a well-organized thing, something to watch on television or to feed neatly into your clean mainframe. It is a useful word.

At certain moments the war became almost literally a war of words. For instance, I recall that the Nixon Administration became rather indignant with journalists who insisted on referring to the invasions of Laos and Cambodia in 1970 as invasions. These were merely "incursions" the Administration declared warmly. Evidently they felt an incursion would be more appealing to the electorate than an invasion, and perhaps they were right. All the same, anyone with a dictionary could have discovered that incursion and invasion are essentially synonymous. The point is that incursion is softer and implies something minor and brief, a headache rather than cancer. Throughout the war the official language game seemed to be to find soft words for hard ones, abstract words for concrete ones, palliative jargon in which to swathe embarrassing facts. And all this occurred at just the moment when television journalism gave the lie to the Pentagon's lexicon of softness, abstraction, and palliation.

Yet television itself, with its battering montage, its vast emptiness full of images, can stupefy no less effectively than Newspeak can. It is this that leads me to complain now and again that one true word would be worth a thousand pictures. Winston Smith, a kind of historian after all, might have felt the same way. He was not a photographer,but a diarist.

Anyway, the specific linguistic perversions Orwell complains about are by now fairly common—though fortunately there are still plenty of people around to complain about them. For instance, in Newspeak, as in the Pentagon, nouns become verbs and vice-versa. In Newspeak there is no longer the word "thought." Its place is taken by "think," as "cut" is by "knife." Already we are practically surrounded by think-tanks and politicians famous for knifing through their own red tape. Orwell predicted that the "ly" ending of adverbs is doomed to be replaced. Madison Avenue became notorious for this two decades ago and the suffix "wise"—if I remember rightly—turns up now and then on the Nixon tapes, which is not surprising, since the president surrounded himself with advertising men like H. R. Haldeman. "Will that story go over well public-relationswise?" they ask, while over at the Pentagon they were perhaps inquiring, "How's that new bomb, killwise?"

It isn't just the government, of course. Students fall into error a good deal, too. For instance, Orwell is very sharp on "un" constructions, as in unfree and ungood. I have often heard students falsely describing absolutely genuine events as "unreal" or things they entirely credit as "unbelievable." This sort of thing ought to be unacceptable.

Orwell complains also of the characteristic Newspeak device of making new compound words: thoughtcrime, goodsex, oldthink, blackwhite. *Time* magazine used to make a specialty of this, inventing cute neologisms like "cinemactress." Agitprop, Gestapo, Comintern, and Nazi are older examples, compound abbreviations that had the original advantage of cutting out undesirable associations. Some years back, Standard Oil Company of New Jersey, which used to go by the Orwellian name of Esso, spent a terrific sum of money to change its name to Exxon and then ran ads selling itself as our buddy, ally, and servant—rather like Big Brother, in fact. Should people have complained that they were selling themselves and not just gasoline?

The distorted languages of business and of politics intersect in the advertising agency, which often aims at the same kind of compliant unconsciousness as the Inner Party favored in its clients. After all, a campaign is a campaign and every election brings us more media consultants. Whether the purpose is more sales or more votes, the methods are pretty much the same: lulling the mind, defusing the sense of reality, invoking authority, bandwagons, nostalgia, and the religion of technology. Consider just the last: nobody uses a razor anymore. We use "shaving systems" like the Trac-2 shaving system in which, of course, Trac is spelled incorrectly. You'd think that this fourth-generation chromium-plated stainless-steel double-edged teflon-enhanced quasi-scientific marvel was too good for merely scraping whiskers or for anything less than slitting your throat in high style.

Like Winston Smith's, our telescreens, albeit still one-way for the moment, are full of Newspeak. Take Orwell's device of the standardized adjective. In Newspeak, he says, there will be precious few of them because this will greatly lessen the chance of a fresh or accurate view of reality. The Inner Party favors stereotyping in particular and muddy thinking in general—or mudthinkfulness—which is greatly furthered by constantly using the same words. The press seems unable to report on a legal brief without putting the word "lengthy" in front of it. Except in underwear ads, there are no brief briefs on television. In the same way, the House Ways and Means Committee is regularly "powerful" while the Rules Committee is always "all-important." Truces in the Middle East are perpetually "uneasy," perhaps because the place is crowded with sheikdoms that are all "oil-rich," and enduring visits from "globe-trotting" secretaries of state who are fleeing "spiralling" inflation (or another "short-term" recession) back home, so that they can "officially" protest "alleged repressive" measures "necessitated" by the activities of "left-wing" guerrillas who are "communist-backed" by threatening retaliation that promises to be "massive."

By all means let us complain with Orwell about such leaden and deadening clichés. It should not be that the very thing most citizens do to become informed about the world should prevent them from thinking clearly about what is going on. Let the machines be the receivers, not the watchers. And let us be grateful to George Orwell for his complaining no less than for his love of the English language.

• • •

So we have made it through both 1984s, still complaining, still free to complain, at least if we live in the right countries. Back in the sixties—when my generation told itself not to trust anyone over thirty—our complaints were memorable when of high quality; petulant, callow, and self-righteous when otherwise. But the habit of griping is hard to break. So now, when we have told ourselves not to trust anyone under thirty, my coevals are complaining still, though the relative complacency of the present rather tends toward the trivialization and narrowing of complaint. Interest rates get more play than social justice these days. In fact, instead of outraged idealism, I hear more outrage *at* idealism. This new hard-headed, bottom-line (or middle-aged) appraisal of life by the baby-boomers casts a curious shadow over the next generation, many of whom are, so to speak, uncertain of just what to complain about for the rest of the century. Their attitude toward those of us who were their age in the sixties remains profoundly ambivalent: on the one hand, I think they envy us our youthful and innocent certainty about our objects of protest, while, on the other, they are quick to see selfishness underlying the apparently indignant altruism of twenty years ago. They also envy our nostalgia, but rightly suspect it is often mere sentimentality and even a way of beating them over the head with the Beatles, Janis Joplin, and Dr. Spock. They wonder at the old far-reaching radicalism, but are quick to observe with a smile that such daring didn't so much fail as it was outlived, as if it were just like any other fad. They marvel at the freedom of the sixties, at the motley variety of lives they spawned, but also understand that the sixties were years of rising economic expectations that could underwrite a kind of luxurious silliness. They themselves do not seem to desire such a wide variety of styles in living, but rather something very particular, something along the lines of what life is like on *Dynasty*, *Dallas*, or other country-club soap operas.

True, these young are modest; they do not tend to formulate grand, far-seeing complaints, apart from a rather hopeless feeling about nuclear annihilation when the thought strikes them, but they are not short on immediate ones: work loads, the weather, criticism. *Non aequus est.* It is not that they are uncritical or inarticulate about the Big Questions, but rather, I think, that they are plainly *fearful*, and fear makes for silence. Paradoxically, a degree of confidence and security is required to complain well. Complaining, like hope, depends on faith in the future. The more protected the child—the more pampered, assured, and the less afraid—the more it is liable to whine. To be blunt, I think the young who are middle-class are afraid of falling out of it, afraid that the system which offers such enormous material rewards may withhold its benefits or might even crush them should they make the wrong move. Given this, it is natural that they should mistrust or nervously mock complaining in the grand style. Moreover, one does not protest a system in which one is striving to triumph.

Even after all this, though, I must admit that complaining may be *almost* pointless, but in this narrow "almost" there remains much to consider. There is in it room not only for whining, breast-beating, the cruder forms of brattish self-assertion; there is also lodging for a proof of life, for sensitivity to irritation, space for the hope that things might be better than they are. I can only think of three sorts of people who do not complain in some way: the smugly complacent, the totally repressed, and the utterly despairing. My great respect for the silence of the Stoics and my detestation of the whining of the well-off notwithstanding, I cannot consider any of these conditions desirable.

Of course spoiled people *do* complain—in fact, they do little else—but not all complainants are spoiled. Besides, there is a purely social element in complaining that should not be overlooked. I believe many close friendships are owing to it. People who go through the truly complaint-worthy ordeals of life together (such as military training or their freshman years) tend to remain remarkably close, for they share the ineffable bond of having griped in common. This discourse called griping ought not to be undervalued as a precious lubricant in slipping us through abrasive times. Indeed, I think many complaints are really only a form of etiquette. One is not expected to like one's drill sergeant, freshman composition class, institutional food, rush-hour traffic, or crowded trolleys. Complaining, like shaking hands, gives one something comforting to do with strangers in barracks, cafeterias, classrooms, and subways.

Complaining will cut us off from others if we only bewail our private fates; but it can connect us with others if we join ourselves to the human condition by it. There is a fine illustration of just these alternatives in the Talmud, an anecdote about the saintly rabbi Hanina ben Dosa, whose complaining prayers were evidently always answered instantly. Here is the whole story:

Rabbi Hanina was once walking along when it began to rain. At once he complained to God: "Lord of the World, all the world is at ease, only Hanina is in distress."

At once the rain stopped.

But when the rabbi reached his house he complained again. "Lord of the World, all the world is in distress, only Hanina is at ease."

And the rain started to fall once again.

Hanina's second complaint is the noble one. In the end, he did not pray that he should be better off, but that he should be no better off than others; not that he should rise above, but that he should share in the common fate; essentially that it should rain on the just as well as the unjust. The second complaint joins him to mankind and, in doing so, cancels the first.

One need not be a prophet to predict that people will go on complaining: no matter how glittering the future turns out to be, it will certainly displease somebody. Besides, as Virginia said, complaining is a fundamental human talent and, as such, necessary and not to be despised. We should develop all our talents. According to Kafka, we humans never cease to complain of the original sin, especially when we are in the process of committing it. And so people will undoubtedly go on complaining no matter what. But we can still choose our objects; we can still perfect our style. If art is complaint, then complaint can be art. So, to conclude, here are two final examples of really first-class complaining. They may stand as models.

The first is one of Heinrich von Kleist's anecdotes:

> A Franciscan, one very rainy day, was accompanying a Swabian prisoner to the gallows. The man complained to Heaven all the way of having to walk so gloomy a path in such wet and unfriendly weather. The Franciscan, wishing to offer some Christian solace, replied: "Lout that you are! How can *you* complain? You have only to get there, but I, in all this rain, must walk all the way back again."

The last is a most elegant and superbly polite complaint which is attributed to no less a personage than Abraham Lincoln:

> Madam, if this is coffee, please bring me some tea; but if this is tea, please bring me some coffee.

A *Parents' Weekend Breakfast Address*

When I was invited to speak to you this morning I felt as I suppose most people would: flattered yet at a loss; eager to please, but anxious about humiliation; chockful of images and void of ideas. In short, I wasn't sure I was up to it. There is a story that Winston Churchill, hearing the Labour Party leader Clement Attlee praised for his outstanding humility, grumbled that Attlee had a great deal to be humble about.

I have a great deal to be humble about too. Here I am, after a dozen years of teaching, still waiting either to be found out for the ignoramus I know I am, or given a dram of hemlock as the corrupter of youth I sometimes fancy myself to be. But perhaps this is not altogether humble. After all, our culture's two greatest teachers, Socrates and Jesus, were not saved by the most sublime student evaluations. I presume I was invited to speak because I received a teaching award, a fact which I am sure astonished my colleagues and students no less than it did me, or will you. Teaching awards always have a touch of irony about them, since our deepest conception of the fate of the excellent teacher remains martyrdom. Prizes suggest virtuosity, but insofar as teaching is, as Socrates said, midwifery, virtuosity seems out of place.

From my point of view, this is a tricky group to address. As freshmen and parents of freshmen, you bring your own generation gap with you. Only some of you probably remember who Jack Kerouac, René Descartes, Spiro Agnew, or Janis Joplin were; to others the names Aristippus, Steven Wright, Duns Scotus, Jan Vermeer, Judy Blume, and Bono may conjure up nothing whatever. Worse yet, I realize not one of you is going to take notes. Finally, like most professors, I am never really comfortable talking to people whom I will not be grading.

So when, in their reckless wisdom, the administration asked me to talk this morning, I inquired what they would like me to talk about. The answer was in equal parts generous and impatient. Talk about anything you like, they said. What a chance they're taking, that made me think, not without exhilaration. However, I can now tell you honestly that there is nothing in the world so difficult to talk about as anything you like.

I figured the idea is for me to be an illustration of a professor in a nine o'clock class. So my first notion was to offer you one of my regular lectures on literature or philosophy. You'll be relieved to hear that I decided against doing so after reflecting that you probably haven't done the reading, at least not recently. True, this has never deterred me in the case of my own students, but still it seemed impolite, since you've never even seen the syllabus.

Therefore, I've decided to talk about education. Education and breakfast are the two things that have brought us all together this morning and I have nothing much to say about breakfast. What I have to say about education will be eccentric, disorganized, and not wholly serious. I will offer no proposals for how to fix things up either. It's not like I'm running for office or anything. Let's just say that, as asked, and as you sip your coffee, I will be talking about anything I like.

In the last decade books, pamphlets, and tracts about education have piled up almost as rapidly as the national debt. It all began a few secretaries of education ago with a report that said our system of education might have been devised by Colonel Khadaffi. I have actually read certain parts of some of these documents. As a rule, they seem to be well-organized, earnest even in their humor, and filled with capitalized nouns, just as if they had been written by German philosophers of the last century. Also as a rule, they say education is in a state of crisis and proceed to blame everything and everybody for it, which amounts to blaming nothing and no one. Most wind up with some sort of ersatz Beethoven ending, bursting with rhetorically irresistible but practically unsupported idealism. They are, in short, terrifically dull, dignified, and depressing documents.

Many of these authors, being educators rather than teachers, declare a special affection for Efficiency, one of those capitalized nouns I mentioned. Efficiency is as good an idol to sacrifice to as any, I suppose, but the trouble is that education is not, by nature, an efficient process. Notice that it is a process and not a result. In fact, a wit once called education a process trying its best to look like a result. The process is not like iron smelting, though. Efficiency isn't all that pertinent to it.

I've also been struck by how many recent works on education are theoretical, especially the practical ones. The curriculum should be concerned more with this hemisphere and less with that one; math should be taught now and not then—that sort of thing. Such treatises tend to leave out all of us pathetically uncapitalized human beings. Theories generally do.

So I have no proposals to make and will concern myself with theories only to trifle with them. This ought to prevent my remarks from running too close to lunchtime.

I'll begin with three popular ideas about higher education, and those who provide it, that I think need correcting.

The first comes from the poet and traitor Ezra Pound. Pound defined a professor as "a man who has to talk for an hour." This certainly sounds like an unexceptionable definition, but in fact it is wrong in three ways.

First, it's sexist. Professors, like police officers and prime ministers, are by no means always men.

Second, it's technologically obsolete. The wide distribution of audio-visual aids means that she or he need not always spend a whole hour talking.

Finally, it's inaccurate. Even without tapes, films, or slides, a professor doesn't actually talk for an hour, but only fifty minutes. Academic time moves faster than normal time. Not only is an hour only fifty minutes, but a week is a mere five days, and a year scarcely nine months. This abbreviation of time is actually one of the great joys of academic life.

The second idea is even more popular than the first because it conceals a little barb of sweet revenge. As every one of us has been a student, every one of us can relish revenge on the expert, the long-winded, the giver-of-grades. The second idea is the cliché that those who can, do, while those who can't, teach—or, to put it a little differently, that it is always easier to talk about a thing than to do it.

The inaccuracy of this idea will appear to you clearly if you take the example of bicycle riding. Almost any ten-year-old can ride a bike, but hardly any adult can describe exactly how to go about doing it.

The example is not all that fanciful, really. As somebody who both teaches literature and attempts to produce more of it, I can tell you that describing what I've done in a story or poem is frequently more of a strain than actually writing the thing was. Besides, universities are not full of people who can't do things; on the contrary, they have become the Renaissance courts of the twentieth century. They are crammed with practicing painters, accountants, musicians, poets, architects, engineers, and doctors.

Incidentally, you might be interested in the intramural version of this idea, which tells us something. This is that those who can't teach, teach education. Then there's the Woody Allen version: that those who can't teach, teach gym. But enough of this.

The third idea is the most popular of all, particularly with students and often with their parents as well. This is the conception of the university as an isolated ivory tower of unreality, while the rest of the world—which generally means the world of commerce and the professions—is the only "real" one. Now, quite apart from the fact that, as a teacher of philosophy, the word "real" has always given me some trouble, I like to disturb my students by simply denying this apparently unassailable bit of wisdom. Where else but at a university, I ask them, do people spend all their waking hours talking seriously about and trying mightily to grasp reality? As for the world they longingly call the real one—if I really want to be provocative, I tell them that that world runs on the illusory lubricants of marketing and advertising, both highly rewarded forms of fibbing. This may be a bit of sophistry, I know, yet a teacher needs to adapt methods to goals. When the object is not to tell students what reality is, but rather to get them to think about what it might be, provocation is the preferred method.

Provocation leads me naturally to my next point, which has to do with a provocative definition of education itself.

All language is metaphor; we speak a tissue of little poems. Etymologies, the genealogies of words, are often startling and invariably instructive poems and stories. A delightful example is the word "daisy." It derives from some Anglo-Saxon horticulturist taking note that the pretty yellow flower resembles the sun, which is the eye of the day, and thus he called it "day's eye," or daisy. Now, if you check the dictionary for the origin of the word "educate" you will find that it derives from a Latin verb, *educere*, meaning to lead forth.

So far so good. To lead forth—that is noble and grand. One thinks vaguely of convincing the ignorant to come out of Plato's cave into the bright light of Truth, Goodness, and Beauty. However, it is the nature of metaphor that its magic must be concrete and not vague. The original meaning of *educere* was very concrete indeed. It meant to lead forth cattle by means of goading or prodding.

Surely this etymology is a mild shock to progressive educational theory, but it at least has the advantage of explaining some of the curious language surrounding education. For example, the words *course* and *curriculum*, which both denote something you run through—or are driven through. Or *discipline*, which takes care of the goading and prodding.

As a teacher, I know that all this is sometimes true enough, that my job may indeed entail prodding some confused and not altogether willing students through pre-ordained courses of study, that the mental equivalent of a well placed kick in the behind is occasionally the best I can do. On the other hand, to reduce education merely to prodding and students to domestic animals would be as foolish as it is undignified. Students are not herds, but individuals; the "class" is really just a legal fiction. A curriculum is something one runs through in order to catch up with oneself. If students are not understood to be individuals and nurtured as such, little of real worth can be accomplished. Big lectures and impersonal exams look efficient, of course, but that's just the trouble with them. Sometimes I think the original sin is our tendency to see people precisely as members of classes and not as individuals. This is a sin we are all condemned to commit on a daily basis. However, if the sin weren't universal and perpetual, it could hardly be the original one.

Those of you who are parents may be interested in the curriculum down which your children will be driven, though, frankly, I doubt it. I seldom encounter parents who care as much about what their children study as they do about what grades their children earn. This is neither surprising nor undesirable. Parents usually want their children to be okay in general—as in "we just want you to be happy"—and avoid dictating the specifications. Besides, most students feel pretty much the same way about their courses. The curriculum is a thing that properly obsesses faculty, much as recipes do chefs. Diners are more interested in the proof of the pudding. Still, there are exceptions. For example, back when I was a new assistant professor a mother of the Mormon persuasion wanted to sue both me and the university for including Aristophanes' *Lysistrata* and Eugène Ionesco's *The Bald Soprano* on my syllabus. Given her beliefs, she wasn't all that bad a critic either. Her complaint was that the first play is obscene and the second meaningless. Nevertheless, academic freedom prevailed. I kept the plays and she dropped her litigious plans.

But my favorite story about parents and curricula is an old Roman tale.

It seems a certain patrician wished to have his son educated and for this purpose visited three well-known teachers in the city. He was a dutiful consumer.

The patrician asked the first what he could teach his son. The teacher replied at once that, for a certain sum of money of course, he would undertake to teach the boy all there was to know about geometry, music, astronomy, and gymnastics.

The patrician then took himself to the second teacher and posed the same question. The second teacher answered promptly that he would teach the boy all there was to know about history, rhetoric, poetry, and engineering.

Finally, the patrician sought out the third teacher and asked him also what he could teach his son. This third teacher thought for a few moments and then replied that he wasn't sure that he would be able to teach the boy anything whatsoever.

According to my source, the patrician was a man of wisdom and courage. He chose the third teacher.

Like the patrician, I think the third teacher understood something about education that is too rarely acknowledged. Just as the first duty of a nightwatchman is not to watch, but to stay awake in order to watch, so the first obligation of a teacher is not to teach, but to put students into a condition in which they can learn. This is a truth from the muddy trenches of education, perhaps, but a truth all the same. What's more, it sometimes happens that more can be taught by putting a student in a proper state of mind for learning than through any erudite lecture or morally impeccable sermon.

This is an idea I sometimes use to get my philosophy students thinking about certain differences between Plato and his pupil Aristotle. Briefly, here's how it goes. Plato believed that evildoing is always a form of ignorance and that knowledge of the good exists inside all of us. Careful Socratic questioning can therefore elicit virtue by addressing a miscreant's rationality. Aristotle was more practical. He thought virtue had something to do with a nonrational element of personality he called character, which is formed by early habit and discipline.

The idea of my class was simply to pretend that one day a bunch of fourth-graders get Plato as a substitute teacher. Spitballs, pencils, and epithets are flying as Plato desperately asks these nine-year-olds whether they have truly considered the nature of justice as the harmony of the soul and the proper articulation of classes in the State. My own students, amused by my rendition of the bald and befuddled sub in his toga, willingly grant that Plato wouldn't have lasted an hour in any of their elementary schools.

All right, I say, the following week the substitute is Aristotle. What would *he* do? My students aren't sure. Probably, I suggest, throw the biggest, loudest kid in the class up against the wall and then ask who's next. Aristotle as Clint Eastwood. Once they are all at their desks, though, Aristotle could address a part of them more receptive to ideas than their backsides.

Addressing character before intellect or the rear end before the cerebrum is a task I can illustrate also from my own experience. I think the story will interest you because it concerns a freshman.

The first year of college is basic training, the initial ordeal. Occasionally it happens that a freshman student will have trouble handling the freedom that is his or her sudden lot. In fact, I am convinced that most of the students who get into early academic trouble do so because of the burden of freedom, rather than that of four college-level courses. In other words, immaturity can lead to disaster.

A few years ago I had just such a freshman. At my school the faculty makes a considerable effort to know each of their students personally. In the case of this young man, though, the problem was less one of knowing than of locating. He began missing classes the very first week. From cutting classes it was a small step to disregarding reading assignments and only a little further to neglecting required papers.

Alerted by the faculty, the counselor assigned to this student met with him and read him a stern lecture on the necessity of doing his work. The counselor omitted nothing, right down to that portentous phrase: "Either you act or you will be acted upon."

But the young man's behavior did not change at all, and so the counselor enlisted his parents in the effort to redeem him. I have no doubt that the boy received a very thoroughgoing sermon from home, but again to no positive effect whatever.

By the end of the seventh week of the semester, the student had failed all his midterms. His faculty met together and the general opinion was that he was a lost cause, the only question being whether to advise early withdrawal or to wait until December to flunk him out.

It was at this meeting that it occurred to me to use the philosophy of Epicurus as a last resort. I am not the first to observe that thinking is what we do only when everything else fails. Epicurus was a Greek philosopher of the fourth century B.C., a hedonist who believed that pleasure is the only good in life and pain the sole evil; however, he also taught that it is far wiser to avoid pain than to pursue pleasure and that mild, long-lasting pleasures, like learning, are preferable to short, incandescent ones, like orgies. Despite Epicurus' false reputation as a playboy and gourmet, he actually accounted prudence the highest of all virtues and bread, water, and fruit the best of all diets.

Now, the reason I thought of Epicurus in connection with my elusive and self-destructive freshman was just this: the student was a foolish and immature hedonist while Epicurus was a mature and wise one. I speculated that it might well be a case of fighting fire with fire. Anyway, there was nothing to lose.

So I arranged to have the student summoned to my office one afternoon. When he came in, looking hung-over and irritable, I asked him to sit down, which he did in a weary, resentful sort of way. I then asked him please to tell me honestly how many parties he went to every week.

He looked at me with surprise. "How do you know I go to lots of parties?" he wondered.

If you could have seen his eyes for yourselves you'd know what a naive question that was.

"Never mind," I said, and again asked him for an accurate estimate.

He thought a little and said defiantly that he guessed he went to about five parties a week.

I nodded casually and asked him please to take out a pencil and piece of paper. He appeared surprised; obviously he had been steeled for yet another sermon.

"I want you to do a couple of math problems for me," I said pleasantly. "Now, multiply seven by five. What do you get?"

"Thirty-five," he said, puzzled, with a suspicious, derisive smile.

"Good, that's exactly correct. Now multiply a hundred and five by two."

"Two hundred and ten," he answered after a moment.

"Right on the nose," I said encouragingly and sat back. "You can go now, if you like." I picked up a memo. He shambled to his feet and got as far as the door.

"But professor," he said, "what's the *point*?"

"You really want to know? All right, the point is this," I said. "If you continue going to five parties a week I can guarantee you'll flunk out in December, which is only seven weeks from now. That's thirty-five more parties. On the other hand, if you begin behaving differently, come to all your classes, do all your work, and cut your partying down to, say, two a week, on weekends, then you have a remote chance of staying here three and a half more years, which comes to exactly one hundred and five weeks, or, as you've just told me, two hundred and ten parties. You can go now."

Well, it was a bit risky, but it actually worked. The student, persuaded by Epicurus' hedonistic calculus in a way that no sermon could touch, got down to work, managed to pass his courses, and finally commenced to grow up. By the middle of the following semester he had learned that there is more to college than parties and that there is a difference between freedom and license. He gradually became quite a good student, in fact, as he always had the potential to, and nothing at all of a hedonist, Epicurean or otherwise.

There is a moral to this story from the cattle runs, and it has to do with the nature of education. The boy's parents and counselor lectured him and in doing so assumed that he was capable of considering a point of view other than his own. However, his inability to do any such thing was precisely the problem. After all, at eighteen hedonism often seems a more persuasive philosophy than it does at forty-five, for physical no less than moral reasons. No frontal assault on what he would have called his "life-style" could have worked. What I did worked not only because I had Epicurus and arithmetic on my side, but because I assumed his point of view. The problem was not to tell him about the shortcomings of his behavior, let alone the triviality of mindless partying, but simply to get him into class, to prod him into the curriculum, if you like.

As with Aristotle and his fourth-graders, however, once he was there education of a quite different order could begin.

• • •

But what is the education that begins then? I have a theory that at any given time answers exist for all questions, but most of the answers are wrong. No doubt the troglodytes had their theories of matter, politics, and cosmogony, just as we do. And this is why the great secret of education is that it consists less in answering questions than in questioning answers. All knowledge begins with ignorance and doubt. Socrates began by admitting he knew nothing and thereby questioned traditional belief. Copernicus began by doubting Ptolemy and thereby began modern astronomy. As a teacher of those inexact sciences called the humanities, I find that skepticism is a far more desirable quality to foster in my students than certainty, let alone docility. For one thing, I know of no skeptics who have been guilty of mass murder. This is not because skeptics are morally superior to mass murders; it is just that skeptics can never be sure enough of a reason for killing large numbers of people. The great virtues of the skeptic are patience and tolerance. Both are good qualities for the pursuit of an education.

Yet skepticism is not merely an intellectual position; it is something besides a patient lack of certainty about what is real or true. It can also be lukewarm, easygoing, overly indulgent. This is skepticism's drawback. After all, not every mass murderer requires reasons of any sort. Some need only to do their job, and this they can do whether or not they are intellectually skeptical. In other words, I'm afraid one can be at once efficient and mindless, and this is surely one of the lessons of the twentieth century. Skepticism makes a good means, but an inadequate end.

Apropos, I'd like to tell you yet another academic anecdote, this time about a course in civil engineering.

Two-thirds of the way through his course, the professor gave his students an assignment to design the best death camp they could, carefully considering all the complex engineering problems of transporting people, guarding them, processing them, and disposing of them. He gave the students one week to complete the task and told them their grades would be heavily weighed. Seven days later he collected the designs from those who had completed them, piled them up on his desk, and announced that every student who had submitted a report in response to his assignment would receive a failing grade.

Outraged, the students protested that they had only done what they were told.

"Right!" cried the professor. "You have only proved that you are good at following orders."

My colleague's object lesson to his engineering students is also an example of what I mean by education being a process of questioning answers rather than answering questions. The latter is too often merely a way of following orders.

• • •

In any case, students certainly do not arrive at the university bereft of answers; on the contrary, they come with lots of them. One of the most common all-purpose answers begins with these words: "Society tells us that . . ."

It is wonderfully convenient to blame things on Society; however, I think it is important to make students aware that society—if such a thing really exists—is always telling us contradictory things. "Obey the rules and be independent . . . don't be prejudiced and stick to your own kind . . . think for yourself and do as I say . . . be well-rounded and learn a trade. . . ." Some of the problems we run into when thinking about education are due to just such contradictions in the messages our culture likes to blink at us.

The way we think and feel about education does not exist unrelated to our thoughts about other matters. For example, how we stand on education will depend on how we think about children and, historically at least, how we feel about nature.

As people of the late twentieth century, we are heirs to two distinct and completely different ways of thinking about these things. The first, and older, view is the one that gave us a word for education that is derived from animal husbandry. In this view, born at a time when technology was crude and cities rare, nature is deemed to be something alien, a threat, or, for certain Judeo-Christian writers, something downright evil. What had to be done with nature was fundamentally to overcome it, to scratch out a corner of civilization from the wilderness that threatens not only from the outside with its storms, wild beasts, and barbarians, but also from within, through our own bestiality, our own nostalgia for the lawlessness of the jungle and the treetops. The very word "civilization" itself suggests this meaning: that a truly human life can only be lived within the walls of an Athens, a Rome, a Jerusalem. In this view, nature and humans by nature are amoral, brutish, and selfish, while the condition of living naturally is one of universal war, as in a western town with no marshal and no school teachers.

The view we take of children has always been conditioned by the one we take of nature, for the reason that children are believed to be closer to nature than are adults. The distance between them is essentially that provided by education.

Given the views of nature and civilization I just outlined, it isn't difficult to figure out what sort of educational theory follows. If nature is brutal, then savages are not noble and children are no more than undersized savages. As the first settlers of New England regarded the Indians as dark men of the wilderness and fought them to the point of annihilation or assimilation, so they regarded their children as uncivilized barbarians needing to be fashioned into suitably disciplined, repressed, and productive adults as soon as possible. We can see this in the Puritans' family portraits, in which

children are depicted precisely as little grown-ups, with the same
black clothes and the same Puritanically serious faces as their elders.
Something like this view of things lies behind traditional opinions
about education. The public high school I attended in the sixties, for
instance, locked its doors from the outside at 8:20 each morning and
employed a hulking vice-principal who fulfilled exactly the same
function in the school as a bouncer does in a nightclub.

And yet our culture has also something quite different to say to
us on the subjects of nature, childhood, and education. Somewhere
around the end of the eighteenth century, coincident with the Industrial, American, and French Revolutions, a wholly new set of ideas
on these matters arose. Jean-Jacques Rousseau had the most to do
with articulating these views, perhaps because he knew both the
urban corruption of Paris and the rural virtue of sturdy Swiss farm-
ers, Madame Du Barry and Heidi. In any case, Rousseau held pretty
much the opposite of the traditional view. He believed that people
are naturally good, sympathetic, even loving, and that all the really
bad things in the world are consequently the result of the corruption
wrought by civilization itself. Now if this is true, then savages are
indeed more noble than the greedy fellows shooting at them with
blunderbusses; and children, so far from needing to be whipped into
little adults, are fine as they are, innocent and sweet. In fact, it isn't
children who should be more like adults, but adults who need to be
more like children.

So childhood was invented. In place of the stern Puritan homun-
culi, we now find paintings of children in a world of childhood. And
nature, as soon as the Industrial Revolution stopped us living in the
middle of it, became something precious, something to be conserved
and visited—in ourselves no less than in the Rocky Mountains.

In this view, civilization, so far from being the necessary repressor
of bestiality, merely masks our natural goodness with its predeter-
mined curricula, interminable tests, and endless disciplines, just as
it does with its oil spills. And so was born progressive education, in
which children are permitted to do more or less as they like, in their
own good time, and, as much as possible, in their own ways.

So we have two views, what we might call the Maybelline school

of thought versus the Ivory Soap school. The first tells us that goodness, like beauty, comes only from covering nature over with social
artifice, that we are what society makes us up to be; the second tells
us that goodness and beauty come only from what is natural and
that social artifice is not glamorous but tends to clog up our pores,
morally speaking.

But we haven't yet reached the end of our contradictions; for we
also have inherited two contradictory views of the purpose of education, going all the way back to the disputes between Socrates and
the Sophists in the marketplace of fifth-century Athens.

Fundamentally, the Socratic position is that there exists a set of
absolute truths, that the purpose of education is to strive to know
them, and that through knowing these things we become better in
our souls. Out of self-interest, if not conviction, this has become
today the doctrine of those arguing for compulsory general or liberal
education.

The Sophists, however, were relativists, holding that there exist
no absolute truths of any sort. Their position is that education is a
matter of learning whatever skills are necessary for making it in one's
society—slick oratory in their day, computer science or business administration in our own.

And so, to go along with our two diametrically opposed views of
nature, childhood, and education, we have two contrasting ideas
about the purpose of learning: what we might call knowing versus
earning, or learning aimed at becoming something versus learning
aimed at having something.

With such a crowd of jostling ideas before you, perhaps you can
appreciate why I encourage a degree of skepticism in my students.
There are too many good and bad points to be found at either extreme
wholly to dismiss or accept the one or the other. Moreover, I have
now lived long enough to watch the pendulum swing once and, with
proper diet and exercise, I expect to see it swing again. But these
swings are not futile; they are frequently correctives, expressions of
political will and, occasionally, of common sense.

We can conclude then that education is neither prodding nor nurturing; it is both prodding and nurturing. It is not either the acquisi-
tion of marketable skills or becoming something grander and deeper

through knowing eternal verities; it is both, or it is much less than it could be. Nor are students either obstinate and intractable savages or heaven-sent, innately wise cherubs; yet education must contrive to take account of them as both. As for those of us who presume to teach, if we do not do so with respect for our students we are not teachers at all, but mere virtuosos and confidence artists. Having everything and being nothing is as bad as knowing everything and being helpless. The purpose of education is not to lead forth cattle into some treacherous pasture called the real world, but to develop inchoate talent and nurture individual potential; not to make disciples, but to produce independent and fully human beings.

• • •

To those of you who are still awake, my sincere thanks for your attention. To those of you who are not, pleasant dreams. And to those of you hovering in between, I believe more coffee is available.

On the Law of Supply and Demand

When I was a sophomore, I ambled through the two-semester economics course offered to undergraduates by the Wharton School of Commerce and Finance of the University of Pennsylvania, dead center of capitalism, Ground Zero as we called the place in those apocalyptic Cold War days. It would be a pleasure to report that the economics course made my fortune, but that would be stretching a point. Anyhow, I had no mercenary motive in signing on as the token liberal arts major in Economics 101–102. I don't suppose that my professors had any intention of making me wealthy either, though their own motives in teaching economics were certainly financial in part, and those of my classmates for studying it appeared to be undividedly so.

Ezra Pound, who also went to Penn, was incorrect—or at least no longer right—in his definition of a professor as someone who has to talk for an hour. Professors only have to talk for fifty minutes. Leaving aside the three unintelligible section men for whom English was not yet a second language, I had two economics professors and neither had any difficulty filling up his allotted time; moreover, both seemed to like what they heard. They were jolly men, possessed by an unbounded enthusiasm for a discipline which, so far as I could see, they believed to be anything but a dismal science. Not only were they cheerful, but they spoke as if they had the inside dope on reality. And, since one of them would occasionally miss a lecture because he was down in Washington telling the Federal Reserve Board what to do, who was I to doubt? Well, being a dilettante, I did doubt. I approached the study of economics earnestly enough, to be sure, but I did so in the same spirit with which I sampled Greek and dabbled in Religious Thought. I meant to be generally educated and let the chips fall where they might. I suppose you could say I was gathering metaphors.

Between them, my two professors taught me three great laws that year, and in this order: the Law of Supply and Demand, the Law of Comparative Advantage, and the Law of Marginal Utility. This was even more metaphor than I had hoped for.

The law of comparative advantage was, so to speak, the Aphrodite of the trio and, had I been Prince Paris, would have had my apple, hands down. So beautiful and seductive is this law, so perfect of feature and symmetrical of limb, that I was dazzled at first sight. It was while contemplating the law of comparative advantage that I experienced, for the only time in my life, some measure of that *furor numerum* of which mathematicians speak with faraway looks, as though gazing beatifically on an elegant Pythagorean god.

Nevertheless, I got over my initial enthusiasm and gradually began to realize that this gorgeous law has in fact almost nothing to do with reality. It is beautiful and serene, but also translunar, or at least nonterrestrial.

According to the law of comparative advantage, it will pay a country to import all of what another country is able to manufacture, grow, or process at a comparatively lower price than it can. In other words, if Italy can produce evening pumps for two cents less a pair than can the United States, we should stop making any evening pumps and buy them all from the Italians. The law proves this mathematically and is therefore as irrefutable as the rules governing ideal gasses and parallelograms. But, so what if the Japanese can build cars better and cheaper than Detroit, or Germans can make steel more efficiently than Pittsburgh? As I thought at the time: nobody's about to suggest dismantling General Motors or shutting down United States Steel. On the contrary. If we were to be governed by this law, the United States would soon produce nothing but soybeans and Big Macs. Thus I concluded that this law's beauty was meant for the endless vacuum of space where the moist reality of earth could not confuse its pure outlines. We have its refutation embodied in no less impressive a figure than Lee Iacocca.

While the law of comparative advantage stunned me at once with its celestial radiance, the law of marginal utility puzzled me and gave me a headache from the inside out. I responded to it as I still do to certain passages in T. S. Eliot—understanding at one instant only to have this understanding drain away in the next, leaving no residue whatever.

Nearly as I can recall, marginal utility is a measure by which prices are determined. The utility, or desirability, of an extra unit of water, for example, when you are no longer either thirsty or dirty, is so low that, fortunately, water is cheap. As I say, this was pure metaphysical poetry, simultaneously precise, analytical, and farfetched. I suppose the law was just too much for me, albeit I was prepared to swear on the exam that diamonds are indeed worth more than water, even in the face of my knowledge that everybody needs extra water and scarcely anybody except Elizabeth Taylor needs extra diamonds.

This leaves the homely old law of supply and demand, the very first subject of the very first lecture, rudiment of rudiments. Still, it turned out to be the most useful metaphor I learned in my study of economics, though neither as elegant as comparative advantage nor as intricate as marginal utility. I'll bet teaching it wasn't easy either, especially for a man fresh from telling the Federal Reserve what was what.

Nevertheless, my professor was a man who grasped the importance of the fundamentals. He was like a triple-A baseball coach explaining for the thousandth time how to lay a bunt down third. He had to present this law to us wisely, knowing that if he were not careful we would ignore what he had to say. After all, if we didn't know about *this* stuff, then we would hardly have gotten as far as we had.

To some extent we were right to yawn through that first lecture. Like the minor leaguers, we knew all about laying down bunts. But this is just the point at which knowledge becomes dangerous, as Alexander Pope once and for all laid down. What we knew could prevent us from learning what we didn't yet know. Or, to put it another and more apropos way, our demand for knowledge fell considerably short of the supply—an endemic classroom situation, in fact.

But we sophomores weren't utter fools. We knew that an excess of supply lowers prices while too much demand raises them. We even knew vice versa. We were, in fact, perfect exemplars of the anonymous epigraph to the chapter on supply and demand in Paul R. Samuelson's famous and immensely lucrative textbook on economics: "You can make even a parrot into a learned political economist—all he must learn are the two words 'Supply and Demand.'" No matter that these are really three words; we knew them inside and out.

However, which of us novices suspected that, as Samuelson declares, "The basic problem of For Whom is the process by which the money votes themselves get determined, which is primarily not by supply and demand in a single good's market but by supply and demand in the labor, land, and other independent factor markets of Part Four"?

All the same, the conditions and provisos of an imperfect world that, for me, had propelled the law of comparative advantage into the blackness of outer space did not at all corrode the iron law of supply and demand. As the attentive reader will have noted in the passage I just quoted from Samuelson, such things merely confirm the law's authority. Those quirky "independent factor markets" likewise run by supply and demand. What doesn't?

The idea is pretty simple. The law works everywhere, like math or music. The complications of reality make only for a sort of accretion, revealing how—if one is but daring enough to follow the trajectory of economic thought—supply and demand govern everything. At any rate, they would, if only we let things alone for a week or two. And that is what I was taught as a sophomore.

But what does this "governing" of things really come down to? Well, first off, the law of supply and demand, despite all the illustrative charts and diagrams which littered our textbook and the professor's blackboard, is ultimately more qualitative than quantitative in the sense that it is supposed to determine *values*.

Now this was a genuinely interesting realization for me. Only the semester before I had taken a course called Ethics which was openly— even shamelessly—preoccupied with values, and yet nobody had so much as alluded to the law of supply and demand. Perhaps this was why my two professors of economics seemed to come out of such a different kettle of fish from the ones who professed philosophy. The philosophers were dour and speculated; the economists were jovial and knew. The proof of this was that the former had to apply for rare and ascetic sabbaticals, while the latter were perpetually being hired as consultants and took fantastically remunerative leaves of absence. Who was worth more? All one had to do was to check out who was in greater demand, of course. What could be more indisputable? How delightful it must have been for the economists to be in such demand, particularly by the government, so delightful that they weren't even arrogant about it. To look at them in those ante-post-Keynesian days one would never suspect they could be charged with hubris; just as to look at the government in those days of the Johnsonian wars on poverty and Asia, one would never think a time like the eighties might arrive when the supply of government could wildly outstrip the voters' demand for it.

Here, I thought at the time, is the eloquence of simplicity; here is the way of the world in the shell of a nut. What couldn't such a law explain?

I recalled an anecdote. The novelist Thomas Wolfe was once asked by an eager student what he ought to write to become successful. Wolfe replied, ''Write a masterpiece. There's always a market for them!'' And there's supply and demand in the arts—the joke, of course, turning on the scarcity in the supply of masterpieces and the inexhaustibility of the demand for them. Little matter that a moment later I realized it scarcely follows that whatever is in demand is therefore a masterpiece. Or that a moment after *that* I recollected at least a dozen examples of masterpieces nobody at all had demanded until those who actually produced them were good and dead. Unwilling to surrender my new enthusiasm, I concluded like a good economist that supply and demand still governed in the long run, or I would never have heard of those masterpieces. You can't pick up a Van Gogh for five bucks these days.

I began to consider that even those factors which most meddle with the law merely confirm it; I mean things like deceptive advertising and socialism. After all, I said to myself, what is advertising but the attempt to tickle the law or socialism but the effort to propitiate it?

No doubt it was true, as I had been told, that the minimum wage indeed disrupted the pristine purity of the labor market, but I countered with the reflection that the minimum-wage law was supplied by legislators only because enough voters demanded it.

So, I was enraptured: demand summons up supply; supply heightens demand. The very neatness of this antithetical sentence structure gives one assurance. Even the historians with their theory of the crisis of rising expectations bow to the law. What I take that theory to be saying is that a moderate supply of reform will lead to an irresistible demand for revolution. Dictators ought to be advised.

Supply and demand are not anarchists; they are merely unruly democrats.

Not only outward events, but even our inmost states of soul could be understood with a new clarity by applying the law. In one sterling passage of my textbook, for example, I found Samuelson inadvertently defining human contentment in his inimitable fashion: "equilibrium can take place only at a price where the quantities supplied and demanded are equal." That is so very much more lucid than what the fuddled old Stoics and Epicureans respectively tagged *apatheia* and *ataraxia*. It is also a good deal more positive in tone, though it means pretty much the same thing. Demand not pleasures the world cannot supply. Live only where thy supply curve crosses with thy demand curve and thou shalt go happily.

Power over ourselves is much the same: the capacity to supply adrenalin, enzymes, eloquence, endorfins, faith, or sexual energy upon demand. What is called self-discipline is nothing more than the ability to demand up to the point at which we are no longer able to supply, to cease demanding as soon as the supply curve is crossed.

Certainly all of elective politics can be boiled down to supply and demand, I thought. The electorate demands this or that; the candidates invariably promise to supply it. Nothing is simpler. Even death is only a sort of biologically final equilibrium between the supply and demand curves of our existence: the body ceases to demand anything at all and the environment agrees to cut off supplies. Or vice versa. As the heart monitor settles into a flat horizon, supply and demand cross at the zero point. Fini. Kaput.

• • •

Well, sophomoric indeed are such metaphoric games. But it is well to recall that only half of the appeal of a metaphor lies with its rightness—the other half reclines in its wrongness. When we say of a courageous man that he has the heart of a lion, for example, we're telling a truth and a falsehood about him at the same time. To make the laws of economics a metaphoric skeleton key to reality may not be so bad a game in itself; however, one must always remember that one has to do with metaphors and not take the game too seriously.

When the temptation to do so is great, it is good to recall such an old saying as this one from the forgotten philosopher Xenophanes:

> No man knows, or ever will know, the truth about the gods and about everything I speak of: for even if one chanced to say the complete truth, yet oneself knows it not; but seeming is wrought over all things.

It certainly *seems* as if the law of supply and demand can be wrought over all sorts of things, that it can really "define values," and even that nothing else can. But is this really the case? Would it be quite meaningless to inquire if to supply a thing is good, even when it is being demanded? Or if to demand a thing is wise no matter how plentiful the supply? If my six-year-old daughter screams for dry martinis, should I supply them, even if I am well stocked with gin and vermouth? Is it prudent for me to demand that my backyard be laced with toxic waste just because there's so much of it around?

In fact, is there not some mystery even in the marketplace? After all, demands do not always arise sensibly, much less rationally or predictably; nor do needs, on which demands may or may not be based, just as the spirit takes them.

Looked at from the standpoint of motivation in general and desire in particular—for which the psychologists, of course, have their own metaphoric laws—supply and demand begin to appear less like the key and more like the lock. Even so simple and so sure a mechanism as the law of supply and demand can break down when fed with human irrationality.

A trivial example of just such a breakdown was provided some years ago when a young New Yorker advertised in the *Times* his willingness to walk dogs in Central Park for a fee of five dollars per day. After running his ad for a week he had no takers. Yet the young man had apparently not studied economics. Perhaps he had been reading Dostoyevsky or Nietzsche. Thus, instead of concluding that there existed no demand for his service, or, with equal economic logic, that his price must be too high, he took out a new ad charging five times as much for the same service. In only a few days he had more work than he could handle.

The system, in short, can be very screwy, as screwy as the perturbed spheres of Ptolemy. I even remember a bizarre announcement made by the Ford Motor Company during the very year in which I was studying economics at the Wharton School. General Motors had recently announced price riseś for its new models. With what I presume was a straight face, Ford's spokesperson announced to the press that his company would likewise be raising its prices "in order to keep pace with competition." And yet we went right on taking notes.

Of course the sophomoric game I played years ago was not an original one. Others had played it, and far more earnestly. Consider the following remarks of Simon Newcomb, an astronomer of the last century who, like me, was bitten by the flea of supply and demand and proceeded to go a little off his scientific nut:

> Let us take up the familiar case of a beggar. A gentleman is implored for relief by a repulsive piece of humanity, enshrouded by rags and covered with dirt. Moved by pity, he gives him a dime and passes on. What is the economical nature of this transaction? We reply that the transaction is one of supply and demand, belonging to the same class as the supply of, and the demand for, personal services. The combined willingness and ability of a number of persons in the community to give dimes to beggars constitutes a demand for beggary just as much as if an advertisement reading "Beggars wanted, liberal alms guaranteed" were conspicuously inserted in the columns of a newspaper.

Newcomb is, I have to admit, ingenious, but nonetheless silly. Yet Newcomb has a contemporary disciple, an economist so respectable that he works out of the University of Chicago, just as Milton Friedman used to. Gary Becker has received prizes and is credited with founding a new branch of economics he somewhat suggestively calls "Human Capital."

Becker is a bold, clever, and obsessed thinker. In the manner of Newcomb on beggary he has analyzed such diverse transactions as crime and punishment, fertility, even suicide. In short, Becker is a man who believes that in the laws of economics we possess a general theory of human action. Those who object to his Grand Unified Field Theory he stoutly dismisses as soft-brained or closeminded reactionaries trying to protect their vested interests in the obsolete—or, as some still call them, liberal—arts.

What I came as an economics student to see as a metaphoric game is essentially Becker's fascinating program of research. Here, for instance, is Becker on the related problems of dating, marriage, infidelity, and divorce, all of which he disposes of with a really breathtaking brevity and neatness:

> Participants in marriage markets are assumed to have limited information about the utility they can expect with potential mates, mainly because of limited information about the traits of these mates. If they could search as cheaply for other mates when married as when single, and if marriages could be terminated without significant cost, they would marry the first reasonable mate encountered, knowing they would gain from even a less-than-optimal marriage. They would then continue to search while married.
>
> Since, however, marriage does limit access to single persons, and termination can be costly chiefly because of children and other investments specific to a particular marriage, participants usually do not immediately marry the first reasonable prospect encountered, but try to learn about them and search for better prospects.

The author of this penetrating analysis is said to have expanded his field. Indeed, he is given prizes for it, which is fine by me because I happen to relish irony.

What is the irony? Simply that what appears to be expansionism is in fact reductionism. Indeed, this is exactly what reductionism in general is: the imperialistic expansion of small insights into omniscient theories, the making of an iron filing into a skeleton key. Becker has invented a deterministic game of which he is, ipso facto, the chief superstar.

It is fun, after all, to make a game of life. It is this popular ludenic sense of things that has made of the late Vince Lombardi our most frequently cited ethical philosopher. But games are played on arbitrarily circumscribed playing fields, like football, or on narrow boards, like Trivial Pursuit. Games have rules that determine and limit the range of behaviors. Life, it seems to me, is not similarly limited. Life is not determined; determinism is only a theory about life. Ultimately, it is a game theory.

The critic Erich Heller once described the deterministic theories of Oswald Spengler, author of *The Decline of the West*, as "correct but untrue." Heller's is a liberating and useful distinction to put beside Becker's economic analyses, or any other form of determinism; for we live in a world where much is correct but little is true and where, for all I know, the demand for correctness may greatly outstrip the demand for truth. I suspect this demand may be in part to blame for summoning up the burgeoning supply of those high-tech marvels called "correct data" or, better still, "true facts," without noticeably bidding up the price of the wisdom needed to sift through them.

But the grander point I wish to make is that the folk of each era entertain favorite forms of reductionism no less than preferred styles of evening dress. Every generation likes to boil things down. In our own times, a fresh insight in economics or sociology is apt to be treated as if it were an all-explaining finding of the physicists; for the social sciences, being inveterately insecure, are inordinately fond of their surname. There is perhaps a wish on their part to emulate the precise and fatal pattern of the physical sciences as observation leads to prediction and prediction to control—and all according to what are metaphorically called "laws."

One of my own reductionist principles is this: whenever you have trouble understanding somebody's behavior, pretend they are six years old. We all know how six-year-olds think of a new toy. Just so, there are always those who get carried away by the excitement of brand-new findings and believe the novelty will account for everything, whether it is Pavlov's slavering dogs, the arithmetic altruism of mud ants, or the spiralling structure of DNA.

But it is economic reductionism that seems to be particularly popular at the moment; and, paradoxically, it is especially persuasive because this is a time when nobody can really explain the economy to anybody else's satisfaction.

In our frustration we turned back to the most rudimentary metaphors of capitalism. The "laws" of Adam Smith, Ebeneezer Scrooge, and Calvin Coolidge made a remarkable comeback at the beginning of the eighties. We have David Stockman to tell us that this resurgence had nothing to do with any actual understanding of economics. Perhaps then the explanation is this. At the end of the seventies, with their intermittent gas shortages, appeals for sacrifices, and wild inflation, it was a profound relief to think that individual selfishness would lawfully lead to collective welfare.

The eighties gave us two new, and not unrelated, stereotypes: the Homeless Person and the Yuppie. Moral responsibility is a fearful strain, and for most people the chief proof that they are being moral is that they are feeling uncomfortable. It really is a relief to surrender to such authoritative comforters as the law of supply and demand, Invisible Hands, and even the apocalyptic Malthusian calculus.

In G. B. Shaw's *Man and Superman* a character recalls the dreadful words Dante had inscribed over the Gates of Hell: ''Abandon hope all ye who enter here!'' ''Just think what a relief,'' the character observes. He is, of course, a yuppie.

That the laws of economics may be entirely correct and nevertheless untrue is, in the present climate, the opinion of a spoilsport, curmudgeonly at best, anti-intellectual at worst. Curmudgeonly too is the opinion that reductionism in any of its avatars—from economic to behaviorist to socio-biological—will never lose either its popularity or its untruth.

To reduce the tangle of human behavior, whether to that of rats in a box, the preprogrammed business of the hymenoptera, or that of a prudential homo economicus, will be perpetually appealing *because* it reduces; while to do so will be untrue so long as there is something *to* reduce. After all, ever since Plato, no devoted theorist has had much affection for human freedom. It is altogether too messy. In a word, freedom is unlawful.

Meanwhile, while there remains something to reduce, we can all reflect on Professor Samuelson's poignant depiction of the tragic complexities and doomed aspirations of the human condition as I found it inscribed twenty years ago in my Economics textbook:

> This limitation on our ability to experiment empirically . . . makes
> it all the more important to be clear in our logical thinking, so that

we may hope to recognize and evaluate important tendencies—such as the effect of P on Q demanded—when other tendencies are likely to be impinging on the situation at the same time.

• • •

Note: I am indebted in this essay to David Warsh's article "Gary Becker, Modern Pioneer," *Boston Globe*, August 25, 1985.

Not Being Earnest: A Lecture

Not long ago I was faced with the prospect of lecturing on Oscar Wilde's *The Importance of Being Earnest*. Now, tragedy is a dignified subject on which to lecture; indeed, lectures almost precisely resemble tragic dramas. But what of comedy? Either the subject evaporates, leaving the lecturer with nothing but his pomposity by way of fig leaf, or, worse yet, the lecturer will foolishly attempt to match wits with Aristophanes and Congreve. Coupled with the clumsiness of my notes and the effervescence of Wilde's play, these daunting ruminations gave me an odd notion: what if I were to pretend to *be* Oscar Wilde? Absurd as it was, the idea wouldn't go away; for if to lecture *on* Wilde promised to be very dull, to lecture *as* Wilde presented itself as a positive liberation, as a completely fitting pedagogical masquerade.

My classes had just finished a week on Henrik Ibsen's *Ghosts* as an illustration of modern tragedy and, before that, we had examined three classical texts, *Antigone, Iphigenia in Aulis,* and *Lysistrata.* Why not have Wilde wind up the unit by giving his views on modern comedy in general and his own play in particular? In the end, it was irresistible.

And so, two days later, I commenced my lecture by explaining my intention to my startled students:

• • •

My inspiration for taking this unusual approach (I said) is the chief theme of Wilde's play, *The Importance of Being Earnest.* This theme is presented succinctly in any number of places but I think Gwendolen puts it best when she remarks: "In matters of grave importance style, not sincerity, is the vital thing." Very well then, I shall be speaking today with as much style as I can, but with absolutely no sincerity— a trait which as invariably spoils the effect of a lecture as it does of a love letter.

To begin with, as I am now Oscar Wilde, let me dispose of my biography as quickly as possible. Biographies of talented people are both irrelevant and trivial, since they merely tell the truth. I owe to my Irish birth my capacity to please others with words, but it is to my emigration from Ireland that I owe the opportunity to use that talent to make money. During my heyday in the 1880s I was the most popular man in London and, I might add, the only imaginatively dressed one. The aristocracy took to me because they instinctively understood how devotedly I took to them. My own form of Bunburying unfortunately came to light during a rather famous court case. A stodgy old hypocrite, a sort of superannuated pugilist, publicly accused me of engaging in certain forbidden practices with his charming, if unreliable, young son, Lord Alfred Douglas. Well, the respectable society I had been doing my utmost to outrage and delight for a decade had its revenge upon me, of course—perhaps more for the delight than for the outrage. In any event, I was sent to prison, then went into exile. The editors of your singularly ugly textbook have the temerity to say that I "died miserably in Paris." But I would like to ask those good professors of literature if there is any *other* way to die—especially in Paris! Surely the important thing is not how one dies, or even where, but how one has lived. And as for my living, well, I accomplished that very much on my own terms. And it is those terms that I intend to reveal to you today.

• • •

Now, it is my understanding that you have just finished studying a three-act play by a contemporary of mine, that frequently stuffy Viking Henrik Ibsen. The chief merit of *Ghosts* is that the first London production was censored on grounds of obscenity. Except for this redeeming fact, which pleases me as much as any shock to public decency, I cannot say that there is one thing in the play itself of which I approve. Moreover, Ibsen's barber ought to have been shot and his tailor (if he had one) drawn and quartered. Really, he was a most unnecessarily frightful looking man.

The two most objectionable things about *Ghosts* are these: first, that Ibsen has written so as to conceal his art, and second, that the play does its utmost to be a tragedy. Well, my friends, art ought never to conceal itself, as if it were a thing of which to be ashamed. Indeed, if art were meant to conceal itself, then we should all be walking about stark naked. Clothes, which do indeed make the man, are an essential form of art; and this reflection teaches us that it is

properly nature which ought to be concealed, particularly in the
cooler nations, such as, for example, Norway. And as for tragedy, it
is a genre which I confess I cannot abide and one, moreover, which
is wholly unsuited to modern life. Tragedy depicts the ways in which
nature defeats art—that is, the way life destroys intelligence, order,
and imagination. Mrs. Alving's plans, the sensible policies of Creon,
the grand ambitions of Agamemnon: all these fine and artistic things
are reduced to ruin, to a very inartistic and inhuman mess, by tragedy. As any fool can see, tragedy is annoyingly concerned with the
truth, and nothing excludes beauty—which is the sole proper aim of
art—more fatally than truth. It is obvious that art ought to have absolutely nothing to do with it.

Comedy, on the other hand, at which I personally excel, exalts
artificiality. It shows us the triumph of human contrivance. *Lysistrata*,
for example—a play very delightfully and precisely illustrated by my
friend Aubrey Beardsley—is one in which the entirely artificial plan
of a clever woman brings a war to an end. There is nothing either
truthful or moral about that play, of course. Aristophanes was a co-
median and so he understood that one cannot hope to eliminate war
by telling people that it is morally wrong to kill one another. So long
as anything is seen as evil, it will never lose its fascination. No, the
only way to eradicate war is by convincing people that it is at once
stupid and vulgar and by laughing it out of existence. So, comedy
shows us the triumph of contrivance and thus, unlike brutal and
inhuman tragedy, is highly civilized and wonderfully social. And
that is why it ends so happily, you see. Happiness, like a good bur-
gundy wine, is a product of civilized contrivance.

Laughter, as you must have observed by now, is a social activity,
like playing cards or lying. No one offers to laugh at the Grand
Canyon or at a sunset—both of which phenomena are, in my opinion,
grossly overestimated by vulgar people who enjoy being made to feel
insignificant. But laughter cannot exist without the sense of our own
superiority; in fact, at base, laughter is nothing *but* an expression of
superiority. Yet superiority is precisely the sensation that tragedy
aims to annihilate.

No, the most important things about life are not its tragic depths,
but its surfaces. A man who does not care about his manners is not

likely to care about anything else; and, take it from me, a woman who does not care passionately about her hair is a most trivial woman. It is our rules, forms, and styles alone that make life worth the living. In a properly conducted life, therefore, real emotion—such as that singularly grotesque display provided by Mrs. Alving at the end of Act Three of *Ghosts*—has no place. All sentimentality destroys good art: Shakespeare's sonnets will be eternally superior to the gushings of Rod McKuen or the sincere optimism of Edgar Guest.

It follows, incidentally, that the only class of people in which there lies any artistic interest is the elite, for aristocrats are the most artificial of people. The lower orders must exist, of course; they are a necessary evil, as they supply servants. The middle class insists upon existing, but such people are continuously concerned with inartistic things like naturalness, earnestness, sincerity, and, worst of all, profit; consequently, this class finds no place in my plays. Nor will you ever discover me doing what that misguided Norwegian did: striving for social reform by attacking the hypocritical morality of our great nation. I am a deal more patriotic than that! No, hypocrisy is the bloom on the cheek of existence; eliminate it and you are left with all thorns and no roses. Only revolutionaries are truly against hypocrisy and revolutionaries are vulgar people. I am sure that you noticed that in *my* play the social rules are all duly maintained. Lady Bracknell, though a dragon, must indeed be satisfied as to her son-in-law's income and family background. She is, after all, a good mother concerned for her daughter's happiness, which is better insured by money and position than by so fleeting a thing as infatuation

As a modern playwright, I did not hesitate in my choice of comedy. Of course, I lack many of the advantages of dear old Aristophanes. For one thing, I cannot write so frankly as he did if I wish to have the income I receive from having my plays produced—without being annoyed by that famous English censor, the man who denied quite a few pounds to Ibsen. Just as modern life does not support the poetical aspects even of tragedy, it does not permit those equally grand obscenities of comedy. And so I am reduced to painting miniatures; but I think I may justly say that my miniatures are objects of aesthetic perfection from which all meaning has been scrupulously eliminated. As a work of sheer beauty, *The Importance of Being Earnest* has no meaning whatsoever. For, you see, the most profound truth about beauty is that it is quite pointless.

Now it is true, as I believe you have learned, that all drama depends upon moving from concealment to revelation. Tragedy revels in its revelations, however, whereas comedy concentrates on its concealments. Moreover, tragedy, being moralistic to its bones, enjoys revealing what it deems to be important things, whereas comedy reveals only the most trivial and frivolous ones—trivial and frivolous, that is, only from the point of view of tragedy. Indeed, *The Importance of Being Earnest* is the best of my comedies because in it I have contrived a plot of impeccable frivolity and have created characters irreproachable in their profound triviality. Tragedy, whether ancient or modern, is hopelessly sentimental and emotional, as I have already said; but in my plays matters like love and death, intrude though they must, alas, are at least not taken seriously. Tragedy, lacking all sense of proportion and order, acts as if love, death, and duty were really significant things and ignores the truly serious matters in life, such as frock coats and watercress sandwiches.

It is certainly true that in our degraded modern world it is occasionally necessary to pretend to be earnest, as my two young men do; but the key thing in life is never actually to be earnest about such trivial matters as love and marriage. To do so is hopelessly middle class.

Now friend Ibsen and I do agree on one point: our hatred for the idiotic materialism of our age. But while Ibsen sought to attack that narrowness and even ended *Ghosts* with a vision of nature outside the window of his claustrophobic little parlor, *my* view is that this narrowness must not only be accepted but enjoyed—and the key to such enjoyment as is nowadays possible lies not in nature but in style and in style alone. My own style is epigrammatic and paradoxical. My contempt for commonness in every form led me to take common ideas, reverse them so as to make them more striking, and then to put them in the most polished and elegant of prose. After all, every common truth is vulgar, no less than every common suit of clothes. Each phrase spoken by Jack and Algernon and Cecily and Gwendolen is, I believe, quite memorable for the simple reason that I spent hours on each phrase to make it so. These people, you see, say nothing that they have not first rehearsed; they say little impetuously and nothing at all that is ordinary. The exclusion of sincerity, as you see, opens the door to wit, to the picturesque, to true distinction of expression. And so, my art does not "conceal itself" like Mr. Ibsen's, as your foolish textbook says. On the contrary, like all perfect things, my art is quite unashamed of itself.

Our one agreement notwithstanding, I dislike Ibsen because, at base, he is a betrayer of art. Art has only its own purposes and every attempt to impose other, non-artistic purposes upon it is a curse to art. Social reform, political propaganda, commercialism, realism and the like produce merely ugliness. Those mountains, those fjords! they are ugly because they are so profoundly inhuman.

I shall now explain why all this is so.

First off, as you must have noticed during the course of your young lives, the more you study art, the less you care for nature. Indeed, it is entirely proper to say that art is itself a protest against nature. And just why is this? Simply because nature hates mind. The products of the human mind—pre-eminently my own plays—reveal design, order, and good sense. In art everything is subordinated to us. In art, if nowhere else, we govern nature herself. Nature, however, is best characterized as that which is inimical to and destroys design, order, and sense.

All true artists know that the core of their art is not some so-called message or theme or subject. None of these matters in the least, except to the middle class, the censor, and the professors of literature—with none of whom we need concern ourselves either here or elsewhere. All that really counts is craftsmanship. *The Importance of Being Earnest* is the ideal illustration of this maxim, for in it I have created a play that is formally perfect but which manages to say virtually nothing. Thus it is not only beautiful, it is purely beautiful. It suffers from no alloy of meaning, no gross taint of emotion, no adulteration of theme . . . and it has no purpose at all.

Let us pursue these invigorating ideas a little further. By definition, art is unnatural. What is unnatural must be learned. Consequently, artists are made and not born. And what artists must learn is their craft or nothing. If artists were born and not made, then the origin of art would be in nature and that is palpably absurd. The source of the artificial can scarcely be the natural.

After a thorough knowledge of his craft, the next thing the artist requires is, as you might guess, imagination. The aesthetic lives on lying and concealment, not on revelation as Ibsen pretends in *Ghosts*. To be beautiful a woman will require a good deal of makeup. Indeed, I need hardly point out that were it not for concealing Oswald's disease, Regina's paternity, Mrs. Alving's past, the Captain's love affairs, and Manders's piddling love for Helen, Ibsen would have had no play at all.

Art and nature, then, are irreconcilable. And so are truth and beauty. The truth is demanded by morality, as one can see in those parodies of Ibsen plays called courtroom trials where everyone ritually swears to reveal the truth, the whole truth, and nothing but the truth (morality is fond of repetition). To be a moralist, like Mr. Ibsen, is to present things as they are. Well, how much imagination does that require? Why, none at all! The true artist, therefore, always presents things precisely as they are not. I feel certain that I have achieved this in my own play, for you may look high and low in London or Boston and never find such perfectly artificial creatures as Algernon and Cecily and Jack and Gwendolen.

Though I have great respect and considerable understanding of the Greeks—in so far as I, like you, was compelled to study them at a university—I must confess that on one essential point they were utterly in the wrong about art and life. You see, all the Greeks believed what that respectable and thoroughly middle-class gentleman Aristotle said—that art is made by *imitating life*. Nothing could be further from the truth! If this were indeed so, then the outside world would have to be artistic in itself—that is to say, well-ordered, lovely, and sensible. However, the merest brush with daily reality forces one to admit that the outside world is a mess and a hodgepodge. Whatever order and sense there are in our lives must be created inside our own minds. And this process of creation is called art.

No, my friends, it is *life that imitates art*. Some years ago I observed, for example, that the famous London fog did not exist until the French impressionist painters created it. Of course, there had been a certain mistiness in the London air before Monet exhibited his work;

however, no one had ever noticed it before. The artist literally teaches us how to look at the world, or at the very least how to look at fog. Moreover, if you will consider for a moment how you have become what you are, you will realize that you have become that way by imitating not life but artistic models. Children imitate what they see on television, adults what they read in books or observe on movie screens. Women make themselves up (a felicitous expression!) to look like the latest Hollywood model of what beauty is; their mates attempt to approximate the paragons of virility selected to appear in cologne commercials. Life consequently always lags behind art and is feverishly trying to catch up with the fashion. It is true that life is continuously seeking to express itself, but for this very reason it is inferior to art, which provides life's sole means for doing so.

I can see that you are still not quite convinced. Well, dear friends, let me tell you that things are never seen as they are; things are as we see them. Our minds are not passive photographic plates, but more or less brilliant projectors. Artistic images are the things we project; form is what we impose. The historian projects cause and effect upon the intrinsically meaningless events we read about in the daily papers, but the artist goes far beyond this and presents a vision of life as truly ordered and lovely, though, of course, it is completely a lie.

Now because beauty is a lie, it must follow that the only beautiful things are those that do not really concern us. Anything that genuinely concerns us has some other than artistic interest about it. In my play I have converted all such things—love, marriage, death, money, family—into mere pretexts for artistic treatment, as bodies are pretexts for the dance. Indeed, what is life itself but the sum of all such pretexts?

And now I shall tell you an academic secret. Here in your university you study not life but art. I do not refer simply to your course in literature. In your other courses you do not study life either; rather you study (assuming you get around to it) what scientists, sociologists, and psychologists have managed to make of life. Life is only a pretext even to the sociologist; though unfortunately, it is a pretext for sociology.

Life then is a pretext and art lives not on life but on artificiality.

At the risk of sounding a bit like Ibsen, I'll repeat myself: the most important thing to cultivate is style. And why is style the most essential thing of all? Because style is our barrier against both nature and life. Without such a defense we might actually be hurt by life, and to be hurt by life is more intolerable than to burp at a dinner party. It is plain bad manners to be hurt by anything; it is, in fact, a sign of poor breeding.

Now because true art is wholly a matter of style, as in my own play, it follows that it can never be a matter of fact. Facts are meaningless, brutal, and disorderly things; facts are very annoying things indeed—particularly on examinations. If one saw only the facts, one would see only meaninglessness. Facts can attain meaning and sense only through our capacity for arranging them imaginatively, like flowers in a vase. This is, once more, what historians are supposed to do . . . arrange the facts interestingly. It is a great pity that they so often fail to do so.

Well, to sum up thus far, what is art? The finest definition is this: quite simply, *art is lying for its own sake alone.*

Now that you understand what art is, you will see how inappropriate it is to judge art by any criterion alien to itself, such as its capacity for telling us the truth, its moral force, its obscenity, or its respectability. No, the sole basis on which art can be fairly judged is on the impression it makes.

The critic himself must be creative in recording his impressions. The role of the critic is not to tell us truths about works of art, you see, but to talk about art in an interesting fashion. His sole duty is not to be boring. Actually, it is my opinion that to be a good critic is much harder than to be a good artist. This is so for the simple reason that it is always easier to do a thing than to talk about it. Indeed, action of any kind is the last recourse of those who do not know how to dream. Action always has something natural about it; thus, to act is inherently inartistic. The man who merely acts makes himself nature's puppet; he loses all his self-consciousness by acting, whereas the man who describes an action does not for a moment lose his balance, his self-possession.

Critics, like artists, then, can only be judged upon their style. This would not be so if art were meant to express something. But, as we

know, all true art, such as my own, expresses nothing at all. It only
is. A diamond expresses nothing, and that is why it is universally
judged to be a beautiful and precious object. And this is precisely the
effect I strove for in my play: that of a perfectly cut diamond, self-
contained, hard, and dazzling in its brilliance.

Everyone knows that beauty is in the eye of the beholder, but few
are willing to admit that meaning and value are as well. In a sense,
my beautiful play does reveal something. Indeed, I believe it reveals
everything just because it expresses nothing. Nothing at all. It is
therefore quite unlimited in its meaning, like a matchless gem. Because, as true art, my play touches on nothing that really concerns
us, neither the crude facts of life nor the brute truths of nature, it is
at once perfectly pure and perfectly trivial. A moment's reflection
will show you that when a work of art means *any*thing it instantly
ceases to mean *every*thing.

Another point for you: given the vast superiority of the artificial
over the natural, it follows that sterile or false emotions are preferable
in every case to real ones. The wonderfully disinterested love of Algy
and Cecily or of Jack and Gwendolen cannot be compared with that
gross, virtually animalistic passion of Mrs. Alving's for poor Oswald . . . who was at least on his way to becoming an artist in Paris
before nature defeated him by way of a spirochete! How, after all,
can we defend ourselves against life's desire to tear us to pieces if we
submit to emotionalism? To care is to be lost, my friends. Personally, I
care only about my wardrobe and my supper.

By now some of you look as if you are feeling rather annoyed by
my ideas. This puckered look is an effect I have frequently noticed
among the public and one of which I am suitably proud. Well, here
is something else to pucker you. I have already said that true art can
have nothing to do with moral intention. That is so, and really to put
the matter more clearly I will say that *all art is immoral.* Not merely
amoral, mind you, but downright immoral. Who, after all, is more
moral and more inartistic than that horrid Pastor Manders? He is a
good example of what I personally find most nauseating in modern
life—to wit, moralism in all its guises, including, I might say, that of
Mr. Ibsen himself, who pretends to dislike Manders but has merely
reinvented him with a fresh set of dogmas.

Because art has no ulterior purposes, nothing to do beyond doing itself, it exists for its own sake and cannot lead to taking moral action. Art is immoral because it lives by concealing the rude facts of life in order to create beautiful illusions and witty impressions. Morality grimly insists on doing just the opposite and hence morality is invariably ugly in its self-expression.

All action, all doing, is vulgar. What could be more common and depressing than that inescapable cocktail-party question: "And what do you *do?*" Foolish people never ask what you *are;* wise ones needn't do so. Now my wonderful characters quite obviously don't do anything. Action is beneath them; they have servants to do things. But just look at what wonderfully graceful creatures they are! And so very accomplished too. For, you see, to do nothing at all is the most difficult and intellectual thing in the world.

And so, my friends, in art and in life form is everything, content nothing; saying nothing beautifully is infinitely to be preferred to saying something clumsily . . . which, in my experience, is exactly how people with a message always deliver it—people such as science lecturers and presidential candidates.

The people in my plays live by a rigid and disciplined code, and I am quite prepared to grant that it is not in the least a moral one. In this code the man who cannot do something is the best judge of it; imagination is invariably higher than fact, art better than life, style superior to truth, and at every point reality must be sacrificed to a good appearance. I am afraid Jack is less true to this code than Algernon, for Jack clumsily endeavors to act in the opposite fashion in his capacity as Gwendolen's guardian. However, I am glad to say that at least he fails in his attempt to appear moral, upstanding, and respectable. Nevertheless, even Algy, I confess, has to make his own little compromise with middle-class morality. There is his invalid friend Bunbury. And yet good old Algy at least raises hypocrisy to the level of a fine art . . . and better than that none of us can hope to do.

Always remember, then, that the really essential thing in life is not your position but your pose. Take the important things lightly and the light ones seriously. Strive with every ounce of your lying imaginations to do nothing, but to accomplish it with great style.

Thank you and good afternoon.

• • •

Note: Apart from Wilde's plays, the principal sources for this lecture are *Intentions* (London: Methuen, 1913), and *The Essays of Oscar Wilde* (New York: Bonibooks, 1935).

Chairness

You teach with what lies, so to speak, at hand. Funny what this can lead to in a classroom.

As part of a big unit on modernism, I began lecturing one day about cubism yet I wound up talking about chairs and that part of ourselves we set on them. I might think of it as the cubism class, but the students referred to it ever after as the chair lecture. Well, in a good class everybody stands to make discoveries, not excluding the teacher.

I started it all off with idealism, sketching the major elements of Platonic epistemology because, as I see it, the abstraction of modern art is idealistic. So, I separated form from matter, drawing a puddle of whiskey beside an empty glass. I explained that, for Plato, true reality is not found in the material world, in the puddle, all natural and man-made objects being mere imitations of a nonmaterial reality of pure forms or ideas—invisible empty glasses. Even at this preliminary stage chairs crept in. Looking for another example to which the students might relate, I observed that, Platonically speaking, the chairs on which they sat were imitations of a single ideal chair, the *idea of* a chair, which on the spot I dubbed "chairness." Everybody found this logism amusing. The students liked to repeat it. When they had calmed down I seized on this hint of interest: "If you see an object with a seat, two arms, four legs, and a back, you recognize it as a chair. Why? You understand the idea of chairness. So to Plato the chair was not invented but discovered. Like the rest of his pure ideas, chairness is perfect, universal, and eternal. It was there before we knew it, before we *were* . . . not only the perfect chair, but perfect justice, perfect love, perfect men and women. The best of us is just a reasonable facsimile."

This led to a brief digression on platonic love, of which all the students had—often to their chagrin—heard. "A union of souls and not bodies," I said.

"All quality and no quantity," one of the young men explained.

This digression prompted a few words from me about how influential idealism has been in Western culture, how it became Christianized, for example, or how Christianity became Platonized when Paul went to Greece and Augustine converted, how it is the root of much of our dualism and many of our characteristic neuroses.

I could see they were perplexed and also wondering what all this ancient philosophy had to do with modern art. At this point I removed idealism from the historical and psychological and moved it up an academic notch.

"Plato's world of ideas is really an intellectual world of abstractions. The best model we have of form without matter would be mathematics."

This, I could see, was worse than Christianity and neurosis. Regarding their darkened countenances, I sensed we were still in the Cave.

"Take 2 × 2 = 4." I wrote it on the board, not only for emphasis, but because I like writing things on the board. "This concept was not invented but discovered. It's nonmaterial and it's true everywhere and at all times. We write numbers on our little space telegrams, don't we, because they'll be true no matter who snags the probes or when. Numbers are forms without matter. You can't smell a 2."

The space example excited me and I returned to the board where I rapidly drew three different types of bridges: a suspension bridge, an arched bridge, and a causeway.

"Look," I said, though they already were looking, "there are thousands of bridges in the world, but all of them have to be engineered in accord with certain fixed laws of structural physics. These mathematical laws are pure and abstract, and they apply to all bridges. In effect, then, the laws are the real bridge. The Golden Gate and the Pont Neuf are, in this sense, merely material imitations of this invisible ideal bridge which is made up of mathematical relations rather than steel or concrete."

Three distinct "huh's" rang out, one for each bridge.

"Of course you don't get it," I said, "and neither do I. This is because we're not engineers. We non-engineers are ignorant of these physical laws, so naturally we take the imitation for the reality. In Plato's terms, that means we are deceived. We depend on our senses and not our minds. Reason sees the true nature of things, while our senses can easily be fooled and mistake appearance for reality, as in mirages or a good deal of social life."

"I don't see, Professor, what all this has to do with modern art—

or did you decide to change this into a philosophy course over the weekend?''

Fell right into my trap.

''Remember last week we talked about perspective, the craft of creating the appearance of three-dimensional space on a two-dimensional surface. This was the great discovery of the Renaissance artists and scientists, who were the same fellows. But what exactly *is* perspective? It's an illusion, of course. It's a trick played on our sense of sight. See? It's just as Plato said: our senses can be fooled, and only reason can present us with true reality either intellectually or morally. Your senses show you your chairs—but your mind reveals . . . ?''

''Chairness!'' came the bemused responsory.

''Forget chairness for a moment,'' one student requested. ''What did you mean about morality?''

This was a digression indeed, but by now I was going with the flow, which is to say with the electrical current of student interest.

''To the idealist truth is absolute and unchanging, like 2 × 2 = 4. True virtue, Plato held, doesn't lie in conforming to local customs or peer pressure, but in acting in accord with absolute, unchanging ideas of goodness and justice. Thou shalt not kill, for example, rather than when in Rome. You see?''

''He's back to religion,'' sighed one exasperated student to her neighbor.

''Well, try applying this to art, then. Can the truth of perception be found in an optical illusion like perspective?''

''But can't art tell the truth by lying?'' wondered a bright fellow with a good memory of something I had said on another occasion.

''Maybe for you or me or Oscar Wilde. Not for Plato.''

''Plato didn't *paint*, did he, Professor?''

''No, but Platonists *do*. In fact, that's what I've been leading up to. One line of modern art aimed at a Platonic reconstruction of space. These artists broke with the long tradition of illusory perspective; they emphasized the flatness of their canvases; they began to analyze objects and space itself into simple, essential forms—or truths. They made modern art look modern.''

I returned to the board and drew a distance runner in a jersey, shorts, shoes. The runner had long, wavy hair.

"Here's traditional art."

Then I drew a stick figure, also running.

"This is stylization."

Finally I drew a curved line, a sort of elongated S.

"And this is abstraction, which means literally to draw away from, in this case away from specifics to the essential form of running. Notice that in this analytic process the details go first—the local color, the ornamentation, all the relative, historical, accidental things like clothing, hair color, gender, age. What's progressively revealed is essential Platonic form, pure gesture. Ideal form is skeletal; in other words, form without flesh."

This burst of eloquence had an effect akin to, say, a bludgeon. The students and I stared at one another, except for a few of the more assiduous and nervous who were dutifully reproducing my cartoons in their notebooks. Looking at these rigid Dutch masters I suddenly had one of those expansive, connective ideas that occasionally visit a teacher who's been with his or her students a good long while.

I reminded them of two texts we had studied the month before, Tolstoy's *The Death of Ivan Ilych* and Kafka's *The Metamorphosis*.

"Tolstoy, the master of the realistic novel, is, you could say, still creating the illusion of perspective, of historical, physical, local actuality. With Ivan he tells the story of what happens to everybody. You may not want to believe his picture, but you couldn't fail to understand it. But Kafka breaks with perspective in his first sentence. He tells us the story of what has never happened to anyone, which, as I recall, gave you fits. Why did he do it? *The Metamorphosis* is every bit as universal as *Ivan Ilych*, for Kafka gives us the *essential* forms of professional, family, and spiritual life. But one thing he never gives us is the illusion of actuality. Ivan dies in Russia in the 1880s. Where and when does Gregor die? In eternity, you might as well say, while the world holds its breath. In the world of ideas. Kafka's story, you see, is like an abstract painting. It's the result of analysis. No loose flesh, just the naked truths of the skeleton, of the X ray."

It was like a presidential press conference. Mental flashbulbs went off all over the room. To be honest, it was an exhilarating moment. I heard the rewarding noises of anagnorisis.

After turning off the lights, I showed some slides of modern sculpture, architecture, furniture, a few Bauhaus utensils, and tried to explain that this same relentless pursuit of pure Platonic form, of basic structures, has given us much of the landscape of our lives, or at least the cityscapes. The students didn't care much for this notion.

"You mean we live in a world made up by Plato and Cézanne and Kafka?" groused one.

"Oh, come on," grumbled another.

"Well, think about it," I suggested. "Don't most modern buildings resemble airports or toaster ovens? Think about how Victorian furniture became modern. It lost its curves and softness, the very things you'd find in Ivan Ilych's overstuffed parlor. Modern rooms are more like Gregor's, with its bare walls and hard edges. Cubist paintings have led to cubist cities. Cézanne's landscapes look a lot like lower Manhattan. The architect Le Corbusier called a house 'a machine for living.' His colleague Mies van der Rohe said 'less is more.' These are the mottos of applied abstraction, of architectural idealism."

"Are you saying this is good or bad?" somebody asked.

"Both," I shot back, and formulated an answer inspired by the question which, to be honest, I had never before considered. "When you apply idealism to objects of use—or paintings, sculpture, even morality or religion—this zeal to seek out the absolute, perfect, essential forms of things has two faces. This goes for *any* kind of idealism. One face is good. You get rigorous, incorruptible honesty; you get simplicity, order, purity, even a kind of serenity. You get, in short, all the virtues of any idealism. You get all the purity and honesty that Ivan's conformist house and conformist life lacked, which makes sense since Tolstoy condemns him for being a materialist and a compromiser, a middleman."

"So what's bad about *that?*"

"It isn't bad. But it can *become* bad when you get too *much* honesty, too *much* simplification, too *much* purity. Take these virtues to excess and you always wind up with something intolerant, inhumane; you get bigotry, self-righteousness, and fanaticism—like Pol Pot in Cambodia. Remember *that?*''

"I don't get it," said one. "Too much goodness isn't good? Is *that* what you're saying?"

This is where the chairs reappeared.

"Take the desk chairs you're sitting on."

"You mean these *unreal* ones?" somebody wisecracked.

"They may not be real, but they're cheap, stamped out of heavy plastic, and serviceable. They're sturdy and uniform. But one thing they're definitely not is *comfortable.*"

The class was over forty minutes old so everyone had good reason to agree with me.

"Your chairs are designed for perfect rear ends, for the Platonic *idea* of a rear end, if you like, and they won't conform to anything else. They have no give in them. They're intolerant."

And here I picked up my own chair which, happily and unlike theirs, had a padded seat.

"Look," I said, and pushed down on the seat. "It's soft. It gives. It's user-friendly. It's forgiving. It's an Ivan Ilych chair. It compromises with all my . . . imperfections."

They laughed, of course. I did too, butt of my own joke, or vice versa.

This left me barely ten minutes to talk about Pablo Picasso's early career, to explain the end of absolutism and the rise of relativism, to point out the coincidence of *Les Demoiselles d'Avignon* and Albert Einstein's early papers, to argue that Picasso, like Kafka, teaches us about reality by leaving realism behind, to lay out the difference between imitating actuality and penetrating it, to note the demise of the omniscient narrator and the rise of multiple perspective.

I didn't come close, but as I rattled on I already knew that what the students would retain from all this was the electrifying concept of a Platonic rear end and the peculiar idea of chairness. I've had worse days.

On Faculty

The word faculty derives from a Latin noun, *facultas*, which, curiously, is feminine. In Latin, as in some other languages not yet dead or even noticeably ill, nouns have gender. Gender is what sex used to be termed only in grammar books but is now called in politically correct intercourse among faculties. It is instructive that in German, for instance, herring is masculine, bankruptcy feminine, while an unmarried woman is neuter. To the greedy Romans *facultas* signified such things as opportunity, capacity, mental or material resources. Upon being imported into English, however, the word took on several different and not always consistent meanings. Ours is a language rich in such confusions. For example, it is neither semantically nor psychologically meaningless to say that a faculty lacks all its faculties.

Time was when whole academic departments were simply called faculties—the faculty of Crypto-Thomistic Theology, say, or the faculty of Flesh Mortification. Nowadays a college prof is called a *member* of a faculty, leading to the arresting implication that faculties can be *dis*membered. As a rule, faculties possess more mental faculties than material ones, the stupendous rise in modern tuitions notwithstanding. Socrates, of course, never charged tuition, so it is a little surprising that he, rather than Protagoras, should be so revered by resentfully underpaid faculties the world over. Perhaps this is because Socrates went barefoot, admitted he didn't know anything, yet always got the better of well-heeled tuition-snaggers like Protagoras. Or maybe it is just irony, of which faculties, like Socrates himself, are uncommonly fond, as people generally are of consolations.

Faculties are seldom portrayed in the popular media (watched closely by many members of the faculty when nobody is looking); but at the beginning of the movie *Horsefeathers* Groucho Marx, playing a newly installed college president, tosses a nub of cigar down in front of his faculty and warns them not to jump for it all at once. Groucho was ahead of his time, managementwise, though he obviously wouldn't have done much to promote a smokefree workplace. Faculties used to be full of superb smokers. Indeed, as I charge my pipe I like to tell my own students that education and fumigation are essentially identical processes.

The quality of a university is not only regularly but piously said to depend on that of its faculty, though administrators have higher ceilings and salaries and, quantitatively at least, students ought really to count for *some*thing. Anyway, the better a faculty the less teaching it does. "Block that student!" as Professor Butley memorably advised. In fact, a nearsighted undergraduate attending a genuinely first-rate institution will never actually see a senior member of its faculty, a sure sign of first-rateness. Immunity from students is a decisive inducement in the recruiting of outstanding faculty. "I won't have to deal with," a slight gulp here, "*students*, will I?" "Oh, certainly not, Professor Optimus! A couple of appearances on campus each semester at the very most." Still, some faculty, quite against their own interests and operant conditioning, will inevitably become attached to teaching, even to students, frittering away valuable hours that should be devoted to the dissection of John Clare's prosody or the larvae of the crested newt. For this they must be forgiven, even if they cannot be heartily encouraged nor frequently tenured.

What Do You Write On?

It was one of those questions on which even stately or vivacious conversations can snag like a riverboat on a sandbar. A breathtakingly intelligent woman in the book trade asked it of me—but what did she mean? The context wasn't much help. We had been talking of writing in the most general and least compromising terms when she suddenly said it, "What do you write on?" For half an instant I thought she must mean what was my subject, what did I write *about*. It would have been flattering to be asked such a profoundly imponderable question, I think. But I saw at once that this wasn't it. After all, the woman had edited some of what I wrote. What did I write *on*?

In the kind of detail that betrays affection and not irony, I described my desk, a flat interior door held up, grad student style, by a couple of two-drawer file cabinets. The door is stained dark mahogany; the files are bright red; my blotter is green. This arrangement affords me, I went on like a Defense Department analyst, a writing surface of $6^{1}/_{2}$ by $2^{1}/_{2}$ feet, or just over sixteen square feet. It is lit by a lamp I made in ninth-grade woodshop. I have literally leaned on this desk and seen by this lamp for twenty years. That, I said, is what I write on.

She let me finish all this before beginning to laugh: "No, ha-ha, no." That isn't what I meant at all—just what J. Alfred Prufrock feared hearing; for when an intelligent woman laughs like that it is hard not to suppose she is laughing at you. My mind raced. Perhaps she meant the type of paper I favored (unlined Hammermill ditto bond). "No, I mean what do you write *on*—you know, *with*. My husband—he's a novelist—still uses an old manual."

"Oh," I said stupidly. Her husband was quaint and I was stupid.

She wanted to know specifically what sort of word processor I employed, what software inside what hardware. She was interested in, well, the means of production—than which, for a writer, no matter is more intimate—and did me the honor to suppose mine were state-of-the-art. Still, I couldn't help thinking, it's a little demeaning that the medium should arouse more curiosity than the message.

As it happens I don't use a word processor at all. I write important things with a fountain pen to begin with (my link to tradition), revise them in the same fashion, then type them up on a machine called a memory typewriter. My machine has a little more memory than a mayfly, but far less than, say, a trout—about eight thousand strokes which comes to roughly four pages of prose or a very short sonnet sequence.

Even though my typewriter is computerized, I have taken some abuse for what they deem archaic working methods from friends and colleagues who extol the virtues of the word processor with the zeal of reformed smokers or Jews for Jesus. Of course they are right. Progress is not only progressive; it is unavoidable. Sooner or later everybody needs to move an entire paragraph from one place to another. You can't do that with a memory typewriter, let alone a fountain pen. Certainly there's no question that retrieval and, above all, revision are made immeasurably easier by the word processor, once you figure out how to use it. Should I desire to revise a text with my obsolete tools I actually have to rewrite it, and the consequence is that I simply don't, except for the most compelling reasons, such as obvious factual errors, egregious misspellings, or potential libel suits.

All the same, I'm not sure I want to give up my disadvantages. My friend X., for example, mastered word-processing years ago. X. can turn out a dozen versions of the same tortured essay in the time it used to take him to write three or four different, albeit underrevised, ones. When X. was being particularly obnoxious about my fountain pen one day, I mentioned this disparity in his then/now productivity and went so far as to speculate that the ease of revision might have made him a wee bit sloppy to begin with. I am ashamed of saying this. It was a low blow, I know, but I was severely provoked. Insult my fountain pen and you insult me. No doubt I was only rationalizing my ignorance of the mysteries of Wordstar and the IBM keyboard. On the other hand, it's true that my golden nib connects me to my writing not only personally but sensually. I must form my letters by hand, just as I did in first grade; and, when I have formed them, they look quirky; they look, in every sense, handmade. Before I type, I try to be pretty sure that I've chosen the best words I can. My last revisions are made, in fact, in the typing itself. Perhaps perfectionism is a compensation for sloth.

What I am hinting at here is an idea I'm deeply ambivalent about:

that, where writing is concerned, the method determines the product. There is some evidence for this. For instance, I find I often write essays or stories in brief segments. I sometimes suspect these are prompted by my machine's niggardly powers of recollection. Also, the memory of my machine allows me to type relatively short items, such as letters, without the distraction of clacking keys or return buttons. Since I got this memory typewriter my letters have begun to flow like a river system in springtime, torrentially quick and riddled with divagations. Consider: poets who compose on word processors may tend playfully to rearrange their syntax, stanzas, and lines more than those who employed sharpened goose quills. It is possible that Ernest Hemingway's famous style is somehow tied in with his manual typewriter. Words beaten into the paper have a different weight from those sprayed on top of it. Already in bookstores I have begun to find volumes that appear more processed than written: bookoids. Fountain pens compel you to inscribe more deliberately than cheap ballpoints, just as hacking words into granite tablets naturally encourages a lapidary style.

Anyway, this is one side of the case. The other is that, where serious writing in concerned, the product transcends the means of production—and this is one way we know it is serious writing. I neither know nor care whether William Faulkner typed or used a headlong scrawl; more worthwhile to know that he used bourbon. It is also less interesting to know whether Schiller wrote a slovenly or an elegant hand than to be aware that to compose at full power he needed the scent of rotting apples. Real writing is a human activity, not a technical one.

More advanced technology does not improve the standard of prose. Nearly all my freshmen come to school equipped with fancy machines that they blindly believe will correct their errors automatically. But the computers, like the students, are baffled by the simplest of homonyms (it's/its *or* there/their/they're). Astonishing typographical errors get through as well, such as that of the student who wrote, "The Supreme Court decision in the case of Schemp v. Abington Township created virtually no pubic response." ("I'll bet" is what I wrote in the margin with a medium red ballpoint.) Nor can high-tech student writers figure out how to break words between syllables or even number their pages.

What you write on is an intimate matter akin to your favorite brand of shampoo or how many pillows you like. I suppose that what you write on is entirely irrelevant—when you are *really* writing. Nobody knows whether Shakespeare would have processed two or three dozen more plays if only he'd had a Macintosh, as a cybernetic acquaintance once suggested. I doubt it, though. Ben Jonson pointed out that his late friend seldom bothered with revisions.

The Unintelligible Hero

The relief of speech is that it translates me into the universal.
—Søren Kierkegaard, Fear and Trembling, *Problem III*

The Telephone System

Let's just say I am preoccupied, no matter with what. All that counts is that I am thoroughly alone in my preoccupation, for even the most humble self always occupies its owner before anything else can. For once I resolve not to break off my concentration on this unnamed preoccupation and, consequently, whenever the telephone rings I do not pick it up. I ignore it. This is no admirable piece of self-mastery on my part, as at other times it might have been. On the contrary, most of the time I barely hear the calls; my phone is one floor, and may as well be seven leagues, away. Nevertheless, my preoccupation goes on for several days; therefore there are many times when I am perfectly well aware that somebody is trying to get me to pick up my receiver. The phone rings as many as seventeen times at once. How do I feel about denying such persistence? After all, I have been conditioned as thoroughly as anyone else to the categorical nature of the imperative: you must always answer a ringing phone! For what is the telephone system but an occasion for bringing all one's social conditioning into play, for fulfilling one's duty to one's fellow men, for meeting the rudimentary demand of all ethical life, which is that one must always be prepared to reveal oneself? In practice, this duty of self-revelation certainly can be taken to mean that one must always answer whenever society rings. Does it matter who in particular is calling? It might be someone selling an *Encyclopedic History of Football;* it could be a desperate friend needing only a word; or (and mark this) it might very well be someone calling expressly to find out if you are all right . . . calling now just because there has been no answer when they rang before. No matter: you must—it is your duty—reveal yourself; you must tell of your intention not to buy the encyclopedic history; you are bound to hand out your best advice to the despairing friend; and you have to explain in negative detail that nothing in the least lethal has befallen you.

Not to answer the phone: what can this antisociability mean? It means not to reveal yourself and it means not to be at the call of the system; it can and does mean to deny your duty. Truly, there is not to be found any more *ethical* document than the metropolitan telephone directory. Where is there another document wherein one can read with such comprehensive precision just who has signed the social contract?

But how can one justify not answering the phone? What are others prepared to accept by way of extenuation, and how will they take the crime itself? It really is a crime since not to answer is not only to refuse to reveal oneself; it is also to allow the creation of illusions. Herein lies one's guilt, what requires justification. True, the illusion will depend on the imagination of those who do the dialing, but the responsibility lies all the same with the one who conceals himself by letting the phone ring and ring into his callers' stimulated imaginations. Thus even the constitutional right to remain silent is limited by the provision that one cannot be required to incriminate himself. This means that our concealment is insured only so far as specific crimes are concerned, while the mere fact of silence invariably implies that we have something to hide. Our silence before a grand jury (or, so to speak, the grander jury of those who possess telephones) cannot help but create the illusion of guilt—if guilt should ever be an illusion—and it will put Them on the scent of our criminality.

One can always lie, of course; but in this case to lie is to become guilty by trying to avoid the appearance of guilt. Thus, when I did finally answer my phone I could have told the concerned voice at the other end that I had not been at home at all, preoccupied with my own concerns. No, I could claim that I was out of town and thus had not refused to answer. Lying like this is a prudent, short-term way out, but not a solution. By concealing myself twice over I can appear to have nothing to conceal at all. Moreover, I could create a new illusion to cover up the old one: that I had not refused to answer the phone and that, if I had been "in" then I surely would have answered it. But such dissembling, even if it is not exactly an obstruction of justice, still begs the question.

So what I did in fact, and in all innocence too, was simply to tell my indefatigable caller the truth, naively expecting to be understood.

But no! Even though he might be one who could hold forth eloquently for an entire evening on the right to privacy, and even though he might be one who has often enough been made the intimate of my secret solitudes, even though he might be an indulgent parent, ever willing to pardon me for much worse peccadillos—my caller's response is nothing at all like sympathy, forgiveness, or even so much as tolerance. Instead I am compelled to listen to an exasperated and indignant accounting of exactly how many times I have been summoned to the phone, a rendering of all his now-unfounded fears and worries on my behalf, and at last I am presented with a display of absolutely genuine anger, a wrath which carelessly supposes my silence has been a refusal to talk to him—just to him—personally. In his capacity as a member of society my caller insists that he is nonetheless an individual, but he does so only the better to bring home to me my guilt in relation to society at large of which he is unconsciously the representative. He will not say, "Of course I might have been an encyclopedia salesman or a wrong number" but, "Why didn't you want to talk to *me*? I was worried sick."

Perhaps he will forget, but for my silence I am never forgiven, and never can be. To be truly forgiven I should have to be understood, but what I need to be forgiven for is not having made myself intelligible.

Interpretation as Mediation, or No One Has the Right to Be Unhappy

It has struck me that a certain truth about interpretation has never been bluntly enough stated. By interpretation I mean what Kierkegaard called "mediation" in *Fear and Trembling*. When he wrote of the impossibility of "mediating" between the knight of faith and God because of their "absolute relation," what Kierkegaard had chiefly in mind was that when you apply ethics to faith you cause Abraham to look like a would-be infanticide and the Virgin Mary a tramp (which is, of course, exactly what they *do* look like from the outside). All mediation is necessarily through the "universal" he says, and he is right. But just as one can have an absolute relation to oneself as well as to God, so too the universal can include more than just ethics. In fact it comprises all the knowledge of all the mental disciplines that can be marshaled to eliminate the noxious peculiarity, or responsibility, of the individual. These sciences can be made to accomplish this task in an infinite number of ways—such as by demonstrating that ontogeny is really only a brand of philogeny or that what we don't know is really only a species of what we already know quite thoroughly. This process is often practiced by means of psychology, as when Kierkegaard's own insistence that his marriage was "vetoed by God" is interpreted to be the result of his mother's early death, the melancholy influence of a gloomy and guilt-ridden father, his inability to form normal human attachments, the fear of physical inadequacy, or even his own unconscious but nonetheless vain and comprehensible ambition to become a famous author. That this commonsense approach makes a mockery of Kierkegaard's whole life and thought is seldom adduced as an argument against it. Nor can it be, for, as Kierkegaard himself demonstrated, there are only two things to be done with such a character: either he must be left alone, or he must be interpreted. The idea that Kierkegaard freely chose the unhappiness of breaking his plighted troth stinks in the universal nostrils. And it is below these same nostrils that the historian pronounces Abraham to be a representative of a superstitious age, that the anthropologist speaks of early Semitic rituals of sacrifice, and the psychologist of forms of religious dementia. Indeed, freedom to choose (which practically means the freedom to choose unhappiness) disrupts all the disciplines. Another way of saying this: the existence of the individual who can choose unhappiness is universally unintelligible. Interpretation is the process by which the universal comforts itself while also taking revenge on that morose and unintelligible lawbreaker who refuses to answer his phone when it rings.

Why Heroes Become Unintelligible

As soon as heroism ceases to be "moral" in any public sense, or in any public interest for that matter; as soon too as the poet ceases to be a public figure dedicating himself to the embodiment or reduplication of pre-existing values; as soon as literature itself ceases to be a reflection of values and becomes instead a fashioner of values (by simultaneously becoming a critic of values)—that may be regarded as the moment when the hero first becomes unintelligible. That is the moment when, so to speak, both the hero and his poet refuse to answer the phone. Now this refusal to answer the calls of the universal may easily appear to be mere mystification, a degrading obscurantism. No doubt it is just this suspicion that first gave rise to the false critique of the Hidden Meaning as a way of mistaking concealment.

The Differences among the Hidden Meaning, the Symbol, and Concealment

The principle behind interpretation in terms of a "hidden meaning" is that nothing is what it is. A ship is a mother, a doorknob is the cosmos, a dog is a woman. Such prestidigitation can only succeed in smirching symbolism's character, not in interpreting symbols; for the first principle of symbolism is that everything must be intensely what it is. Even so, the symbol can be successfully mediated and may even be said to have been created for that very purpose. This is because the symbol, at which the hidden meaning method is aimed, is not really a form of concealment. At most it is the aura thrown around the concealment practiced by the individual hero or his poet and marks the supreme lyrical effort of the unintelligible to clarify itself to others without at the same time betraying itself. Therefore, the symbol may be successfully interpreted without destroying concealment. But the concealment of the individual that makes him unintelligible is most recognizable in its resistance to any satisfactory mediation at all. In practice, since mediation possesses, for all its insistence on finitude, infinite resources, concealment may become apparent when there are too *many* interpretations. Where there are a score of diagnoses the disease may reasonably be said to have escaped any one of them. Moreover, who would dare speak of the "levels of meaning" of a disease? Well, concealment is a disease too. Certainly one can imagine a virtuoso diagnostician or exegete, but who can achieve virtuosity in disease or in concealment?

The fact that concealment can be interpreted in manifold ways proves nothing in favor of interpretation, though it does prove something against concealment—namely that concealment allows for the creation of illusions. The interpreter, bent on filtering what is concealed through his mesh of intelligent and universal principles, creates this illusion and, in so far as he then values his own interpretation as highly as its object, he may be said to suffer delusion as well. For his delusion concealment is also to blame.

Five Kinds of Unintelligible Hero

How can there be a taxonomy of the unintelligible? It doesn't seem very likely because classification is itself a sort of interpretive mediation and depends on seeing things from the outside (even if it should occasionally become necessary to vivisect a specimen). But this is a literary essay, limited to examining the literary embodiment of the unintelligible; that is, to exploring the paradoxical act of revealing concealment. By virtue of this technical paradox, then, a taxonomy is possible since a plot invariably reveals the nature of the concealment, albeit without disclosing the content of what is being concealed. One can therefore classify these literary heroes from the standpoint of the universal by seeing what it is about them that the universal finds the most nonsensical. And so we can isolate:

A. The hero who does things that apparently make no sense.

B. The hero to whom something happens that makes no sense.

C. The hero who is able to make himself intelligible to himself but is nonetheless unable to make himself comprehensible to others.

These are the three genuinely unintelligible heroes, and to them we can add a couple more who are not authentically unintelligible—at least to begin with—but for whom unintelligibility is an essential motive and a possible fate:

D. The hero (or poseur) who tries to appear unintelligible.

E. The hero who is secretly intelligible enough, but who must act as if he were not.

It may be added that heroes D and E who act at unintelligibilty risk becoming unintelligible in fact since an ironic poet might elect to punish them for their false concealment by making it real.

Now we need to get down to some cases.

•   •   •

A. An example of the unintelligible hero who does things that apparently make no sense—i.e., appear to others to be nonsensical—would be the narrator of Fyodor Dostoyevsky's *Notes From Underground*. Take for instance this account of the visit to the billiard room that results in the absurdly drawn-out *affaire d'honneur* with the tall officer:

> One night as I was passing a tavern I saw through a lighted window some gentlemen fighting with billiard cues, and saw one of them thrown out of the window. At other times I should have felt very much disgusted, but I was in such a mood at the time, that I actually envied the gentleman thrown out of the window—and I envied him so much that I even went into the tavern and into the billiard room. "Perhaps," I thought, "I'll have a fight, too, and they'll throw me out of the window."

Now, this is no uncharacteristic or inconsequential passage in the *Notes*. It occurs towards the beginning of part two and marks the first embodiment in narrative of the ideas expressed more discursively in part one. If in part one human freedom was spoken of as "whim" and "caprice," in part two the doctrine of this "most advantageous advantage" is illustrated by just such a curious piece of masochism. The narrator's perverse desire to be thrown out of a tavern window is, in effect, the counterargument to utilitarian utopianism, to mathematical ethics, to all rationalizations that allow predictions of human behavior and of life. If a sane individual can choose unhappiness, then the monolith of universal psychology crumbles. Existence is once more an open question, ethics are once more problematic, heaven and hell spring to life. At the same time this passage reminds us of an often overlooked truth about this notorious narrator—that, like ourselves, he too has been well educated in all the interpretations of the universal. He knows just as much psychology as does Jeremy Bentham: indeed it is Bentham's psychology that he knows. "At other times" he says it would have gone differently—that is, when he is as much within the universal as other people and has nothing to hide; "at other times" the observation of a taproom scuffle should have "disgusted" him. His distaste would probably have been for the sordid violence of potentially rational and useful creatures. However at the moment he feels differently; for he is "in such a mood."

Now a mood also can be a form of concealment. "Mood" expresses vagueness of emotion and sensibility, a nebulousness that can reach unintelligibility when it is made the motive for an action, as it is here. In contrast to the eminently comprehensible and gentlemanly motivation of "rational self-interest," then, Dostoyevsky logically opposes irrational self-harm . . . or unintelligibility. It might be objected that the narrator is after all intelligible enough because he knows he is motivated by a chance mood. But this is contradictory. The passage makes it clear enough that this character's reason for doing what he does is not clear at all. To ascribe one's acts to a mood is really to deny that there is any explanation for them at all. It is a form of concealment practiced often by each of us. But the narrator's remarks not only conceal his motives from the reader but show further that his motives are also concealed from himself. All of part two is a flashback to the narrator's youth; that is, all this occurred long before he had figured out the doctrines of part one that he does not even bother to tell us he is now illustrating. How could he know yet that he was a seminal anti-hero and the author of an existential classic? No one would understand him if he were to say so, if he were to attempt his duty of self-revelation in this case—certainly not the "gentlemen" in the tavern, nor those other "gentlemen" (the universal ones, the good liberals, ourselves) to whom all of the *Notes* are addressed.

And yet the narrator seems to try for revelation. The pronoun "I" appears fifteen times in the first paragraph of the *Notes* and is the subject of every sentence save, pointedly enough, this one:

That you probably will not understand.

Indeed, the *Notes* begin with a parody of self-revelation, and so readers have been beguiled into regarding the whole work as *simply* a "confession." But everything the narrator reveals about himself is contrary to universal laws: in short, the narrator answers his phone but only in order to shout into it his wonderfully subversive jibberish. B. The hero to whom something happens that makes no sense is perhaps the most common and sympathetic of all unintelligible heroes. Our sympathy with him is caused by the immediate thought that such things could happen to ourselves also—and, as if to remind us of this, the hero himself often wonders if his private ordeal could occur to others too. This is true of Leo Tolstoy's Ivan Ilych and of Franz Kafka's Gregor Samsa and Joseph K. Sometimes such a hero or heroine just seems to have been caught up in the extraordinary, like Heinrich von Kleist's Marquise of O—— or Albert Camus's Meursault. It is not their selves that are unintelligible so much as their fates, fates that are incommensurable with the universal, lacking any common measure or ground. Because of this, mediation tends even to become a part of the story, as if the work could hold within its narrative a number of false interpretations of itself. Tolstoy's travesty of medical diagnosis in *The Death Of Ivan Ilych* is a good example.

The best example of all is probably Herman Melville's "Bartleby the Scrivener: A Story of Wall Street." Here it is of course Bartleby who is unintelligible, but then Bartleby exists primarily as a literary symbol of unintelligibility. The repeated attempts to interpret, to mediate between Bartleby and his unintelligibility on the part of the Master-in-Chancery, or master-in-perplexity, are precisely synchronized with his efforts to save Bartleby's life. One is as futile an effort as the other. It is true that if Bartleby could be successfully interpreted economically, biographically, ethically, anthropologically, historically, psychologically, or sociologically, he could indeed be saved— but only by being "translated" back into the universal, and thus losing his right to unhappiness, to silence and, in short, his right to be Bartleby the Scrivener. At best Bartleby might then join in with Turkey and Nippers and become that mockery of the unintelligible, a grotesque or eccentric. As his employer well knows, any eccentric who is predictable in his eccentricity is infinitely more useful than one who is entirely unintelligible and springs surprises. So mediation fails the narrator. But neither will Bartleby offer any revelation on his own, as is his duty to society. He will not even advance a reason for his negative "preferences." Well, preferences are, after all, as non-rational and as inexplicable as moods. So Bartleby reveals absolutely nothing of himself. In his despair he will let the phone ring as many times as it likes . . . all the while staring at and even dying beside his extremely blank wall. Naturally, when the time comes for the Master to betray Bartleby—denying denial—he does so to the authorities and to his clients; it is to the universal that he does so. To deny responsibility for Bartleby is the only way to save his own beloved and ironically lamented "office," his place, his listing, his sanity. This denial is a concealment too; yet the Master's concealment does not rest on unintelligibility but on his vital need to fight it off before unintelligibility taints him and ruins his business. That in the end he can see in Bartleby all the misery of "humanity" is by no means a revelation of Bartleby the Scrivener, but a redemption of himself. It is even perhaps to equate humanity with concealment, the right to remain silent—to prefer not to answer the phone. There is then, the Master discovers late in his life, something beside the phone system, something concealed that is walled in on Wall Street and walled up in the Tombs.

So a peculiar fate can render one unintelligible—but why? Just because of the absence of a common language. "That was no human voice," cries the Manager after hearing Gregor Samsa's long explanation of his unprecedented plight. And, in fact, Gregor twitters and is an insect. That is his fate and no one shares it with him. Everywhere the lack of common experience undermines the meanings of words. In Gregor's case it does no good to seek after the "universally human," since the universal is just what his experience has ruled out. Between young and old, rich and poor, living and dying lies some form of this same unintelligibility: the young man is unintelligible in his youth, the poor man in his poverty, the dying man in his death.

C. Now for the hero who is intelligible to himself but cannot make himself understood by anyone else, because he is unable to or must not. First off, such a hero has to get over thinking himself crazy. If, as Kierkegaard says, faith is what justifies concealment, then this faith must be in oneself as something apart from what others understand about oneself. In the absence of universal validation, one must have faith in himself, whether or not he also manages to have faith in God; otherwise unintelligibility would be unendurable.

In symbol and in narrative the situation of this hero is best represented by a physical withdrawal from the universal, but such a withdrawal as will, so to speak, continue to adhere to him should he return. This is the case with Fred Daniels in Richard Wright's *The Man Who Lived Underground*. Fred is a Black man who is being hunted for a murder he did not commit and who takes refuge in the sewers of an American city. In the sewers Fred sees the unspeakable and gets in touch with the unintelligible; yet Fred is all right until he decides to attempt the fulfilment of his duty to the universal by coming up and revealing himself to others. When he does so he is thrown out of a Black church, for the filth of his sewer sticks to him. In the end Fred is shot by a policeman to whom he is a threat. Were Fred's unintelligible language to become intelligible to the Police Commissioner, the officer might be held criminally liable for the death of a suspect and for other irregularities. And yet Wright allows this policeman to express his own selfish obstruction of justice (concealment of the concealed) in universal terms. This guardian of private property says over Fred's body, dying now and spinning away in the effluvia of the city, "You've got to shoot his kind. They'd wreck things." Exactly. Whenever the truly unintelligible threatens to communicate itself it is bound to overturn "things," to be revolutionary. This must be because what gets communicated can only be a truth that is wholly new. All unmediated truths are revolutionary. If Bartleby dies because of his concealment, Fred dies because he will not persist in his concealment, but tries to reveal a new truth which he himself barely understands. He cannot find the words. Nevertheless, the effort to find them and to speak them makes him not just a revolutionary (since, after all, most revolutionists mediate everything through ideology), but a messianic messenger. Always the great miracle occurs when the unintelligible is freely revealed. No wonder Wright has Fred dream of walking on water.

The dialectic of universal revelation and messianic concealment is nowhere more clearly or brilliantly expressed than in Dostoyevsky's "Legend of the Grand Inquisitor." The ninety-year-old cardinal is, in fact, the greatest mediator in all literature. His view of Satan as "the terrible and wise spirit" indicates that the universal is, from the standpoint of the individual, the Adversary—for this Satan holds doctorates in all the Arts and Sciences, not excepting Religion. He can mediate any individual out of himself by sheer talk. However Jesus, the Cardinal insists, must remain silent. Both know this is the rule and the Grand Inquisitor justifiably objects to the two miracles at the cathedral steps as breaking the rules. Since Jesus stands for freedom—of which "freedom of faith" is only one dimension—he can make no objection. Indeed, any word or act stands to be a revolutionary compulsion ("hindering our work," as the Inquisitor complains); it would be a revelation of the unintelligible.

So the Inquisitor is right in accusing Jesus of giving men no clear or intelligible guidelines and of effectively undermining those they already possessed in the Mosaic codes. Jesus has even chosen to appear (but not to reveal himself) in Seville the day *after* the burning of a hundred heretics. So even this tentative revelation is still concealment: is Jesus' appearance a mark of approval or the opposite? And so too Jesus makes no verbal reply to all the Inquisitor has to say, all the universal can say, but only offers a kiss on the lips. Is this acquiescence in or annihilation of the cardinal's monologue? No matter, for the "the kiss burns in [the Inquisitor's] heart but the old man adheres to his idea." Naturally; the universal has framed its arguments over against the heart and such things as the kiss that forgives the sinner but not the sin. The universal prefers its ideas, which are more intelligible and indulge the sin while having contempt for the sinner. Indeed, it is hard to see how ethics can speak of sin at all without undermining itself.

D. It will immediately be seen that the hero who tries to be unintelligible is not so much a hero at all as a poseur around whom a comic action ought to, and usually does, revolve. Kierkegaard remarks that all drama depends on the tension between concealment and revelation—fantasy and significance, intrigue and discovery. From this it follows that no truly unintelligible hero can be dramatic. Heroes A,B, and C above can hardly be brought on the stage, which is an arena for the revelation of the universal. In fact the whole emotional raison d'être of the drama, whether comic or tragic, *is* revelation, as Aristotle pointed out twenty-three hundred years ago. So it follows that for drama revelation must at least be possible, which entails that what is concealed must be—whether trivial or tragical—intelligible to everyone both on stage and in the mezzanine. Under dramatic conditions then, this kind of character cannot be really unintelligible at all; rather he is only concerned to play at unintelligibility for a while. What he desires of unintelligibility is its power of illusion. He smiles to himself as he lets the phone ring and ring: he himself is imagining what he wants his caller to imagine about him. He merely toys with concealing himself, since his purpose is not really to conceal himself but to reveal himself falsely—as "interesting," as "mysterious," as "too busy to bother answering," as off in some palace, or what not. And if he succeeds in concealing anything it is only that he has nothing interesting, mysterious, or deeply preoccupying to conceal. Thus, the dénouement.

However, one must examine a little the motives of such a character. While he is by no means an unintelligible hero to begin with he may still be on the point of becoming one—out of sheer will power. How might this happen? In literary terms one might discern such a tale in one of those modern bildungsromans that detail the course of an adolescent rebellion into young adulthood. The tale must be developmental rather than dramatic. Beginning with a barely understood but highly characteristic revulsion from the universal as it is disclosed to him at school, in church, at home, or with peers (that is, starting from a revulsion only barely understood by the adolescent himself; any developmental psychologist would smile at it quite knowingly), the adolescent may strike the pose of a Stephen Daedalus, of a Bernard Profitendieu, of a Holden Caulfield. He may pretend that he has within him such private chasms that no one could begin to plumb them. Thus the universal is correct in the way it interprets adolescent withdrawal, saying that it marks a stage in negative self-definition during which, more or less pathetically, the adolescent will insist on his own unintelligibility. He rebels instinctively against being understood, though customarily he also enjoys complaining about it too. However, if the stage should somehow be prolonged to the point where the adolescent can never completely reintegrate himself into the universal (as psychology legally insists he should and scientifically predicts he will), *then* he may indeed become an unintelligible hero. It is the possibility of just this special fate that tantalizes a reader at the end of *Huckleberry Finn*, when Huck "lights out for the territory." The open west is a good place in which to conceal oneself (it has no phones as yet), particularly if one has chosen forever "Hell" over "Heaven" because one can no longer bear those Aunt Pollys of the universal nor the thought of someday being comprehended by them.

E. The hero who is secretly intelligible, but who must act as if he were not, would appear to be the opposite of the last case. Indeed, the two would be antipodal if this hero really desired to make himself intelligible, as often happens. On the other hand, a man in such a position might also come to relish his own unintelligibility, if only because it gives him so totally to himself. Also he might become lost in his role. These possibilities do not exclude one another and for this reason: the unintelligibility of this sort of hero is, to an even greater extent than for all the others, a social need. True, heroes A–D appear to be concealed only because they exist within a social setting, but even if they were alone they might still be regarded as unintelligible . . . to their own reasons. This hero, however, assumes unintelligibility as a disguise, as a discipline, because he must, being under a direct threat from the outside. All individuals are under indirect threats, yet for this one the threat is special—say, that he will be murdered if he should for a moment reveal himself. So here it is more a question of at whom the unintelligibility is aimed.

The finest example of this kind of hero is Hamlet, who assumes the unintelligibility of madness to protect himself from his uncle—and, because his uncle happens also to be a king, from the whole of the Danish court as well—from Rosencrantz and Guildenstern, from Polonius, from Gertrude, even from Ophelia and Horatio. Since his unintelligibility is so inclusive one might well wonder whether Hamlet can remain intelligible to himself. The evidence is that he certainly begins that way, since his unintelligibility starts as a rational stratagem, as craft. Nevertheless, the question is reopened in the very places where one might expect self-revelation to assert itself (that is, his intelligibility to himself): in Hamlet's soliloquies.

The soliloquy, once just a means of informing the audience about a dramatic character's motivation—therefore as a way of presenting a revelation that is always more narrative than dramatic, as in act one of *Richard III*—becomes in *Hamlet* something quite different. Instead of serving as revelations, Hamlet's speeches become instead *attempts* at remaining intelligible to himself. They are therefore less and less addressed to the audience (the universal beyond the end of the stage) and become, as we now say, more and more "psychological." At this "level" they fail, though only to succeed at deeper and higher ones. Even in the first of his soliloquies Hamlet is on the verge of the unintelligible; his revelation of himself is already equivocal, calling as it does for the opposite of revelation, silence:

> It is not nor it cannot come to good:
> But break, my heart; for I must hold my tongue.

In his next soliloquy, after the conversation with the ghost (and what is it to converse with a ghost but to leave the universal?), Hamlet explicitly gives himself at once to the task of revenge and to that of unintelligibility, of forgetting all mediation, as if one demanded of him the other:

> Yea, from the table of my memory
> I'll wipe away all trivial fond records,
> All saws of books, all forms, all pressures past,
> That youth and observation copied there;
> And thy commandment all alone shall live
> Within the book and volume of my brain
> Unmix'd with baser matter . . .

Thus, like the narrator of the *Notes*, Hamlet must act *against* his education, which is all that can make him intelligible. Those "saws" and "forms" that others can comprehend are no use to him now that he is to become incomprehensible. They are "baser matter," and he has been transmuted.

In the soliloquy of act two, concerning the actor and his passionate Hecuba, Hamlet explicitly describes his inability to make his own strong emotion intelligible. It seems that, paradoxically enough, dramatic revelation is not available to the greatest character in all drama:

> Yet I,
> A dull and muddy-mettled rascal, peak,
> Like John-a-dreams, unpregnant of my cause,
> And can say nothing . . .

Still, he attempts (like his own critics) to mediate himself, to interpret not his behavior, which would be dramatic, but the absence of any behavior, the defeat of drama. He perceives that in relation to his duty he is either guilty or inexplicable:

> Am I a coward?
> Who calls me villain . . . ?
> . . . it cannot be
> But I am pigeon-liver'd and lack gall
> To make oppression bitter . . .
> Why, what an ass am I!

From considering the emotional revelations of a dramatized Hecuba, then proceeding through the cold illusions of his own concealment, Hamlet hits on the irony of seeking a secure revelation through yet another play. After all, even the ghost cannot be trusted to reveal the truth as well as drama can. But this ''Mouse-Trap'' is not intended to reveal Hamlet, who is not intelligible, but Claudius, who is. Perhaps when Claudius is revealed, Hamlet may then reveal himself as well, and become not an unintelligible hero but a dramatic and a tragic one.

Oddly enough, it is the famous ''To be, or not to be'' soliloquy of act three in which Hamlet reveals himself the least of all. This is paradoxically one cause of its fame, for how could the unintelligible become universally famous? The key is all in the pronoun used by the poet, which is never ''I'' but rather ''we.'' Hamlet speaks in the universal all right—he even speaks *for* it—but for that very reason he does not speak for himself. Yet this speech is also another effort to make himself intelligible to himself once again. The idea that Hamlet is the "man of intellect" who cannot become the "man of action" is not an idea of the last century, but of Hamlet himself in this speech. It is a theoretical attempt to mediate his silence, his inaction, his unintelligibility; to find the golden words that will "translate him into the universal." By saying "we" he is trying to take the universal by storm. However, Hamlet cannot be "we" and still be Hamlet. So this soliloquy neither reveals motivation nor the hero's peculiar psychology; rather, it is a kind of formal essay.

By act four Hamlet has increasingly lost the sense of his own condition and has become thoroughly unintelligible to himself. Mediation fails him, or rather he no longer has even a little conviction in it:

> Now, whether it be
> Bestial oblivion, or some craven scruple
> Of thinking too precisely on the event,
> A thought which, quarter'd, hath but one part wisdom
> And ever three parts coward, I do not know . . .

Whereupon, to bring home the gap between the intelligible, the universal, the obviously heroic, the active, the clear, the *not*-Hamlet and Hamlet himself, we are given the prince's envious/contemptuous account of Fortinbras, that other

> delicate and tender prince

who can act even for "a straw," an "egg-shell." Those who are willing to die for "a fantasy and trick of fame" are intelligible as possessing true "greatness." Consequently, they are applauded and will come to inherit the universal kingdom. Hamlet has only Hamlet and is the last of his line. After all, marriage too is a way of being "translated into the universal." But was there ever so unintelligible a lover as Hamlet? And yet he can say, so concealed is this love, so intense, and yet (and here is the really miraculous thing) still so near the surface and potentially intelligible:

> I loved Ophelia: forty thousand brothers
> Could not, with all their quantity of love,
> Make up my sum . . .

Here we see that the tragedy of Ophelia lies entirely within the unintelligibility of her lover, and that he knows it. Even at the moment of his death, which in tragic drama is apt to be one of general self-revelation, Hamlet still conceals himself. He speaks of the election falling on Fortinbras; he puts Denmark's affairs in order, but as to Prince Hamlet the Concealed and Unintelligible, he confides nothing: "The rest is silence."

A note on the above: Hamlet is tantalizingly unintelligible and therefore has undergone more "mediation" than any other character in literature. But why should he have been so constructed? One answer: Hamlet's unintelligibility is an antidramatic solution to a dramatic problem. The problem is simply put: how to delay the consummation of what would otherwise have been a conventional Elizabethan revenge tragedy; and then, how to avoid the anticlimax of, say, Thomas Kyd's *Spanish Tragedy*? It is often said on this score that Shakespeare's solution lies in making the avenger question the propriety of revenge itself, as if the play and its hero marked some new ethical refinement of their age. But this is not so. Hamlet never doubts the rightness of revenge; rather, he perpetually questions whether or not he will be able to carry it off. At first, on the apparently lame pretext of making certain that the ghost's information is correct, he disguises himself in a cloak of madness in order to observe Claudius; later on, the cloak adheres to his skin in the form of real unintelligibility. Having been given information from outside the universal (though his heart has been prophetic), he is called upon to act within the universal. This is already a paradox. But Hamlet lives in paradox; thus in silence and concealment. Hamlet is called on, but not through the phone system. Rather he is called on to make a call himself. What the play shows is his reluctance to climb the stairs and place his finger in the dial. The man who lets the phone ring is not so very different from the one who will not himself make a call.

The Critic on the Telephone

R. P. Blackmur once defined criticism in a lovely phrase, "the learned discourse of an amateur." Faced with an unintelligible hero, what discourse is likely to come from this amateur, this disinterested lover of literature? That is doubtless where the learning comes in. More exactly, the learning is what comes in between, is what mediates. It mediates between the amateur and the incomprehensible object of his love; it mediates between the critic and his reader; between the poet and his hero; but most of all it mediates between the hero and himself. Learning turns the unintelligible into the intelligible, the individual into the universal; it renders the preoccupied and the concealed fit for the telephone system once again. Learning is the answering service.

Some examples:

Historical mediation: the hero is the way he is because of when he lived, or when he was written.

Anthropological mediation: the hero is this way because he is involved in such or such primitive ritual, or driven by this or that archetypal model.

Sociological mediation: the hero acts this way because of the position he occupies in the society he inhabits.

Ethical mediation: the hero acts this way because he sees it as his peculiar duty, or because he is really a villain and is acting contrary to his duty.

Philosophical mediation: the hero behaves as he does in pursuance of this or that system of metaphysics.

Literary mediation: the hero acts in this way because his poet was influenced by certain other poets, whose heroes behaved likewise.

Economic mediation: the hero acts as he does because Marx explains it is inevitable that he should do so.

Psychological mediation: the hero acts this way because his behavior is symptomatic of a certain condition he has that was described by Freud.

In such fashions might the discourse of the amateur show learning. We demand it of him and he asks no less of himself. We all have a great stake in such universal mediations. Without their assurances the ground slips from beneath us. It is not that unintelligibility is *contra naturam*, but that it undermines our security and peace of mind. We dial and the phone is never answered. The doctor is called upon to mediate between us and our disease, why not the critic to mediate between us and our malaise? The disease must at least be diagnosed; the unintelligibility of the hero must at least be explained. And yet . . . no disease can be diagnosed away.

Imagine the absurdity of a critic who resisted every temptation to mediate. He would appear to be a fool and could yield up only a criticism that looked like the ignorant discourse of puppy love. But then too his words might be vastly sophisticated, despite appearances—like the work of those elegant painters who strive to do consciously what three-year-olds do thoughtlessly. Worst of all, such a critic might seem unintelligible himself, and of what possible use is an unintelligible critic?

Why has the lyric mode prevailed so thoroughly over the dramatic and narrative in recent years? Perhaps it is for the same reason that writing itself is now glibly designated "self-expression" in the schools. With the loss of a common ground what, after all, is the great challenge to those who deal seriously in words? An answer was suggested earlier in this essay: that the challenge is to reveal the unintelligible without betraying it. In other terms, the task is to manifest the individual in the language of the universal without robbing him of his uniqueness, including his rights to unhappiness and silence. Without a God to underwrite the sanctity of the individual, one may be forced to this line of thinking: sanctity is a form of unintelligibility, a mystery; therefore may not unintelligibility itself serve as proof of the existence of this mystery?

Kierkegaard, who provided the starting point for this essay and perhaps too much of its terminology, argued that only an "absolute relation to the Absolute" could save the individual. That Absolute is God or the Absurd—but also oneself. The unintelligible hero can be above or below the universal (that is, everybody else, the phone system), but he cannot be like everyone else and still be himself. This is always the rock on which mediation founders. It is just those things about ourselves that we cannot shout through the phone system that matter the most. If Kierkegaard was right that it is when we feel least a part of the congregation that we are closest to God, then it is also true that it is when we are most unintelligible that we are closest to ourselves. It is then that we remember we can have selves, and, enthralled with this sublime preoccupation, so near to mere selfishness, so close to absentmindedness, we may easily fail to notice the ringing phone.

Ex Nihilo, or For Openers

God made everything out of nothing.
But the nothingness shows through.
— *Paul Valéry*

Can nothing really come from nothing? It looks as if the physicists have extended their explanations down to an inconceivably tiny fraction of a second after the Creation; that is, just as soon as there was something, they are now able to account for everything. This is a most impressive achievement, fully justifying the positivistic awe it inspires in those with a feeling for it. But what if one should be looking for something other than an explanation of the laws of nature, something beyond even the Grand Unified Field Theory? What if somebody should want to know why there is anything at all? "Yes, yes," says the ungrateful child. "What you physicists say is astounding; but could you please tell me how everything got here in the first place and what was here before that?" Children have a knack for the unanswerable question.

• • •

In his "Tlön, Uqbar, Orbis Tertius," Jorge Luis Borges explains the sudden worldwide popularity of a fantastically detailed fiction, that of the imaginary planet Tlön, and how this fiction actually comes to replace our old nonfictional reality:

> How could one do other than submit to Tlön, to the minute and vast evidence of an orderly planet? It is useless to answer that reality is also orderly. Perhaps it is, but in accordance with divine laws—I translate: inhuman laws—which we never quite grasp.

Is Tlön what the bibliophilic Borges understands as literature? Very likely, given his next sentence, which epitomizes the Master's work: "Tlön is surely a labyrinth, but it is a labyrinth devised by men, a labyrinth destined to be deciphered by men." In other words, Tlön's origins, laws, and history are knowable, while ours, comparatively speaking, are not. Tlön is a product of human artifice. Indeed, Tlön *is* human artifice and, in the twentieth century, the science of exegesis has flourished right next to the art of astrophysics. Borges confidently declares that what is devised by persons must be "decipherable" by other persons, while what is brought into existence by nonhuman agencies is as fundamentally unknowable as Immanuel Kant said all things ultimately are. However, if this is really so, then literary explications would have a much better claim to precision than such vague speculations as physics, chemistry, or biology are capable of carrying out. An odd conclusion.

Borges's theology is unobjectionably orthodox, at least. He implies that humans *devise* while angels (or whatever) *create*. Creation cannot be a capability of mere creatures, despite the brash Renaissance boast of Marsilio Ficino that human artificers could do as good a job of creation as God if they "could but get hold of the heavenly stuff." Indeed, the whole notion of human artists as "creators" got its start as a metaphor in the salad days of hubristic Renaissance humanism. Nowadays we use the term all the time, albeit rather uncritically. When we speak of somebody *creating* an advertising campaign, for example, do we mean real creation or just what is vaguely called "creativity" in psychological profiles? Do we mean creation out of nothing or do we mean only Borges's "devising" which—whatever it entails—is a lesser activity than creating? What do we mean, in fact?

• • •

Even in the Bible itself creation is a vexed matter. In some important places creation is conceived not so much as making new stuff as arranging chaotic stuff (as in Genesis 1:2 or The Wisdom of Solomon 11:17). But in 2 Maccabees, chapter seven and Hebrews, chapter two, the doctrine of creation ex nihilo is stated for Jews and Christians, respectively. These are relatively minor sources, with a prestige well below that of Genesis or Matthew. Maccabees is not even in the Bible proper, but the Apocrypha, while the author of Hebrews is unknown. Nevertheless, there they are.

In Maccabees, a summary of Jason of Cyrene's multivolume history, the doctrine of creation out of nothing comes up in a context fitting for Jewish history. A woman's seven sons are being tortured and executed by King Antiochus, all in one day. The mother encourages her dying sons with noble theology stated in Hebrew so that the Syrio-Greek overlords will not understand her. Her fortitude is praised as patriarchal: " . . . she fired her woman's reasoning with a man's courage," says the text. When only one son remains alive, Antiochus promises him pardon, riches, and power if he will only recant his faith. The King then orders the mother to persuade the boy to do so, ignorant all the while of the purport of her Hebrew words. The woman agrees, but says just the opposite to her son, exhorting him to remain steadfast. She includes the following sentence:

> I beseech you, my child, to look at the heaven and the earth and see everything that is in them, and recognize that God did not make them out of things that existed.

This is the first mention of creation ex nihilio, not out of chaos, as in Genesis.

Hebrews is not so dramatic, though it too is a piece of theological exhortation. The epistle is one sustained argument, the longest in the whole Bible. It is aimed at certain early Jewish converts to Christianity who were having second thoughts. Chapter two is on faith and says right off:

> By faith we understand that the world was created by the word of God, so that what is seen was made out of things which do not appear.

What these invisible things (Ficino's "heavenly stuff"?) might be is not revealed. But the point seems to be that the whole matter of creation is to be taken on faith, which here, as later in Kierkegaard, is itself also a sort of something-out-of-nothing or a belief in the scientifically absurd. So *creation* is an equivocal term, biblically speaking. It can mean organizing what is there but formless, or it can mean making something out of nothing. The first meaning is easily grasped; the second is not. What about human "creations" then?

Are they also equivocal? I pose this in a playful spirit, though perhaps to ask is also marginally blasphemous. Certainly creation out of nothing *is*, in a scientific sense, an absurdity; but, in a religious or metaphysical sense, it may only be a redundancy. For example, *The New Encyclopedia of Philosophy* defines the term "creation" unequivocally and emphatically:

In the first meaning it is the production of something, with its entire substance, from nothing. If one does not consider that act of creation, then nothing is left, not even an uncreated matter or material, from which it would have been made.[1]

By this definition at least, if we insist on imputing creativity to our species, we must be equal to the wonders of creation ex nihilo.

The *Encyclopedia* goes on to add a Thomistic corollary about creation ex nihilo which is no less relevant to the rating of human productions:

The philosophical concept of creation . . . does not necessarily mean: began in time. Time is . . . co-created. Creation can therefore not be compared with a fact which happens in time, but forms the basis on which all the happenings of facts appear in time.[2]

In other words, a creative act is not a chronologically fixable one because time begins simultaneously with the act. Any creative act occurs at zero o'clock, so to speak. Moreover, what follows after creation is called "the creation." Cause and effect earn the same name at the initial moment; verb is at one with noun. The timebound, composed, linear, plotted, stanzaed, painted, erected, constructed, grandly unified and explicable—all exist in time *only* because they were preceded by creation ex nihilo.

• • •

Like the universe, a good deal of literary criticism has sped away from the bang, from the inception of its object of study. Not construction but deconstruction is the current game. To deconstruct predicates a prior construction of some sort, a "creation," but need not concern itself with exactly how it got there. Instead, criticism can, with an intelligence as dazzling as physics, delve into the recesses of everything but the inexplicable, breaking down the ingeniously combined elements, turning up the deep structures, elucidating prejudices, celebrating the interpenetration of this creation by that one, but always stopping short of the daunting nothingness out of which all this issues.

Do artists create merely in the sense of juggling elements, rearranging the furniture of actuality, casting unexpected alloys, and do it all in one continuous time? Or, can we—playfully, metaphorically— understand the commencement of a work of art as a sort of creation ex nihilo? The "playfully, metaphorically" may preserve us from undue absurdity, pompousness, and sacrilege. After all, metaphorical play cuts two ways. If, for example, the work of Shakespeare is compared to that of God ("After God, Shakespeare has created most," quipped William Hazlitt), it seems equally fair to say that our conception of God's creativity may be modeled on Shakespeare's. If the one is equivocal, why not the other? What is indecipherable in the one is so also in the other. Analogies may not be understandings, but they are generally the next best thing. How good an analogy is creation ex nihilo for literary work? Or, to put the question a great deal more concretely, what can be learned by looking at opening sentences? In the most inspired cases, these sentences may be little big bangs, beginning universes with their own "co-created" time. Consider the criteria of creation ex nihilo as we have thus far developed them:

1. not made out of existing things (Maccabees);
2. made out of things not apparent (Hebrews);
3. in its absence there is nothing, not even uncreated stuff (*Encyclopedia of Philosophy*);
4. time begins with the creative act—or, conversely, creation does not occur in time (ibid.).

Though I insist that my aesthetic metaphor is playful, it is not necessarily ludicrous. We can examine the limits of the playing field by applying these four criteria. First, without doubt stories are made out of "existing things" (ideas, images, memories, language). Oscar Wilde called literature "the supreme representative art" because it can represent so much of what exists, and so it must use what exists. On the other hand, it seems no less true that each genuine work comes out of nowhere and catapults into existence (for the writer no less than the reader) something that was not previously there. An anthology is made out of previously existing things too, yet it is not a work of art. Only plagiarists write fictions without creating. In this sense, then, we can partially satisfy the Maccabeean criterion. The satisfaction is partial, even in the case of the wholly fantastic or surreal, and yet the creation of a work of art is still the making of something wholly new, something never before seen. Even artists are "creatures," and all metaphors have their limits. Indeed, all metaphors tell truths and falsehoods at the same time.

Less ambiguous is the satisfaction of the second criterion. A story can certainly be made out of "things not apparent." This process is what we commonly mean by imagination, the capacity to conjure up that which does not appear before us physically. Where has a traveling salesman transformed into a gigantic bug ever "appeared"? Where can I discover portraits from the life of Mesdames Bovary and Defarge? Note that this is not to claim with even a little high seriousness that Kafka, Flaubert, and Dickens had nothing out of which to make their characters. I only mean that these writers possessed imaginations that were what Samuel Taylor Coleridge called "esemplastic"—able to gather disparate elements (salesmen and bugs, for instance) into organic, convincing wholes. Still, it is a special kind of creating. What these writers have accomplished is different in quality from the work of, say, an investigative journalist who gathers data for an exposé or a scholar accumulating quotations for a monograph. If we want to, why not call this special, nonjournalistic, nonscholarly activity "creation"?

Third, were there to be no *moment* of creation—no first pen-stroke to propel a work into the ambiguous existence of which literary productions are capable—then there is indeed "nothing." Every writer knows this nothingness. It is that of Bartleby's blank page, of the whale's vast whiteness, perhaps that of the universe a moment before the Creation. "What is the matter, Bartleby, you scrivener?" Nothing is the matter.

Finally, there is the vexed question of time—vexed because hardly anyone understands what time is. If we assume a Newtonian view, with a single and regular continuity of time, infinitely and regularly divisible—no perturbing bumps, accelerations, bends, or gaps—then of course there can be only a single act of creation at its outset, only one mysterious bang after which the chronometers and exegetes take over. We have then a sort of explosive form of deism. All our so-called "creative acts" are not creative; they are merely historical. There can be only one act of creation, the one occurring (so to speak) in the unimaginably infinitesimal fraction of an instant when time itself begins, because there would be only one sort of time.

But what of, say, the time that begins here?

> In a village of La Mancha the name of which I have no desire to recall, there lived not so long ago one of those gentlemen who always have a lance in the rack, an ancient buckler, a skinny nag, and a greyhound for the chase.

Is it illogical to say that a narrative like Cervantes's "co-creates" its own time? Indeed, in the second part of *Don Quixote* we find fictional characters reacting to a prior fiction (part one), and this priority itself must be wholly created by Miguel de Cervantes. That narratives create a time of their own is the common experience of readers. To be immersed in a story is to exist in two kinds of time: the normal time in which you are reading for an hour in your chair, and the fictional time during which you travel the roads of sixteenth-century Spain. What is obviously true of space ("I felt I was there") is no less true of time ("I felt I was then"). From the writer's point of view as well, a peculiar sort of time commences with the first sentence. Thus, once he or she has begun, the writer can leave the manuscript to fetch a cup of coffee or check the mail, then return to a universe in chronological suspension. The pen alone can kick the pendulum back into action.

• • •

Most readers want to know what happens in a novel, how a story turns out. They are like those thoughtless but human historians who judge Alexander great because he conquered the world, rather than because he set out to do so. More devoted readers and most writers, though, are bound to be fascinated by opening sentences. They will know that here is the really miraculous moment—the instant of artistic chutzpah that causes heaven and hell to spring into life, when the Muse smiles and the game's afoot, when another little bang occurs and a potential universe begins its expansion. Besides, openings are more difficult to achieve than endings; the former require all one's energy and nerve, the latter are often achieved effortlessly, by the trajectory of all that has come before. Opening sentences make a splendid study indeed, for they accomplish so many different purposes and come in such a variety of styles. Most are commonplace, of course, and paltry; but the great openers, like high poetry, are scarcely biodegradable. "In the beginning was the Word," St. John resonantly starts off his testimony. It is a sentence in which form and content are indistinguishable.

Words, including those in opening sentences, reflect individuality, where there is some to reflect. Moreover, fashions in opening sentences change over time. Henry Fielding's openers are wonderful examples of the rational dignity of the early eighteenth-century style of beginning a narrative, which is generally with a whole prefatory essay, even after the extensive dedications. These openings are like the lugubrious introductions with which Haydn liked to precede joyous first symphonic movements. For example, this is the rather unpromising way the subsequently lively *Joseph Andrews* begins:

> It is a trite but true observation that examples work more forcibly on the mind than precepts: and if this be just in what is odious and blamable, it is more strongly so in what is amiable and praiseworthy.

The ensuing chapter is short and, before it is over, filled with creeping comedy, including that old London sport: Colley Cibber bashing.

A much more famous first sentence, one which might at first glance appear similar to Fielding's, is the opening of *Anna Karenina*. It is a decidedly nineteenth-century beginning, unimaginable in the late twentieth not only because of its tone, but also due to its content.

It is not the start of a slow windup, like Fielding's, but is given great weight all its own. Tolstoy does so by making it also his entire first paragraph. It is a sort of sociological aphorism presented as an advance moral:

> All happy families resemble one another, but each unhappy family is unhappy in its own way.

Nearly a proverb, but this generalization is not permitted to hold us back for long; an instant later we are in medias res: ''Everything was upset in the Oblonskys' house.'' How different, and how much less Tolstoyan, the beginning of Anna Karenina would be were this the first sentence. The point is that Tolstoy creates a world in which such absolute generalizations are possible and one in which the norms of family life will be rigidly established over against the exigencies of passion. In short, here is the universe in which Anna's fate will work itself out. Already in the first sentence we know what she is up against, into whose hands she has fallen.

The first sentence of Philip Roth's early novella ''Goodbye, Columbus'' makes an instructive comparison to the Tolstoy. Like most great openers, Roth's operates, so to speak, both linearly and spatially—getting the story rolling but, once we have finished reading and can look down on the whole like a map, full of anticipatory significance:

> The first time I saw Brenda she asked me to hold her glasses.

The heart of ''Goodbye, Columbus'' is the complex romance between Brenda Patimkin and Neil Klugman. Roth's first line not only marks the initial moment of this doomed relationship; it also reveals in advance what that relationship is to be and why it is doomed. Brenda will want Neil to be her servant; Neil is also required to do her perceiving for her, while she carelessly goes off to play in her cushioned and chlorinated suburban world. Even Neil's characteristic irony (an important element in dooming the romance) can be discerned in this brief and retrospective sentence; for he already knows what the reader has yet to learn, the gap between Brenda's beauty and her narrow soul, his desire for her and his repulsion. The sentence, then, is momentary, just the first second of the narrative and in this respect like Tolstoy's *second* sentence. But it is also outside the flow of the events it sets in motion, outside their time, itself a kind of generalization, like Tolstoy's *first* sentence. However, unlike the aphorism that begins *Anna Karenina*, Roth's is a generalization that is not abstract but particular and symbolic. For both Tolstoy and Roth the ethical aspects of their tales are paramount; the worlds they create are moral ones, fixed between polar values and soaked with opposed sensibilities. While Tolstoy commences with a magisterial abstraction—solidly impersonal as a Victorian couch—Roth begins with the shifting modern "I" of an alienated narrator whose relativistic world is morally blind and who thus must see twice over: once for himself and once for others.

Formally, the most astounding of all first sentences is probably the celebrated one that begins Heinrich von Kleist's story "The Earthquake in Chile." Here we explode out of a calm *Nihil* before the story begins into the center of a starburst that douses us with data and leads us by means of ever-decreasing turns, like the coils of a great python—spirals of space, time, and catastrophe—until, at its breathless end, we arrive at a single point of crisis about whose meaning we are constrained to be fascinated. At once we know we are in a universe where order and disorder are in battle, one in which events will occur with the shattering speed provided by a zoom lens:

> In Santiago, the capital of the kingdom of Chile, at the very moment of the great earthquake of 1647 in which many thousands of lives were lost, a young Spaniard by the name of Jeronimo Rugera, who had been locked up on a criminal charge, was standing against a prison pillar, about to hang himself.

Kleist's story itself is the perfect example of logical and symmetrical means employed to undermine the logic and symmetry of a providential, rational universe. Beautifully organized, like this first sentence, the story is filled with horror and misleading hope, social irony, private love. The realms of nature, society, and intimacy are arranged in curious relationships that cannot be naively assessed, and all this is announced here, in the great expository sentence; the elements of this world tumble down upon one another: the kingdom of Chile, nature's earthquake, the fate of Jeronimo Rugera. Kleist's sentence is perhaps too detailed to be recalled verbatim, although one never forgets it; but there are many great opening sentences—or opening sentences to great works—readers ought to be able to identify on sight, just as they might a place or a face from childhood. Each marks a moment of creation—in effect, ex nihilo—of an intensely rendered world, the start of a fictional time co-extensive with the pages of the ensuing narrative. Here are a dozen distinctive examples on which to try your memory:

Robert Cohn was once middleweight boxing champion of Princeton.
Once upon a time and a very good time it was there was a moocow coming down the road and this moocow that was coming down along the road met a nicens little boy named baby tuckoo.
Gustave Aschenbach—or von Aschenbach, as he had been known officially since his fiftieth birthday—had set out alone from his house on Prince Regent Street, Munich, for an extended walk.
Towards the end of a sultry afternoon early in July a young man came out of his little room in Stolyarny Lane and turned slowly and somewhat irresolutely in the direction of Kamenny Bridge.
Under certain circumstances there are few hours in life more agreeable than the hour dedicated to the ceremony known as afternoon tea.
To Sherlock Holmes she is always *the* woman.
On May 15, 1796, General Bonaparte made his entry into Milan at the head of that youthful army which but a short time before had crossed the Bridge of Lodi, and taught the world that after so many centuries Caesar and Alexander had a successor.
It was a bright cold day in April, and the clocks were striking thirteen.
Someone must have traduced Joseph K., for without having done anything wrong he was arrested one fine morning.

Through the fence, between the curling flower spaces, I could see them hitting.
In my younger and more vulnerable years my father gave me some advice that I've been turning over in my mind ever since.
It is a truth universally acknowledged that a single man in possession of a good fortune must be in want of a wife.[3]

• • •

Can something come from nothing? In a sense, every one of the above sentences marks the sudden transition from nothing to something, a sort of plunge into waters that did not exist before the dive itself was attempted. Each calls us to attention like a ''for instance'' in a dull lecture; or, to put it differently, with amazing individuality, each constitutes the first brush stroke on an empty canvas.

The urge to ''create'' is not necessarily fused with the desire to create anything in particular, yet creation cannot function in general. Thus, the blocked writer would willingly sell his or her soul for a fine first sentence, were there a soul to sell. Johannes Scottus Eriugena's name for the divinity that preceded Creation was ''Nihil.'' Before the first sentence, the writer too is nothing or, at the least, not a writer. For such people creation is both identity and deliverance.

Notes

1 *The New Encyclopedia of Philosophy* (New York: Philosophical Library, 1972), 93–94.
2 Ibid., 94.
3 Here are the sources of the unidentified first sentences listed in this essay:
Ernest Hemingway, *The Sun Also Rises*
James Joyce, *A Portrait of the Artist as a Young Man*
Thomas Mann, *Death in Venice*
Fyodor Dostoyevsky, *Crime and Punishment*
Henry James, *The Portrait of a Lady*
Sir Arthur Conan Doyle, ''A Scandal in Bohemia''
Stendhal, *The Charterhouse of Parma*
George Orwell, *Nineteen Eighty-four*
Franz Kafka, *The Trial*
William Faulkner, *The Sound and the Fury*
F. Scott Fitzgerald, *The Great Gatsby*
Jane Austen, *Pride and Prejudice*

Six Meditations
on Letters

1.

The five thousand Akkadian letters discovered by André Parrot when he excavated the 3,700-year-old palace of Zimri-Lim all start off with the ritual phrase "To my lord say," just as we might begin, "Dear Ms. Smithers." From the first, letters have been extensions of the human voice. These Akkadian letters were meant to be *said*, rather as a musical score is intended to be *performed*. The ancient letters are matter-of-fact reports and yet they are already touched by the physics of the imagination; that is, by the rearrangement of physical conditions. For instance, I suppose that the writing of letters was initially aimed at obliterating both distance and time. Perhaps the convention was that the writer was actually present as his writing was read aloud to the king. But of course space and time were as relative before King Tut as after Doctor Einstein. To erase distance is simultaneously to join times. Through the medium of the letter the past becomes the present. If a letter could place his front-line commander in Zimri-Lim's presence, then as the king heard the letter from the frontier he was also, in a sense, on the Euphrates; moreover, he was there as the commander wrote the letter.

> To my lord say . . . Yapoh-Adad has made ready the settlement Zallul on this side of the bank of the Euphrates River, and with two thousand troops of the Hapiru of the land, is dwelling in that city. . . . The security forces which are stationed within the brick-enclosure are numerous, and, lest they wipe out the troops, I did not draw near the city. This tablet of mine I send to my lord from the bank of the Euphrates River. The troops and cattle are well.[1]

But while letters undoubtedly bring correspondents closer, this being no less than their original purpose, they cannot help but express distance which, being only imaginatively obliterated by the letter, is also confirmed by its existence. So, in a letter the present indicative is also the past tense. The letter itself proclaims that time has elapsed, distance has been covered. The troops and cattle *were* well when the tablet was inscribed. Thus, a letter always preserves what Nietzsche, in another context, called "the pathos of distance."

2.

According to Angela Pandri, the lifelong friendship of the T'ang dynasty poets Po Chu-i and Yuan Chen is "the most memorable relationship in the literary history of China."[2] This friendship was
conducted almost entirely through letters—and also through dreams,
which themselves may be only the extremest form of the inwardness
of a real correspondence like Po's and Yuan's. Po even wrote letter-
poems about these dream-meetings with his exiled friend, these in
addition to their many exchanges about each other's lives and work.

Of course literary letters written only out of the pretension of the
writers are no more real letters than the ones we get from Ed McMa-
hon or our congresspersons. In considering this sort of falseness one
might recall Madame Stavrogin's devastating retort to Pyotr Stepa-
novich in Camus's version of *The Possessed:* "Twenty years of vanity
and posturing! Even the letters you sent me were written for posterity. You are not a friend; you are a stylist!" However, that Po and
Yuan were not guilty of such counterfeiting in their letters ought to
be clear from one of Po's most beautiful poems, which is, in fact,
about receiving a letter from his friend Yuan. It is entitled "The Letter" and is itself a letter. I think all those who understand what it is
to receive a real letter, to wait for it, looking forward eagerly to the
daily mail and searching through the flyers and bills for something
that promises to be genuine and inward, will be touched by Po's
verses:

> They came and told me a messenger from Shang-chou
> Had brought a letter,—a single scroll from you!
> Up from my pillow I suddenly sprang out of bed,
> And threw on my clothes, all topsy-turvy.
> I undid the knot and saw the letter within;
> A single sheet with thirteen lines of writing.
> At the top it told the sorrows of an exile's heart;
> At the bottom it described the pains of separation.
> The sorrows and pains took up so much space
> There was no room left to talk about the weather![3]

Was it for a weather report that Po leapt out of bed and undid the knot with hurrying fingers? Of course not, for Po knew that in a genuine letter the inward should displace the outward. That is, perhaps, what people mean when they refer to "real" letters. One can understand what is real about real letters simply by reflecting on what is not real about other kinds of letters. But this reality lies not only in the letter itself, nor even in the intent of the letter writer. It rests also with the reader, a reader such as Po. The reality of a real letter is bound to the interest and sympathy with which it will be read, also perhaps the degree to which its honesty flatters the recipient. A dead letter is one lacking a reader.

3.

The lesson called for Mrs. Rodgers to teach us third-graders how to write letters. She began by describing the two kinds of letters that existed in the world. These she denoted the Friendly Letter and the Business Letter. On the blackboard she outlined a Friendly Format and a Business Format and set us to practice writing imaginary letters of both sorts, filling these dry bottles with our weak grape juice.

Even at the time I wondered whether this division of letters into only two varieties might not be a little too categorical. Indeed, since then I have become familiar with many genres of correspondence: the letter of inquiry, the letter of application, the letter of recommendation (or "wreck-emendation" as I sometimes think of it), the satirical rejoinder, the angry riposte (I mean the one you write then prudently throw away), the thank-you note, the academic memorandum, the letter to a parent, the letter of condolence, the billet-doux, the travel letter, the letter of rejection, the letter of credit, even the suicide note. Though this list is long, I wonder if Mrs. Rodgers may have been more right than wrong. Hers is as good an organizing schism as any. Friendly letters are not businesslike, and vice versa, at least not usually. An exception may be the letters I got from my father when I was a child at summer camp.

My father, a lawyer who could type faster than the first generation of IBM printers, was a whiz at the business letter. What he sent to me at camp puzzled and disappointed me because they were all precisely in Mrs. Rodgers's business format. Even the language was businesslike: "Hoping you are well, I am . . ." Though my father had a sharp sense of humor, these were not ironic letters with a content running counter to their form. In fact, I would say the one fit into the other just so. Grimly in the woods, I imagined my father writing them—one draft, maybe two or three minutes of machine-gun tapping. Was it Friendly or Business? Had the composition of thousands of lawyers' letters bound my father so strictly to one format that he could no longer fall into epistolary informality even with a child? His feeling, I had to suppose, lay *behind* these letters of his, since there was none to be found *inside* them. Function, I hoped childishly, did not follow form.

The formulaic nature of letters is, after all, peculiar. We customarily begin by assuring people, even those whom we don't know, that they are *dear* to us and close by asserting that we have been *sincere* with them (my father favored "very truly yours"). It is as if this rigmarole were essential to reinforce the idea that the letter is in fact written to its addressee and that it means what it says, though often neither is the case. For instance, a letter can be the means by which a crank lets off steam in the direction of a newspaper editor, or a letter might be a missive from self to soul—in each case the addressee being merely the public occasion for private ruminations.

Letter form is strict enough that one can play with it. In my misery during last summer's heat wave, I took to replacing the date at the upper right of my letters with "Neo-Jurassic Period." Robertson Davies's alter ego Samuel Marchbanks is a great master of the pointed sign-off: "Yours in a very limited sense" for instance, or "Yours with warmest admiration down to the ankles." Rigidity of structure—indeed, rigidity of any sort—positively provokes the spirit of parody, and letter form (friendly or business) is no exception. One can play such games with one's letters as no mere telephoner could imagine. I once made up a literary agent for myself who both wrote and negotiated like an entry-level mafioso. Of course the genteel editor for whom I playfully created this barely literate ruffian knew that Luigi Swarthrectum was only a figment of my silly capriciousness, but the correspondence proceeded amusingly on that basis for several weeks. I could never have had such fun over the phone.

Compared to letters, virtually any conversation is grossly inarticulate and bumbling. Remember the Nixon tapes? Ever read the work of a court stenographer? The friendly letter is not really ''conversational''; Mrs. Rodgers was right. It too has its form. Is it not a foolish prejudice to insist that the prattling of a telephonic dialogue is more genuine than a witty letter on the assumption that what is clumsy and halting must be more sincere than what is formally considered and amusingly expressed?

Still, one can carry respect for the purely formal aspect of letters too far. In effect, the form letter is what you get when you do the carrying. While all form letters are by no means written by machines, they all *could* be. But is a mechanical letter a ''real'' letter at all, one worth springing out of bed for? If it were, why would corporations spend so much on machines whose chief talent is to create letters that appear not to be machine-made, right down to the fake ''signature'' in blue ink? Would anyone hasten to open the knot on such a letter? Is anybody fooled or flattered? Is anyone not disgusted by the masquerade? No, a good letter, like a good sonnet, ought to do something individual within the form of the universal.

4.

''I am extremely concerned, my dearest friend, for the disturbances that have happened in your family.'' So begins the letter from Miss Howe to Miss Harlowe that opens Samuel Richardson's spacious epistolary novel, *Clarissa*. This is almost what any eager reader might say to any sympathetic protagonist. Oedipus, I'm concerned. Hamlet, I'm worried. Miss Bennet, I'm on the edge of my easy chair. Madame Bovary, watch out! You too, Anna Arkadyevna!

That letters can rise to the level of literature or that literature can enact itself in the form of letters is hardly to be doubted. We have not only epistolary novels, but verse epistles, story-letters, famous ''open'' letters, prison letters, the collected correspondence of gifted writers. A more daring and capacious thought is to wonder if *all* of literature may not be conceived as letters—daring, but not original. One of Emily Dickinson's most famous and touching poems begins:

> This is my letter to the World
> That never wrote to me . . .

Her letter is her oeuvre. The poem ends with the quite personal plea that we, her "sweet countrymen," her readers, judge Emily "tenderly."

The idea of imaginative literature as a letter to a world that does not always open—let alone answer—its mail is also embodied in Herman Melville's "Bartleby the Scrivener," which on an autobiographical level is surely the tale of the apparent failure of Melville's novels to interest those same "sweet countrymen." The fire at his publisher's that consumed the plates of his earlier books, his artist's despair, his deeply depressed desire for "motionlessness," even his later renunciation of fiction are all in Bartleby, whose baffling negative preferences are nearly explained at the end by the "rumor" that he used to work in the Post Office's Dead Letter Office.

> Dead letters! does it not sound like dead men? Conceive a man by nature and misfortune prone to a pallid hopelessness: can any business seem more fitted to heighten it than that of continually handling these dead letters, and assorting them for the flames?

After all, the transaction of a letter is a *correspondence*, and a living letter must have its reader. The same holds for poetry and novels, except that poets and novelists generally do not know the name of the addressee (though the persistence of the old custom of dedicating a work to an individual endures and vestigially suggests the idea of a letter). But writers who do not know their readership need not for that reason entirely ignore their audience. Many may even imagine, however vaguely, sentimentally, or megalomaniacally, an Ideal Reader—perhaps some graduate student in the twenty-first century. Writers who get a million readers in one year (and none the second) know their correspondents in about the same way a marketing analyst knows his or her consumers. But those writers who only get their million readers over a century are more like those correspondents whose letters achieve genuineness and depth by, so to speak, ignoring the addressee. Ignoring the addressee does not mean one doesn't need one, of course. If there were no readers there could be no writers, even if those both turn out to be the same person. One can write letters to oneself as well as to the world.

The words *literature* and *letter* have the same root and so, I am suggesting, do the concepts for which they stand. Both begin as extensions of the voice over distance and time. The pleasure and interest with which we read worthy personal letters are not so different from those with which we pore over our favorite authors. In both we find a voice we like, news that concerns us, a communion that broadens and deepens the scope of our experience. In both we are struck by qualities of form, by individuality harnessed to the universal, by messages that seem intended for us, as only we can bring them to life. For all such letters, even if it is impossible to write back, we ought to be grateful, we ought to judge tenderly.

5.

Why did Franz Kafka write so many letters?

Though I think this is a new question, a great deal has been written, virtually all of it incisive, about Kafka's letters. Erich Heller's introduction to the massive volume of *Letters to Felice* is a subtle analysis not only of Kakfa's love life but of his entire situation as a human being. Willi Haas, in prefacing his edition of *Letters to Milena*, tells us not only what manner of woman Milena Jesenska was but also about Kafka's ambivalence toward his Jewishness. Elias Canetti has devoted an entire book, *Kafka's Other Trial*, to the author's on-again, off-again engagement based on the letters to Fraulein Bauer. The volume of collected *Letters to Friends, Family, and Editors* is as fat as the *Letters to Felice*. So, despite the demands of his job, his illness, his fiction, and his diaries, it looks as if Kafka must often have written half a dozen letters a day, none of them merely formulaic or thoughtless, a large proportion of them several pages in length, all of them as distinctive as his stories.

Why so many?

One might be tempted to answer such a question stupidly, for example by remarking that the postal services of central Europe in the first two decades of our century were highly efficient, and that Kafka's letters are really the last flower of a dying technology, as the telephone was on the point of superseding the post when he died in 1924. Nowadays, one might confidently suppose, Kafka would occupy his afternoons and evenings on the phone to Berlin or Vienna.

Only a little less stupid is the answer that Kafka was, after all, a man of letters and, as such, was bound to favor the written word. If his letters are distinguished this is only because, being Kafka, he was incapable of writing anything undistinguished. "All that is not literature bores me," Kafka once confessed. Very well then, his letters *are* literature. They are characterized by that thrusting, almost pedantic precision about the inner life that one finds everywhere in his work. The letters are as much a part of his oeuvre as *The Trial* or the *Diaries;* thus they are not only letters to Felice, Milena, or Max but—incidentally, so to speak—letters to the world. In them Kafka covers over his correspondents with words as a landscape is transfigured by snowflakes. In the case of Felice Bauer this transformation by Kafka's imagination seems really to have taken place. In describing his first meeting with Felice, Kafka writes in his diary of "an empty face that wore its emptiness openly." Heller comments on the torrent of letters thrown at this face in the last months of 1912:

> Empty: thus it offers as much room as an empty page to the expansive imagination. And indeed, this imagination instantly falls in love, and before long word-storms, let loose in Prague, will blow around the beloved empty face in Berlin.[4]

The greatest number of letters are written to women. It is only too clear that the letter form is superbly suited to Kafka's approach/ avoidance behavior with women. To write is to make contact, but also to preserve distance, to be and not to be on the Euphrates. Kafka's struggle to be married was never a struggle to wed any particular woman; it was a battle with his talent and with the world itself, to which marriage represented the most ethical and natural bond. If Kafka's work is dreamlike and neurotic, then Felice symbolizes health and reality. Here is Heller once again:

> It is moving and at the same time terrifying to watch his words—
> how, in their entrancing dexterity and calculated helplessness, they
> woo this "reality" of hers, those fragments of reality he gathers in
> through this correspondence, and how they maintain the precarious
> state of balance between the "real" and the "literary." And all the
> time they are on the verge of becoming literature themselves. . . .

True, true, except that now they really *are* literature. Why should
the *real* and the *literary* be balanced against one another? Which one
imitates the other is a perennially vexing question, after all. Kafka's
letters contain a surprising amount of comic invention that one could
see as "literary." This sheer playfulness may not constitute fictional
escapes from the real questions of marriage and bachelorhood. Often
it is enchanting entertainment, for the letters to Felice and Milena
are obviously a means of seduction. They are seductions but also
deceptions, though it is a very odd kind of deception that comes from
telling more of the truth than any correspondent could be expected
to take in. There is a great deal in these love letters of angling, of
playing the correspondent on the hook, which is all the harder to do
when the fisherman is deeply undecided about reeling in.

Why did Kafka write so many letters, then? Because he *liked* writing them, because the form was so congenial. Kafka certainly appears
very much himself and even at ease in his letters. It seems to me he
expresses himself in many of them at greater length and with more
facility than in his diaries. So it is not surprising that he chose the
letter as the form in which to explain such deadly things to his father
who, living a mere few steps away, could only be addressed at a
distance and in a form that allowed of no interruptions. Though
Kafka does not omit to invent his father's interruptions in the famous
Letter to His Father, it is, after all, Kafka who invents them, so they
are not truly interruptions but parts of the flowing dialectic of this
critical autobiography. The letter to his father was never delivered;
in fact, it is the most notorious dead letter of twentieth-century literature.

But the fluidity and volubility of Kafka's letters suggest also that
letter writing must have been for him a relief, a discharge of tension
and feeling. In fact, Kafka's letters are wonderful in part because

they so often begin with something decisively human and inward, whether fear ("Dearest Father, you asked me recently why I maintain that I am afraid of you.") or love ("Today Milena, Milena, Milena— I can't write anything else. But I will.") or anxiety ("Where is the doctor? I'm searching the letter without reading it just to find the doctor. Where is he?"). Moreover, the letters allow him to enter with fantastic zeal into the lives of his correspondents—though always preserving a distance, of course—just as he records the trivial round of his own days in phenomenal detail and with athletic inventiveness. The sheer pleasure Kafka must have taken in writing is more evident from these letters than even from Kafka's "real" work.

No doubt a part of this pleasure came from the escape provided by letter writing; I mean the escape from what one might call the nonreality of the actual self into the solid reality of the imagined correspondent. Kafka wrote so many letters because he found them easy to write. In one sense, it was easy because he was not a writer when he wrote them and his stern Flaubertian demands on himself could be relaxed. In what sense not a writer, though? In the high sense Thomas Mann gave the title when he said that "a writer is a person for whom writing is more difficult than it is for other people."

And there is one other reason why Kafka wrote so many letters. Love for his correspondents and for receiving *their* letters. All prisoners rush for the mail like Po Chu-i, and worry when there is nothing for them. To Milena, Kafka wrote reproachfully:

Please write the address a little more distinctly, once your letter is in the envelope it's already almost my property and you should treat other people's property with more care. . . .

And a few weeks later, still more charmingly:

The addresses are again unclear, Milena, written over and completed by the postal authorities. The addresses, after my first plea, were wonderful, a model collection of beautiful, varied, although not always legible specimens of handwriting. If the post office had my eyes, it would be able to read almost only your addresses and no others. But as it is the post office—

By the way, while letter writing is not a frequent theme in Kafka's fiction, there is one crucial exception. "The Judgment," his breakthrough story, was written in one night in September 1912; that is, just after the first meeting with Felice Bauer and during the period when he was beginning to snow her under with letters. Here Georg's letter to his friend in Russia is the fulcrum on which the story of father and son turns.

Georg, out of misplaced thoughtfulness or perhaps guilt, does not want to write his suffering and lonesome bachelor friend out in Russia about his engagement (the fiancée's initials are, of course, F.B.):

> So Georg confined himself to giving his friend unimportant items of gossip such as rise at random in the memory when one is idly thinking things over on a quiet Sunday. . . .

In other words, Georg writes a sort of form letter; he writes idly of externals. When his father suddenly rises up to condemn Georg it is not only over the issue of the engagement; it is initially for having carried on such a mendacious correspondence:

> that's why you had to lock yourself up in your office. . . . just so that you could write your lying little letters to Russia.

And, as if the power of letters were, like all other powers, being wrested back again from son to father, the old man reveals that he has been keeping the friend better informed all along, that each of Georg's letters has been dead, as he too will shortly be:

> He knows it all already, you stupid boy, he knows it all! I've been writing to him . . . in his left hand he crumples your letters unopened while in his right hand he holds up my letters to read through.

The power of letters is great for Kafka, but ultimately he judged it to be a negative power. The logophagous ghosts that haunt the postal system, the nothingness of the spaces between letters, these became for him the very image of the impossibility of honest human contact and of love. Already in 1920 Kafka predicted that the new technologies—ever faster and more deviously and desperately immediate—could not change this. Here, in one of his last letters to Milena, and surely one of the most shattering, a letter written after their impossible relationship had cooled, Kafka undoes the fantasic knot of all his letters and condemns letter writing itself as humiliating, forlorn, and even worse than futile:

It's a long time since I wrote to you, Frau Milena. . . . Actually , I don't have to apologize for my not writing, you know after all how I hate letters. All the misfortune of my life—I don't wish to complain, but to make a generally instructive remark—derives, one could say, from letters or from the possibility of writing letters. People have hardly ever deceived me, but letters always—and as a matter of fact not only those of other people, but my own. In my case this is a special misfortune of which I won't say more, but at the same time also a general one. The easy possibility of letter-writing must—seen merely theoretically—have brought into the world a terrible disintegration of souls. It is, in fact, an intercourse with ghosts, and not only with the ghost of the recipient but also with one's own ghost which develops between the lines of the letter one is writing and even more so in a series of letters where one letter corroborates the other and can refer to it as a witness. How on earth did anyone get the idea that people can communicate with one another by letter! Of a distant person one can think, and of a person who is near one can catch hold—all else goes beyond human strength. Writing letters, however, means to denude oneself before the ghosts, something for which they greedily wait. Written kisses don't reach their destination, rather they are drunk on the way by the ghosts. It is on this ample nourishment that they multiply so enormously. Humanity senses this and fights against it and in order to eliminate as far as possible the ghostly element between people and to create a natural communication, the peace of souls, it has invented the railway, the motor car, the aeroplane. But it's no longer any good, these are evidently inventions being made at the moment of crashing. The opposing side is so much calmer and stronger; after the postal service it has invented the telegraph, the telephone, the radiograph. The ghosts won't starve, but we will perish.

It is ironic that in his final illness Kafka, no longer able to speak and barely able to swallow, had to substitute for his voice little letters directed to those gathered around him. Even the tiny space between a deathbed and the chair beside it gaped wide and had to be traversed by letters, by these haiku-letters. The very last of these slips, drily interpreted by the editor as a response to the doctor's leaving the room, reads as follows:

So the help goes away again without helping.

6.

I have made this letter longer than usual because
I lack the time to make it short.
—Blaise Pascal, *Lettres Provençiales*

Kafka, the great letter writer, deconstructs not only letters, but even telephones and telegrams. Ghosts suck the life out of our disembodied voices, he says in his alienation. He was right. It is the twentieth century and, even if we are more crowded together than ever, and communication over vast distances is increasingly an "easy possibility" in this global village, actual communion does remain pretty tough.

But letters are not always meant to be transparent or messages from the soul, let alone eaten. Some letters are like solid, indigestible objects—bricks, for example. I am not excessively proud of my professional correspondence; however, after receiving a lengthy and bitterly reproachful letter from me (the kind one is supposed prudently to throw away before mailing) a college administrator reportedly said, "Wexelblatt shouldn't be let loose behind a typewriter." I think this is the finest compliment I have ever been paid as a writer. I would be honored to have it for an epitaph.

There is a poet I once knew who, driven to distraction by scores of rejection letters, mimeographed a few hundred copies of a letter of his own. As I recall, it began like this: "I am sorry to have to send you this form letter, but I receive so many rejections that I am unable to answer each of them personally. . . ."

The spirit of letter writing survives, but has letter writing itself become obsolete? It may have, though it is still widely practiced. After all, when a technology becomes superseded it may avoid oblivion and instead achieve any number of nonutilitarian destinies. It may become quaint (like blacksmithing), an art (like calligraphy), an eccentricity (like fountain pens), an affectation (like celluloid collars), a proof of dogged resistance to progress (like manual typewriters), an expression of elitism or affection for tradition (like sailboats). In short, the aesthetic may replace the useful.

In a sense, letter writing has become obsolete since the technology used to produce and move letters has been largely superseded by electronic media. The proliferation of greeting cards, condolence cards, birthday cards, of computer-generated "personalized" advertisements and junk mail in general, bank statements, bulletins, bills and invoices, boilerplate legal correspondence—all mass-produced and inauthentic letters—suggests the letter's lack of vitality. Who can deny that more personal communication is now conducted by telephone than by letter? The telephone, of course, promises an immediacy the letter cannot; it overcomes distance and time more thoroughly. Better yet, it doesn't even require literacy.

Yet in every gain, a loss. To some the loss may seem negligible, so slight as to be no loss at all, while to others what is given up may appear irreplaceable and the gain hardly worth the candle. The telephone's instantaneousness cancels out the letter's pathos of distance in which more may transpire than time.

For example, the distance preserved in the letter allows for more dignity on the part of both the writer and the reader than does a telephone call. Dignity is a thing we begin to learn with our toilet training; we apprehend it in the twin demands that we *wait* and exercise *self-control*. Those who can wait and control themselves have the rudiments of dignity. The letter is more dignified than the phone call in the sense that a letter compels us to await a reply and to control ourselves, not only as we wait, but also in our answer. In a letter, one must choose one's words, while, relatively speaking, phone conversations tend to be reflexive and slovenly. Since the whole appeal of the telephone is its instantaneousness, we quite naturally resent being put on "hold" or, worse yet, interrupted by the besieging clicks of "call waiting." But these are only the measure of the impatience that afflicts the entire telephone network, a cacophony of clamoring voices, urgent and summoning, like the undignified child trying to compel his mother's attention: "Talk to *me*. *Now!*"

The same contrast holds with respect to individuality and personality. Many telephone conversations are only *shallowly* personal. Since there is an immediate exchange of voices, there is an apparent personality in the transaction, perhaps even a degree of sincerity that one might question in a letter. And yet most phone calls are really generic and one can even more easily cultivate an insincere telephone manner than a distanced literary style. Between the ritual "Hello" and the conventional "Bye-bye" not everything that is said truly expresses the speakers. There is more often an exchange of facts, needs, news. The interlocutors may not even be paying the sort of attention that one must in reading a letter. One or the other may be putting away groceries, watching television, painting toenails. The mind divides; all one needs to keep many phone conversations afloat is an occasional "Um-hum." One could even go so far as to say that we tend to communicate *externals* over the telephone, while a genuine letter is genuine in so far as it expresses *internals*. The exception here may be, oddly enough, teenagers. Though most of their distended telephone conversations are inarticulate and many downright inane, sometimes they go on so long because of the adolescent urge to express feelings: "Like, I mean, you know?" More dignified and more punctilious in their language because of their adulthood, grown-ups commonly object to this not only on account of the grammar and the phone bills, but also because they cannot see that the teenagers are talking *about* anything—that is, about anything of external significance. In an earlier era, the emotional teenager might have kept a diary, to which the traditional form of address was that of the letter: "Dear Diary, today Victor smiled at me across the gingham in the dry goods store. It made me go feathery all over." True letters are always potentially intimate things.

Letters, therefore, are also more private forms of communication than telephone conversations. That is why we still feel it a worse crime to read someone else's mail than to eavesdrop on their phone calls. The envelope, like the old wax seal, is a sign of this inviolability of the letter. Postcards, of course, are all faintly ridiculous nonletters. There is nothing to *seal*.

To sum up, here are some of the advantages of the phone call over the letter:

a. immediacy (e.g., one at least knows the other is alive during the phone call);

b. hearing the voice of the other (frequently this is all one really desires);

c. the impact of intrusion (as in "telemarketing," more favored by sellers than buyers);

d. nonchalance, ephemerality (one is freed from the awful responsibility of choosing one's words, or consulting one's lawyer about them).

Here are some of the advantages of the letter over the phone call:

a. You can read a letter whenever you want. It is not an intrusion. You can even throw it away without reading it.

b. You needn't reply to a letter. It never *rings*.

c. You can save a letter.

d. If you do choose to reply to a letter, you can look closely at what you are replying to.

e. Letters allow us the chance to see even the long-gone and immensely dignified with their pants at least halfway down.

Notes

1 James B. Pritchard, ed., *The Ancient Near East* (Princeton: Princeton University Press, 1958), 261–262.

2 See Greg Simon, "Seeking Kindness from the Dust," *Northwest Review* 19, nos. 1–2 (1981): 265.

3 Ibid., 266. Translation by Arthur Waley.

4 Franz Kafka, *Letters to Felice* (New York: Schocken, 1973), xx.

.

Invasion of the Bourgeois Snatchers

Civilization has always meant walls, which is to say distinctions. Somebody discovers agriculture and that leads to the granary, followed rapidly by the walled village, a protection against distinctionless nomads. Later come the fortress, the castle, the villa, the hacienda, the chambered house, the apartment, the study, the office, bathrooms and bedrooms, locked cars, sealed crypts. Civilization defines spaces; it makes insides and outsides.

Literature, I think, often takes up an ambiguous relationship to this making of enclosures. A lot of it is devoted to undermining walls. Poetry and narrative often work by artfully confusing what is inside and outside. You could say that in one of its impulses literature is primitive, casting back before the walls to a less differentiated sense of things, or, if you prefer, sympathizing with the nomads. Even though the nomads did not build walls they certainly told stories, a habit that persisted when they conquered the granaries and became the overlords of the walled cities. The nomads, now aristocrats, celebrated their warrior virtues in epics like *The Iliad* and *Beowulf* in which the distinction between inner life and outward activity is minimal, where handsome is and handsome does. As Hamlet notes when preparing himself for princely action, epic contests are properly "between the pass and fell incensed points of mighty opposites"—Achilles versus Hector, Aeneus versus Turnus. In the heroic drama of neoclassicism honor and love collide with a nearly tedious regularity. The Achaean kings, whose fathers were northern marauders and whose sons succumbed to the next wave of the same, achieved their destinies by combat outside the walls, though they might be fighting over what lay inside. This aristocratic literature celebrates risk, power, domination, ruthless prowess. It provided Friedrich Nietzsche with his model of Master Morality: "My best friend is my worst enemy. He keeps me on my toes." Patroclus brings out the best in Achilles only when he is killed by Hector.

"Working-class literature" is a too-small quilt of a phrase; it can't cover all it is meant to. Loads of things that heroic literature pretends to disdain—history, ethnic origin, economic determinism, generational differences, the critical role of protagonistic women—here become so important that universality cannot be taken by storm and simple categorization is far too simple. Moreover, its study is a new field with open questions to resolve, such as whether an educated and literate writer of working-class background is still a member of that class at all. Such literature is also a new phenomenon because only recently has literacy been available to the working class. Still, a few generalizations may be gingerly advanced, so long as one is ready to take them back quickly enough. For instance, conflict in working-class narratives tends to be played out within the family. Characters have a heightened sense of dominance and oppression. The antagonists are systematic and structural, like poverty, racism, sexism, and internalized class consciousness itself. Also, many stories imply a sort of secondary conflict, a choice not between love and honor, but between rootedness and escape, life within the walls (other people's walls, mostly) or flight into a wilderness or an education. Suffering here is grinding and inevitable, not sudden and honorable. Life is insecure not because risk is demanded by a heroic code but because of marginal economic or social status and the ills that go with them. Nobody is offered the neat choice of Achilles, whether to live long and dully or briefly and gloriously. Conditions are in the saddle and so the stories tend to be about the collective impact of these conditions often as seen by one who, like the writer, is half inside and half outside, one foot planted in the material, the other in the means of its expression, as in *How Green Was My Valley, A Tree Grows in Brooklyn,* or *Sons and Lovers,* each with its loved, hated, oppressive, nostalgic, constraining village walls. The sheer humanity of this literature is stunning. This is humanity naked in the wind; Lear humanized by deprivation. What is true of the best working-class literature is what Lawrence Ferlinghetti said about Francisco Goya:

> In Goya's greatest scenes we seem to see
>
>   the people of the world
>
>   exactly at the moment when
>
>   they first attained the title of
>
>   "suffering humanity"

This suffering comprises, as Anton Chekhov insisted in the teeth of

Tolstoy's elitist romanticization of the Russian peasant, drunkenness, bigotry, and brutality,.

The kind of recurrent tale this essay is about is altogether different from the above. That it is a middle-class story and that it belongs to the last century and a half is, I think, pretty clear. What I want to claim is that it has become both *the* middle-class story and one of the typical modernist fables. Unlike the characteristic narratives of those originally at the top or the bottom, this bourgeois story does not celebrate the values or experience of the class it describes. On the contrary, it is the self-critical nature of the story that, for me, confirms it as bourgeois through and through.

In China and Japan, the novel was born as an aristocratic form, but in the West the rise of prose fiction paralleled the rise of the middle class. Broadly speaking, in the West aristocrats favored poetry, the working class plays, but the English shopkeeper of the eighteenth century, his wife and children, preferred something in plain language and about people more or less like themselves. To avoid the immoral and perilous stewpots of the theaters, they wanted something to read alone in the secure confines of that little castle which is every middle-class Englishman's home, a drama to play out in their private heads or to read to the family circle, like the Bible. The stories should be edifying, secular, and ought to supply some of the same demand met by the new gossip broadsides. (An old professor of mine speaking of Thomas Mann: "All novels are at least eighty percent gossip.")

The middle class rose with industrialization and urbanization. The novel is tied to the city, which provides its typical setting but also the model for its web of characters and coincidences. We can say, then, that prose fiction in the West is nonaristocratic, tied to the world of commerce, that it stresses bourgeois individualism both in its themes and, just as essentially, in the mode of its consumption. From *Robinson Crusoe* through the novels of Samuel Richardson and Henry Fielding up to *Pride and Prejudice* and *David Copperfield*, the English novel in particular treated the aspirations and peregrinations of middle-class characters making their way in the world, making their way above all to financial and marital security.

Once the middle class had really made it, however, things began to change. Security itself is criticized, for example in the great nineteenth-century novels of adultery, *Madame Bovary* and *Anna Karenina*. The quest to rise, to build up the walls of the bourgeois home and the stolid values of middle-class regularity, is displaced by another story, one that shades into the fable of modernism itself. It is a story of invasion, of stability called into question and undermined by antithetical forces. Explosion becomes implosion. Moreover, the origin of the nomads who invade this middle-class space is ambiguous at the root; they come from the outside and the inside at once. The story, therefore, often takes the form of a double tale, Jekyll the respectable, Hyde the invader from within.

Most of the examples I have in mind of this story about the undermining of the middle class, of its invasion by the subversive, disruptive and nomadic, are not English, but American, Russian, or German. Georg Lukacs began his essay on Dostoyevsky with this sentence: "It is a strange, but often repeated fact that the literary embodiment of a new human type with all its problems comes to the civilized world from a young nation." He offers the illustrations of Werther and Raskolnikov. Now whether America, Germany, and Russia are to be deemed young nations may be less important than that they were, in a sense and for a time, peripheral ones. Lukacs carefully distinguishes between works of such cultures that present the merely exotic and those that embody the totality of questions affecting the core of a culture. I don't know if there's much to Lukacs's idea; perhaps it is only a matter of illumination. The lamps that light up the baseball field are never on the field itself.

In any event, the rudiments of the invasion story are simply stated. A middle-class character situated securely within the walls of home, job, and self, nestled in a rationalized and limited vision of life, has these walls breached by a character or a force that is alien and disruptive. But this outside is somehow also an inside, so that the invasion is presented as a crisis of self-doubt. Thus, the outside force, though dangerous to health, social position, sanity, and self-concept, grows in intimacy with the middle-class character and the process has the effect of revealing previously concealed or repressed truths or broadening the range of compassion and the scale of feeling. The middle-class character may be changed or even destroyed, may cut himself

off from the alien threat in order to save himself, but will not be the
same afterwards. The nature of these changes is suggested by a list
of adjectives describing the middle-class character prior to the crisis:
secure, temperate, calculating, routinized, complacent, self-seeking,
conforming, repressed, prudential. Some examples: Herman Melville's "Bartleby the Scrivener," Tolstoy's *The Death of Ivan Ilych*,
Chekhov's *Ward Number Six*, Mann's *Death in Venice*, lots of Kafka—
The Metamorphosis, The Trial, and such short works as "An Old Manuscript" or "The Burrow," Joseph Conrad's "The Secret Sharer,"
Lionel Trilling's "Of This Time, Of That Place," Joyce Carol Oates's
much-anthologized story "Where Are You Going, Where Have You
Been?" Variations on a theme.

As if it were a maze, "Bartleby the Scrivener" is crammed with
walls, from its subtitle and setting—"A Story of Wall Street"—to the
carefully described subdivisions of the lawyer's office, the "dead-
wall reveries" of the despairing Bartleby, down to the thick Egyptian
walls of the Tombs, where Bartleby at last curls up and dies. Why
does the forlorn scrivener prefer not to write, eat, or live? "Don't
you see the reason for yourself?" he replies, staring at a brick wall.
Here is the once-nomadic Melville's protest against cities, blind critics, American business, even the confinement of his own art. All the
same, the story is not primarily Bartleby's but the narrator's, the
Master-in-Chancery's. In it can be found all the elements of the invasion fable, already in 1853. The narrator's walled-in quarters and
walled-up self are invaded by a spirit of pure negativity—an "incubus," he calls Bartleby—and the story turns from realism and thus
turns on the unexplained fact, not of Bartleby's preferences, but that
the narrator is unable to throw Bartleby into the street. The reason
for this debility rests in the inner state of the narrator, who responds
to Bartleby with guilt, protectiveness, increasing intimacy. From the
first he places Bartleby on his side of the major interior wall of his
office:

> I resolved to assign Bartleby a corner by the folding-doors, but on
> my side of them. . . .

And yet this man who boasts that his two great points are prudence
and method preserves his distance:

Still farther to a satisfactory arrangement, I procured a high green folding screen, which might entirely isolate Bartleby from my sight, though not remove him from my voice. And thus, in a manner, privacy and society were conjoined.

Notice that last phrase about privacy and society; in it the inner and the outer begin to penetrate one another. Later on, in his remorse and compassion, the narrator will actually offer to move Bartleby into his "own dwelling."

The Master-in-Chancery begins by giving himself the character of the perfect bourgeois bachelor, hating Byron, admiring Cicero, exploiting his employees, rationalizing their low wages, praising himself as "an eminently safe man" who is fond of "the cool tranquillity of a snug retreat" in which he does "a snug business among rich men's bonds, and mortgages, and title deeds." Papers and not people. Smugness and property. Safety, prudence, method. He is content even with the lifeless view of walls that surround him, for these walls make for snugness as his business does for smugness.

In a sense, Bartleby undermines the walls that kill him, that symbolize what kills him, what he is up against. As the embodiment of the American nightmare, his presence undercuts the narrator's realization of the American dream (in the 1980s *The Wall Street Journal* openly took to calling itself the daily chronicle of the American dream). Everybody in the office starts using the nonrational verb "prefer," and the narrator's reason itself begins to totter. He loses even his masculine identity before the passive Bartleby, whose resistance he twice says "unmanned" him, as though there were a feeling woman inside a Wall Street lawyer. But then Bartleby is the female here, as Billy Budd is in his story.

The emotional climax of the tale comes when the narrator discovers Bartleby living alone in his office on a Sunday morning, a discovery so spiritually important that it prevents him from going to hear a famous preacher:

> For the first time in my life a feeling of over-powering stinging melancholy seized me. . . . The bond of a common humanity now drew me irresistibly to gloom. A fraternal melancholy!

But enough explication. The story is well known. The narrator, fearing to lose his reputation as the rumors spread, betrays and denies Bartleby Saint Peter-wise; the scrivener is taken away, dies, and we feel so strongly that the narrator has been humanized in the process that we look back on the description he had given of himself at the outset and see that it is riddled with irony:

> I do not speak it in vanity, but simply record the fact, that I was not unemployed in my profession by the late John Jacob Astor; a name which, I admit, I love to repeat. . . .

This is that same Astor who came to the New World and despoiled the continent's furry animals, bought up large tracts of Manhattan island, and established what became the New York Public Library, where you can read all the Melville you like. The Master-in-Chancery (lost in the perplexity of a spiritual Chancery Court) does not aspire to leave the walls for the wilderness, as Astor did to become a grandee; he is middle-class, after all, "unambitious" and "snug." As the putative author of "Bartleby the Scrivener," though, he makes a mockery of the values by which he has lived. Psychologically, Bartleby has been his passive, infantile, rebellious, pessimistic self; in fact, all the selves he has buried to become so . . . snug.

Things happen *to* such characters as the Master-in-Chancery. They are not properly protagonists at all. Action is initiated against them, so to speak. Their walls are assailed. But they must defend these walls as much from fifth-columnists as from the invader at the gates. As in the famous Cavafy poem, the final fear may be that the barbarian nomads will never come, or even that the true barbarians are the people huddled so snugly inside the walls.

But where is Melville in all this? Where is the bourgeois artist? In the interior drama of "Bartleby," Melville's despair over the failure of his novels, the destruction of their plates in the fire at his publisher's, his distaste for the yes-saying world of Wall Street and the dehumanization of cramped cities put him on the side of Bartleby, who is less a character than a gesture. Melville shows us that the middle-class writer is himself an invader of bourgeois consciousness, bringing messages that may, like dead letters, not be received. This is likewise, I think, why the nomads from the north in "An Old Manuscript," Kafka's concentrated blueprint of the bourgeois invasion story, "communicate with each other much as jackdaws do." *Kafka* means jackdaw. It is as if he were saying that his own works are so many nomads at the wall of normality: "A screeching as of jackdaws is always in our ears." Had Max Brod followed his friend's directions, we would have missed the screeching.

This view of the artist as nomad and marauder helps to account for the sheer persistence of the invasion motif in middle-class literature. How, after all, do middle-class adolescents, bound for law, business, medicine, housewifery, turn into writers? Isn't it by withdrawal outside the walls, outside the world of security and common sense, of "prudence and method" ordained for them, by a sort of sympathy with the nomadic? These talented adolescents may build walls too, a shell of isolation and pride like Stephen Dedalus's, so that life can invade them too in all its fullness and turn them away from the constraint of the parental parlor. From the stronghold of their art they then march on the world into which they were born by the act of writing scathingly about it, like Nathan Zuckerman in *The Ghost Writer*, who also wants to forge an uncreated conscience.

The ambivalence that results from all this inside-and-out business seems to be essential. *Death in Venice* could, one feels, almost have been written by Gustave von Aschenbach himself—the style is certainly his—but for that official "von" he got as fiftieth birthday present from the northern, fatherly world he so doggedly defended with the talents of the southerly mother. That the artist's is a divided soul seems to be one of Thomas Mann's axioms; you find him hammering away at it from *Tonio Kröger* to *Doctor Faustus*. Mann's artists are always symbols.

Tolstoy was no bourgeois, yet it is his own obsession with death that invades the orderly and meticulously ridiculed world of Ivan Ilych Golovin, that utter middleman. The invasion story is always, at some level, personal. In *Ward Number Six*, Chekhov divides himself even more neatly between the bourgeois doctor, Andrew, and the visionary madman, Ivan. Did he himself not say that medicine was his wife, while literature was his mistress? The one is legitimate,

then, and the other implicitly beyond the pale of respectability, nomadic, unsettled.

The invasion theme is ontological, and not merely sociological. It
has its origins in the source of the bourgeois artist's own identity, in
the very experience of becoming a writer. Such an artist, like the
invader, is bound to be a disruptive force, an intimate alien and
incubus revealing what his or her readership has often been at pains
to hide from itself. By virtue of being a "bourgeois writer," however,
the middle-class artist is never purely villager or nomad, but something curiously in between the two.

The version of the invasion story most of us hear first is that of the
Little Pigs, middle-class homeowners all three. The fairy tale might
resonate for a reader through all these stories, from Kafka's "Great
Wall of China" to Joyce Carol Oates's "Where Are Your Going,
Where Have You Been?" But Oates's story differs in interesting ways
from the others I have cited. For one thing, the main character is a
teenaged female rather than a middle-aged male; moreover, the invasion here seems to present a less ambiguous threat of evil and violation.

To use Coleridge's word for the magical process, the three elements esemplastically combined by Oates are the actual story of
Charles Schmid, twenty-three-year-old murderer of teenaged girls in
Tucson back in the 1960s, Bob Dylan's "It's All Over Now, Baby
Blue," and finally fairy tales and folk ballads. The author informs us
that all three constituents were quite consciously used, and the last
seems to mark the story out as aiming at something typical of female
experience. Here is Oates herself:

> Arnold Friend is a fantastic figure: he is Death, he is the "elf-
> Knight" of the ballads, he is the Imagination, he is a Dream, he is
> a Lover, a Demon, and all that. The story was originally called
> "Death and the Maiden," but I thought the title too pompous, too
> literary.

And all that. Eliminate the r's from Arnold's name and you get what
is gradually revealed to Connie: an old fiend. In the male cases the

invasion usually bears some possibility of humanization or transcendence, even in such lethal instances as *The Death of Ivan Ilych, Death in Venice, Ward Number Six,* or *The Metamorphosis.* Even if Arnold Friend is connected to fantasies of ''elf-Knights,'' the female case as presented by Oates bears a heavier burden of destruction and violation, murder, penetration, rape. This is not surprising if the prime sexual fear of the adolescent male is inadequacy and that of the young female violation.

Irreligion, consumerism, flirting, and dependence on rock 'n' roll leave Connie with little resistance; in fact, it is Connie's emptiness that dooms her. Her heart seems as ramshackle and impermanent as her parents' flimsy house:

> She was hollow with what had been fear, but what was now just an emptiness.

Big Bad Nomadic Wolf Arnold Friend knows how to breach walls:

> ''I mean, anybody can break through a screen door and glass and wood and iron or anything else if he needs to, anybody at all and specially Arnold Friend. . . .''

And he knows also the resourcelessness of his victim:

> ''Now put your hand on your heart, honey. Feel that? That feels solid too but we know better. . . .''

Like the other invaded bourgeois, Connie also has within her that which would fling open the gates. In fact, there are explicitly two Connies, impatiently obedient villager and would-be cool nomad, so to speak:

> She wore a pullover jersey blouse that looked one way when she was at home and another way when she was away from home. Everything about her had two sides to it, one for home and one for anywhere that was not home.

172PROFESSORS AT PLAY

It is the experimentally nomadic Connie who actually initiates the catastrophe by leaving the safe, permitted walls of the mall of middle-class consumerism and crossing the perilous highway to the drive-in of cheap romance, which is forbidden terrain. It is here that Arnold Friend singles her out like a predator looking over a herd for vulnerable young: "Gonna get you, baby." The prolonged crisis of the story is also spacial: will Connie leave her middle-class home, flimsy and void of support as it is, for a "land that [she] had never seen before and did not recognize except to know that she was going to it"? Inside is a vacuous safety, and outside everything from Imagination to Death.

In these stories the life of the middle class is presented paradoxically as full of emptiness, like the crammed vacancy of Ivan Ilych's knickknack parlor, the collected works of Gustave von Aschenbach, or the yellowing mortgages and title deeds of the Master-in-Chancery. The stories reflect deep anxiety; security seems assured but is illusory. All walls are pregnable. The invader is, in a sense, the creature of the quest for security, called up by it, longed-for as much as feared. Is Gregor Samsa fleeing his job or just losing it? Does Dr. Andrew Ephimich Ragin not find the paranoic Ivan Dmitrich Gromov better company than the sane postmaster? Is Connie not more than a little intrigued by Arnold Friend? Isn't Joseph Howe drawn to his student Tertan, making allowances for his madness as the Master does for Bartleby's uselessness? Only the profound ambivalence of the middle class towards its material achievements and spiritual failures, best shadowed forth by its writing children, could have made *The Death of Ivan Ilych* an international bestseller—ambivalence and perhaps an inexhaustible well of self-deception. How many little Ivans read the indictment, saw that "reproach and warning to the living" on Ivan's dead face, but said with Peter Ivanovich, this does not apply to me; Ivan has made a mess of things but I have not? Always looking, never learning. Almost perceiving, but eager to play bridge.

Still, the anxiety persists, even in the castle keep of the bourgeois den. In Kafka's long story "The Burrow," the nameless creature who all his life has pursued snugness in constructing his fantastically ramifed den, security through his ingenious system of defenses,

thinks always of that other burrower, the unseen nomadic invader
for whom he does his work, and confesses:

> For to be honest I cannot endure this place, I rise up and rush, as
> if I had filled myself up there with new anxieties instead of peace,
> down into the house again. . . . Up there under the moss no change
> touches one, there one is at peace, uplifted above time; but here
> every instant frets and gnaws at the listener.

Kleist, Kierkegaard, Kafka, and Marriage

Among the several motifs that congealed into the story of Faust there is one equally ancient and persistent. It is to be found, for instance, in the old tales of Saints Theophilus and Basileus. The tradition is that the devil argues against a marriage desired by his contractee. Christopher Marlowe continues this tradition in *Doctor Faustus* and even lays a certain stress on it by having the episode occur immediately after Faustus has signed the blood contract with Mephistopheles:

> FAUST. But leaving off this, let me have a wife.
> The fairest maid in Germany
> For I am wanton and lascivious
> And cannot live without a wife.
> MEPH. How, a wife?
> I prithee, Faustus, talk not of a wife.

And a bit later:

> MEPH. Tut, Faustus,
> Marriage is but a ceremonial toy.
> If thou lovest me, think no more of it.[1]

L. W. Cushman, the venerable scholar who is my authority on this tradition, says of it that the devil argues against marriage not because it is a route to salvation, but merely because marriage happens to be a sacrament.[2] Yet whatever orthodox intentions the original hagiographic and homiletic writers may have had, later understandings can be different. Besides, the moral nature of literature is such as to allow everything to live in a story. Here, in the case of Dr. Faustus for instance, we see that to the hero of knowledge and consciousness, the newly-damned professor mirabilis, marriage itself appears to be a temptation, the act of one already lost, even another way of selling one's soul, sacrament or not. Furthermore, a Freudian Age might remark in the episode not only the suppressed libido but also the naiveté of John Faustus, lifelong grind, who must learn some sexual sophistication of his pander. (What, sex without marriage? I can have Helen of Troy?) It is almost amusing that the middle-aged academic should think himself so dreadfully "wanton and lascivious," while he shows himself an obvious newcomer to the sexual banquet. Even so, Mephistopheles is made to argue the point with some heat and, as noted, with a weight of tradition behind him: "If thou lovest me, think no more of it." Marlowe's devil seems to be aware of how downright indecorous, not to say threatening, a behest this is. Just as if to wed were indeed to risk selling one's soul all over again—but to Satan's Rival.

This "complex," which I have come at so obliquely, is what I believe distinguishes each one of my three Ks in what deserve to be called his marital relations. That is, all three share an apprehension of marriage as selling one's soul to salvation, while simultaneously (it is a sale, after all) marriage is feared as a special temptation of the high-minded "intellectual" hero. Is this not, for instance, rather precisely what one infers from Kafka's (Kafka! the author of "Bachelor's Ill-Luck") remark that to have married a good woman is already to have fulfilled the Law?

Wilhelmina Zenge, Regine Olsen, Felice Bauer—these are names one connects to the authors' with some compunction. After all, these women are the cast-off, the sacrificed, the impossible-to-wed. Indeed, the three stories are remarkably congruent. As Kafka put it in 1913:

Today I got Kierkegaard's *Buch des Richters*. As I suspected, his case, despite essential differences, is very similar to mine, at least he is on the same side of the world. He bears me out like a friend.[3]

For that matter, so did Heinrich von Kleist, always a favorite of Kafka, "bear him out like a friend." In one of his letters to Fraulein Zenge, Kleist wrote as any one of the three could have written:

I have often wondered whether it is not my duty to leave you . . .

And from Kleist's last letter of all to his fiancée:

There is one term in the German language most women will never

understand. That is the term ambition. . . . Don't write to me again.
My only wish is to die.[4]

But isn't all this fear of marriage really just a cliché? Or, better still, is all this stale gossip really worth dredging up? I would say not, unless the rather special bachelorhoods of Kleist, Kierkegaard, and Kafka have something to do with their work. But, as to that, I am not at all sure that anything could have been more important than the ways in which these men did not get married. Of course, the reverse is just as true: nothing could have had more to do with the broken engagements than their work.

The usual way to consider this thrice-repeated ritual, myth, or experiment is to see these "solitaries" more or less as subtypes of the poète maudit. And certainly one may say on good evidence that they feared marriage, respectability, the "bourgeois style," not being alone, not being unhappy, not being special, and—most of all—not writing. The distinguishing element, though, is that all three should have so much wanted to be married that they began to look on marriage seriously as a salvation forbidden to them. Of course this wish of theirs to marry could never have been simply wholehearted: you just do not look for undivided hearts or simple minds in such a quarter. But who can imagine the work of these three (all of whom appear to have undergone virtual creative explosions because of their doomed betrothals) without the engagements? What else is at the core of Kierkegaard's wonderful *Fear and Trembling* and then, still more explicitly, his *Repetition*, or Kafka's own "breakthrough" story, "The Judgment," and then "The Metamorphosis"? As for Kleist, Thomas Mann describes his decision to break off his engagement as the epitome of the whole crisis that turned his life around and around and made him into a great poet instead of a mediocre mathematician.

As it happens, Kierkegaard himself has a word to say about Faust, Goethe's this time, and in *Fear and Trembling* at that. As usual, it is his own case he is rehearsing, and what he here calls his pseudonymous author, a *tortor heroum*, describes fairly exactly what he is doing to himself. He supposes Faust to fall deeply in love with Marguerite (Faust now sees her "not in the concave mirror of Mephistopheles but in all her lovable innocence'') and then to say nothing about it. In this self-imposed silence we are to note that Faust is as unintelligible as Abraham, not merely shy or uncommunicative. Faust's silence, Kierkegaard tells us, is due to his being an "ideal doubter." And such a doubter, Kierkegaard confesses over and over again, "hungers just as much for the daily bread of joy as for the food of the spirit."[5] So much for a trite choice of Art over Life, spirit over matter, productivity over sex.

Common wisdom says that complex men make for complex problems, but can such men then really be said to "have" their problems? From one viewpoint there could be nothing simpler than the bachelorhood of the three Ks. All we need to see, and there is plenty of bright evidence by the light of which to see it, is that their "work"— however defined—was perceived as antithetical to their marriages— however valued. As we have to do with three modern geniuses and not what Kierkegaard himself called "Fausts in carpet slippers," the work won out. As for the rest—for all that subtlety, all those explanations—it is justification, rationalization, masochism, resignation, neurosis—what you will. Under this analysis, the close connection between the marital crisis and the literary career of each man is ultimately nothing more than the consequence of turning self-justification and self-laceration into one's natural materia poetica, a kind of stock-in-trade. Therefore, even in their work everything can repeat itself. Kleist writes of his Marquise of O——, Kierkegaard of the similar fate of Mary, Kafka of Gregor Samsa's metamorphosis. The baroque prose and furiously micronometric sense of justice in Kleist's *Michael Kohlhaas* become the astonishingly alert, lucidly composed peregrinations of Kierkegaard's scruples in his journals, the ins and outs of guilt in Kafka's *The Trial*, the precise rending of his *Diaries*. The religio-aesthetic faceting of Kleist's "Catholic" stories turns into the theological lyricism of Kierkegaard's *Fear and Trembling*, and culminates in Kafka's *Castle*, his late allegories, and sets of aphorisms. Kleist's gorge instinctively rises against the Enlightenment (once he digested Kant in 1801); Kierkegaard sends the greatest intellect of his generation into battle with the intellectualism of Hegel; while, piercing even further into what enlightened intellect had buried, Kafka sums up his writer's "fate" in the idea of a "talent for portraying

[a] dreamlike inner life [that] has thrust all other matters into the background. . . . ."[6] Kleist refuses to settle down to being a Privatdocent at Königsberg; God himself lodges an absurd "veto" against Kierkegaard's marriage, and Franz Kafka cannot bear to lose even the bitterest dregs of a loneliness that might cause him to write. These men didn't marry because they didn't want to. Marriage simply wasn't good enough for them.

But what presumption it is to say all this, and of what men! No, the reverse holds better: complex problems choose complex men. Marriage was too good for them. They didn't marry even though they wanted to, wanted to more than anybody, more than their fiancées, for example. *Fear and Trembling* is *Fear and Trembling*; it is not a work of self-service or rationale. Worldly wisdom is useless when even the creator of Adrian Leverkuhn admits that Kleist's "combination of ambition and desire for annihilation is difficult to comprehend. . . ." As for Kafka, isn't he always ahead of his critics and biographers, though his being ahead only spurs them on? Already in 1916 he was accusing himself of "infantilism," and in the very context of the reduplications of literary history:

> Give up too those nonsensical comparisons you like to make between yourself and a Flaubert, a Kierkegaard, a Grillparzer. That is simply infantile.[7]

There are no self-fulfilling prophecies here; there is no self-dramatizing. In fact, these men acted in the usual tragic way, at least in one sense: they expressed their freedom in a context of necessity, a necessity of which they were effusively, blindingly conscious. *Nullum exstitit magnum ingenium sine aliqua dementia*: Kierkegaard called this Roman saying "the worldly expression for the religious affirmation that the one who is blessed is also cursed." You could say that Kierkegaard was too smart to get married, but too dubious also not to want to. In this respect, of course, all three Ks were "ideal Fausts."

Divided and doubting these men may have been, yet all three seem to have looked upon marriage, philosophically, quite positively and in much the same way. For instance, they all acknowledge marriage as the fulfilment of an ethical commandment—if not as a categorical duty, then certainly as a paradigm. To Kierkegaard, for example, married life constitutes almost the whole content of the ethical stage of life described at length in part two of *Either/Or*. Moreover, the condition of being married appears to have struck all three as being therapeutic. That is, marriage would not only be a sign of mental health, but to marry would be a substantial aid to achieving physical well-being. All three were sick men, remember, betrayed by their bodies; each could have benefited from the care and regularity marriage might have provided. Thus, to these men marriage to a good woman would be to fulfill not only the moral law but also nature's.

Nevertheless, all three men felt themselves prevented from marrying by more than just their own perverse natures, wishes, or drives. Kierkegaard and Kafka are especially close in the language they use to express this sense of intervention. As Kierkegaard could write in his diary that "God has lodged a veto," so Kafka would write to Felice Bauer: "I am held back by what is almost a command from heaven. . . ."[8] But here too one can see into certain differences. For Kierkegaard the divine veto entailed a vocation that formed the basis of his life's work, to translate the passion of faith into discursive prose. But for Kafka, the religious element is by no means so easily distinguishable from the psychological, nor, of course, so certain as it was for Kierkegaard. Whereas to Kierkegaard marriage was plainly "vetoed" from on high, Kafka characteristically enough feels what is "*almost* a command." Moreover, the rest of this sentence in Kafka's letter places "apprehension" in apposition to this command—just as if a "command from heaven" were really the same thing as "an apprehension that cannot be appeased. . . ." After all, in Kafka's work it is often so.

This peculiar mixture of apprehension and vocation, also of desire and duty, comes up more than once in Kafka's thinking about marriage. A month and a half after the remark about the heavenly command, he was writing to his fiancée:

What is stopping me can hardly be said to be facts; it is fear, an insurmountable fear, fear of achieving happiness, a desire and a command to torment myself for some higher purpose.[9]

I think this remark can be applied to all three men. For, what really distinguishes them is this relation between desire and command, that desire and command should coincide on the side of not marrying, while all three see marriage in general as both desirable and mandatory. The plots of Kleist's "Marquise of O——" and "The Duel," for instance, can be understood as elaborate engines for forcing young women out of premature spinsterhood. In this regard, these stories, which question so much, have a clear ethical element, an ethic in favor of marriage.

Now, a man who has only the *desire* not to marry is what Kierkegaard designated (in the first part of *Either/Or*) a seducer, a Don Juan. On the other hand, a man who feels only a *command* not to marry is enduring a fate that has nothing directly to do with his character. Such a command could be that of the priesthood, a monastic order; or, more arbitrarily, it might derive from the provisions of a father's will or an accidental castration. But neither of these alternatives can be applied to Kleist, Kierkegaard, or Kafka. Kierkegaard actually attacked monasticism in *Fear and Trembling*. Of Kleist and marriage Kafka wrote:

> perhaps Kleist, when compelled by outer and inner necessity to shoot himself on the Wannsee, was the only one to find the right solution.[10]

Failing such a solution, however, there remains the need to "torment" oneself, which is both a desire and a command.

Of the three, Kierkegaard went the furthest in analyzing this special torment. Though he wrote that to enter the ethical stage (i.e., marriage) was to "choose oneself," Kierkegaard makes it clear that the final proof of inwardness is its isolation from the social values of ethics, its outward unintelligibility. As he insists, either there is something above the explicable, universal, and moral, or the individual is lost; the outward will defeat the inward. Thus, it is the very incomprehensibility of the decision not to marry (to sacrifice Isaac) that may be most important; for the necessary condition of the individual's existence is, if one likes, literally to be misunderstood. "You misunderstood," Kafka wrote to Felice, "if you imagined that what keeps me from marrying is the thought that in winning you I would gain less than I would lose by giving up my solitary existence."[11] One wonders just what else she could have imagined.

• • •

I have only two conclusions I wish to draw from all this. The first is that, for each man, the crisis over marriage made everything bloom, and suddenly too—as when Kafka stayed up the whole of one night writing down "The Judgment," or when Kierkegaard's *Fear and Trembling* and *Repetition* were completed so rapidly that they could be published on the same day. I suspect that the case of Kleist was similar. And, after all, it is not so surprising. There is hardly anything in them, in their experience, their understandings, that is not fully and intensely engaged in the matter of their engagements. And this may be affirmed both of their personal lives and even the most impersonal aspects of their work. It is therefore no accident that the family situations of these writers, situations that become so much *the* pattern in their writings, are intimately tied up with the question of marriage. How crucial for Kleist is the whole of his relationship to the "House of Kleist"? How frequent are his efforts to prove himself before those exemplary Prussians, and perhaps to make more of them? Doesn't this turn into the plots of "The Marquise of O——," "The Duel," and even "The Prince of Homburg"? For Kierkegaard the family crux is the great and melancholic secret of his father's life, the need to hide which he even catalogues as one motive in breaking off his own engagement. It is more than a clue to the same connection when Kafka comes to write his own explication of "The Judgment" and remarks that:

> the bride . . . lives in the story only in relation to . . . what father and son have in common. . . . [She] is easily driven away by the father since no marriage has yet taken place, and so she cannot

penetrate the circle of blood relationship that is drawn around father and son.[12]

The duty of the last of a family is, of course, to be the last. Isn't it mostly the deliberate not giving up on their family struggles that gets men like Kleist and Kafka accused of real "infantilism"? And isn't it perhaps true that to continue to be a bachelor is also to continue to be a son? Yet without their consciousness of such a choice, where could we locate the elemental response their stories of family life elicit from us? In short, the three Ks have bent their astonishing geniuses to the work of redeeming (not "rehabilitating") the problems they are said to suffer from. This leaves their analysts and accusers the task of turning intricate silk purses back into useless sow's ears.

My second conclusion has to do, more generally, with the view of marriage as an impermissible, interdicted variety of salvation. What did marriage really mean in itself for these men? and what, beyond itself, did marriage represent? First and maybe last of all, marriage is the possibility of happiness. These great distinction-makers (all three are really either/or men, Kohlhaasian terrorists with themselves) somehow did not distinguish between an unacceptably complacent "happiness" in marriage and a higher "happiness" as bachelors. Did they really fail then to grasp how trite their cases were? No, their more courageous choice was one between kinds of unhappiness. They elected the sort that precluded happiness in their relations with women—the good women with whom marriage would be no less than fulfilment of the Law. For these law-abiding men, then, the choice was virtually a form of lawlessness. They confess it everywhere. The idealization of spontaneity (Kleist), of the "universal" (Kierkegaard), and of "the commonplace" (Kafka) is deliberately offset by the uniformly anguished but even more forceful idealization of (respectively) consciousness, the Absolute or Absurd, and what Kafka came to call "the Indestructible." From the viewpoint of the first set of ideals, these men appear to be neo-Manichaeans. But that is clearly not *their* point of view, or not the whole of it. Perhaps we can attempt to glimpse this through a figure.

Imagine that these men lived in such a way as always to remain teetering, like eggs precariously balanced on a rooftop, full of the potential energy of a fall. On one side there is Something, on the other Nothing. For them, to marry would be to float miraculously free of the rooftop, to be wafted down to the welcome ground of Something—perhaps they could land softly on Kierkegaard's carpet slippers. On the other hand, for them entirely to deny the salvation to be found (found by them, if not others) in marriage would be to tumble off into pure Nothingness. That to move either way would be to fall, to make an end of the predicament of their lives, is true; but also it would be to expend in one vertiginous moment the energy each man felt the need to husband. We can say that they preferred to crack their shells from the inside, as in a real birth, rather than to be smashed from the outside by either the joy or despair of the world. And so these writers speak to us from "on high," each in his unique voice. But, for all their unprecedentedness, they speak more humanly than we begin by supposing. Or, should we only cast our eyes down, we will see them as in a reflecting pool: they appear to speak from down below, in their murky bachelor's hell, and the thrust of their always threatening fall we mistakenly interpret as a rising to the rippling surface of real life.

Notes

1 *Doctor Faustus*, act 5, lines 157–162, 170–172.
2 L. W. Cushman, *The Devil and the Vice in the English Dramatic Literature Before Shakespeare* (Halle: M. Niemeyer, 1900), 15 et passim.
3 Franz Kafka, *Diaries* (New York: Schocken, 1948), vol. 1, 298.
4 Cited by Thomas Mann in his foreword to the English edition of *The Marquise of O—— and Other Stories* (New York: Signet, 1962), xii.
5 Søren Kierkegaard, *Fear and Trembling*, trans. Walter Lowrie (Princeton: Princeton University Press, 1941), 116–119.
6 Kafka, *Diaries* (New York: Schocken, 1949), vol. 2, 77.
7 Kafka, *Diaries*, 2, 164–165.
8 Franz Kafka, *Letters to Felice* (New York: Schocken, 1973), 288.
9 Ibid., 314.
10 Ibid., 316.
11 Ibid., 334.
12 Kafka, *Diaries*, 1, 279.

We and Kafka

The bachelor-genius Franz Kafka, who writes like no one else, who sees like no one else, the German Jew in the Czech capital, the poet in the house of business, the brother in the family of sisters—this is the lonely writer who, at the end of his life, says *we*. He means it, too, though one cannot think of another writer more constrained by temperament and circumstance to isolation. It is as if Kafka's insularity, without being overcome, or even by being intensified, has imploded and become its opposite, allowing him to speak for a great deal more than himself. For example, in the very middle of his last work, "Josephine the Singer, or the Mousefolk," there occurs this moving sentence:

> This piping, which rises up where everyone else is pledged to silence, comes almost like a message from the whole people to each individual; Josephine's thin piping amidst grave decisions is almost like our people's precarious existence amidst the turmoil of a hostile world.[1]

At this point in the story, readers may be feeling fairly secure in the opinion that they are in the midst of a fable about the individual artist in his or her relation to the group—the audience, the people, the race, the species. They will not have been troubled by the rather unusual point of view: evidently there is a mouse-narrator of some sort, an *I*, though this narrator is by no means reluctant to speak for the group, for all the generations of the Mouse Folk. He or she says *we* far more frequently than *I*: "Tranquil peace is the music we love best . . . we are wont to console ourselves . . . we are quite unmusical . . ." and so forth. One might easily suppose the story is about Josephine. After all, it is her intense individuality that illuminates the mousy qualities of her people. Josephine, in short, is the exception, the only vivid *I* among this vague collective *we*, the Mouse Folk. It is her unique love of music and her capacity for performing it that elevate Josephine to individuality. So, like "A Hunger Artist," with which it appeared, "Josephine" would seem to be another tale about the artist, with all the artist's self-consciousness, vanity, neurotic arrogance, and renunciation. It really looks as if Kafka has simply found another extended metaphor with which to rehearse his own case: Josephine K. this time, instead of Joseph; "piping" rather than fasting; the Mouse Folk instead of the Samsa family.

Yet there is something not quite satisfactory in this comfortable view, perhaps even something fundamentally wrong. Should we hurry over the tiny stumbling block of Kafka's peculiar angle of narration, it leaves some slight effect nonetheless, as if we had lightly stubbed our toe. This insistent *we* begins to call attention to itself. For English-speaking readers in particular, it is an odd way to tell a story. The *we* is alien to a consciousness built upon such things as the Reformation, which set each soul on its own in a landscape of pitfalls; British Empiricism, with its atomized sensorium; the American Dream, which is not the dream of the American People but of people who live in America one at a time; travelogues, with their first-person Crusoes and Gullivers; Romanticism, with its cult of private experience and personal vision; Capitalism, with its regard for calculating self-interest. The Preamble to the Constitution is one thing, but there are few authors who pronounce themselves a genuine, collective *we* in English or American literature. Eliot said of Yeats that it took him more than half his life to achieve the freedom of speech really to say *I*. Here, in his last story, in a fable of a singer written just as his own voice was about to fail him, the author of "He" and creator of the two Ks does not struggle at last to say *I*; Kafka says *we*. He has not taken the point of view of Josephine the Songstress, but of all the Mouse Folk who are *not* Josephine. Kafka's last word is not, after all, about an art of the stifled, isolated ego, but one which is "almost like the precarious existence" of an entire species. True, for him there is no alternative to the isolated ego, even a stifled one; yet here he invokes its very opposite. Thus he also does not say that Josephine's art is a message from the individual to the group, or even a piping-for-piping's-sake which the anxious, utilitarian group can take or leave; in fact, he says the very opposite. In a reversal of expectation, if not of logic, Kafka writes that this art of Josephine's is "almost like a message from the whole people to each individual." The group speaks through the individual to the individuals who constitute the group . . . almost. Kafka is hardly ever without this "almost," and one should not forget it.

Kafka's strenuous and even athletic agnosticism does not admit of
many certainties. All the same, Paul Goodman saw in "Josephine"
something sublime, virtually a final redemption for the guilty artist,
for all who are guilty over their art:

> *Josephine* . . . demonstrates a beautiful Kafka-like possibility for fin-
> ished art, as he says: "Our relation to our fellow man is prayer."
> The songstress melts back into her people and atones by proxy for
> the arrogance of art. It is such a conviction, that their art is really
> universal, it is really only human speech, however incomprehensi-
> ble, that lightens for many artists their heavy guilt.[2]

There is no evidence in the story of Josephine's sense of guilt. Nevertheless, the narrator believes in her redemption, and thus in her need
for it. This redemption occurs not in spite of the forgetfulness of the
Mouse Folk, but just because of it. In this way, her *I* is subsumed in
the *we*, but only as she rises "to the heights," which are not to be
confused with immortality. Oblivion is up there.

"Josephine" can certainly be classed with Kafka's other tales about
artists, but it belongs equally to another and rather small group of
stories, most of which are late works—those told in the first-person
plural, each of which strives to become "a message from the whole
people to each individual."

Kafka is careful about pronouns. Even in his first published work,
"Meditation," several of the inchoate lyric pieces are directed at a
you or refer to a deliberately indeterminate *one*. He is already, one
senses, restless with the lyric ego, something suggested also by such
an early effort as the dialogue "Conversation with the Supplicant,"
where the confident *I* encounters its suffering alter ego. The bound-
aries of identity are already in some question there, though the *we* is
only parenthetical and limited: "Why indeed should I feel ashamed—
or why should we feel ashamed—because I don't walk upright and
ponderously, striking my walking stick on the pavement . . ."

A writer says *we* decisively when his material calls for it, when the
matter is of a collective character for instance, when an individual
subject can best be illuminated through the more objective opinions

and memories of his people, or when, among the tensions between individual and group, the group is to be given a chance to express its opinion. However, in the case of Kafka, a story is frequently like a blueprint of experience, a plan that can be used to construct a great variety of interpretations conforming to the same structure.[3] In his work, then, the *we* is as likely to represent the fate of an individual as a group, an inward state as much as an outward condition; or rather, the story may express all these things simultaneously.

"An Old Manuscript," for example, a symbolic story of invasion, is just such a blueprint. A people's land—even their capital city—may be invaded by unruly and carnivorous barbarians, but so may an individual's consciousness be invaded by the repressed impulses his defenses are not strong enough to hold back. The Emperor may be an emperor indeed or a version of, say, the superego, guarantor of order and degree, of cleanliness and obedience. Of course, "An Old Manuscript," like "Josephine," is only equivocally in the first-person plural. There is a particular narrator, an *I* who is a cobbler. And yet the cobbler speaks for his fellow citizens. He is only one of those "artisans and tradesmen" to whom the salvation of the nation is being ineffectually relegated. He is the norm, the one who is moved in on, the firstborn child, the bourgeois, the homeowner, the man of this world who wishes to establish a sealed-off reality and believes himself secure behind his Chinese Wall; he is the lover of order, the anxious ego caught between Emperor and barbarian. The invasion is not simply a catastrophe for the cobbler; on the contrary, he concludes that "it will be the ruin of us." The story is as collective as, say, a psychological theory. In this sense, the *we* is by no means inappropriate. It is precisely *we* who try to screen out the unreal, to suppress the "nomadic" in ourselves, to defend ourselves against the inexplicable—even, let it be said, the terrifying and barely intelligible messages of a Kafka. (The barbarous nomads, Kafka writes, "communicate with each other much as jackdaws do." *Kafka*, you remember, is Czech for *jackdaw*.) We all like to think ourselves safe if we live "far from the frontier," huddled before the very gates of authority. The story is about us, and the collective narration, without falling into abstraction, universalizes it, confirms it. The angle of narration is itself a sign of Kafka's sureness here, of the precision of his blueprint. If we have read it properly, then the story has indeed become "a message from the whole people to each individual." Perhaps that is one definition of a masterpiece.

"An Old Manuscript" is to be found in the volume *A Country Doctor*. The story that Kafka insisted should lead off the collection is an even briefer plural narrative, "The New Advocate."[4] The collective point of view is not insisted upon here, as in "Josephine," yet it sets the story's chief idea in motion:

> We have a new advocate, Dr. Bucephalus.

It is not enough to say that Alexander the Great's old warhorse has become a lawyer. Kafka implies that he is, so to speak, *our* lawyer. The "we have" is a clear sign that the story is to be an expression of "our" condition, and, indeed, the parable is little more than a contrast between then and now, which is to say between them and us. It is an ancient enough theme, the common complaint of today's inferiority to yesterday; but Kafka elevates this complaint from private, querulous nostalgia to the dignity of a spiritual judgment. Kierkegaard once remarked, "That past which cannot become a present is irrelevant." History which cannot repeat itself recedes into dusty tomes that may, in the course of time, come to resemble Bucephalus's thick law books. But what of a past we cannot succeed in making a present? The irrelevance then may lie more with us than with the past, which, like the Gates of India, will have receded, not into dusty tomes, but "to remoter and loftier places." And why should this be?

> Nowadays—it cannot be denied—there is no Alexander the Great.

Paul Goodman was so taken with one of Kafka's late aphorisms that he called a section of his book after it. "Such freedom as is possible today," Kafka wrote, "is a wretched business." Here in "The New Advocate," what is possible for us is pointedly expressed by indicating what is *not* possible for us today. Yes, murder, wanderlust, and the hatred of fathers all are flourishing, even perhaps to excess, but no one, no one at all, can blaze a trail to India.

Of course, Dr. Bucephalus possesses "such freedom as is possible today"; that is, with "his flanks unhampered by the thighs of a rider . . . far from the clamor of battle." But there is nothing grand for him to do with this unbridled freedom. Instead,

he reads and turns the pages of our ancient tomes.

Without that initial *we* to set the pitch of the story, one might think with some amusement of Kafka preparing for his irksome law examinations, writing up his detailed briefs, or compiling his compulsive annual reports for the Workman's Accident Insurance Company. With the direction of the pronoun, however, we must think of nothing less than the conditions of modernity, a period that substitutes anxiety, dissociation, and lawbooks for ambition, integrity, and the imperial ego's bold cavalry charges on the Absolute. "The New Advocate," for all its brevity, has as much to say on these modern-classical contrasts as "The Waste Land" or *Ulysses*. To have left out the *we* would not perhaps have altered the meaning of the story, but it would have altered its effect and restricted its scope. The distance would be by that much the greater between ourselves and the parable, which is truly a serious one only if it is about ourselves. Without the *we*, not only would the story become a more private matter—the spiritual sentimentality of an implied *I*—but its playfulness (a horse is reading the law, not the King of Macedon) would then take our eye to such a degree that the earnestness behind it ("yet the King's sword pointed the way") might wholly escape our attention. After all, Kafka is seldom more in earnest than when disporting himself among his metaphors, his fortified similes.

The simile of "The Problem of Our Laws" is a complex one and yet, underneath superficial differences, not without resemblances to "The New Advocate." Both are collective narratives; both speak of an essentially ahistorical predicament in historical terms; each invokes Kakfa's typical infinite regression to express the distance of the Absolute (the vanishing origins of the laws, the receding Gates of

India); moreover, both conjure up the image of the Law itself—in one case as an unworthy and pedestrian substitute for the lawless greatness of Alexander's ambition, in the other as a mysterious or even non-existent source of redemption entrusted to unworthy and lawless substitutes (the earthly nobility) or made up by them. The question of "that freedom which is possible today" arises in both stories. "The Problem of Our Laws" is, certainly, no less explicit:

> though there is still a possible freedom of interpretation left, it has now become very restricted.[5]

The condition of the people among whom Bucephalus has taken up the practice of law is given no positive expression whatever. It is conceived essentially as a lacking, a debility that draws Bucephalus to their law courts. In "The Problem of Our Laws," the same is true to the extent that the people's whole condition is solely the result of not knowing the laws by which they are ruled:

> We are convinced that these ancient laws are scrupulously administered; nevertheless it is an extremely painful thing to be ruled by laws one does not know.

So it was also for Alice in her Wonderland, where too "the nobles" seem an oppressive law unto themselves. But then again one of the chief differences between Alice and Kafka is the latter's willingness to say *we*. Lewis Carroll's rationality precedes the dream, whereas Kafka's reflections (and ours) can only try to catch up to it. Kafka's stories will never become entertainments for children, even though the condition of the people in "The Problem of Our Laws" is not unlike that of children, assuming for the moment that the nobility are like grown-ups. For both spirited children and the dissatisfied people, the thought of a real insurrection is equally impossible. After all,

> The sole visible and indubitable law that is imposed upon us is the nobility, and must we ourselves deprive ourselves of that one law?

The *we* here is the common people, perhaps mankind, but these people are not completely unified. There are two factions based, of course, on their response to the problem of the laws. The narration is at first impartial between the majority and the minority parties: the former believing in the existence of the laws and in their ultimate discoverability, the latter only in the "arbitrary acts of the nobility." Finally, however, the narration sides—provisionally, at least—with the majority who hope to discover the Law and be rid of the nobility. They do not hate the nobles, however:

> We are more inclined to hate ourselves, because we have not yet shown ourselves worthy of being entrusted with the laws. And that is the real reason why the party which believes that there is no law has remained so small . . .

In either case it does not matter, for the narration is all-inclusive when it concludes that "we live on this razor edge"—no matter which of these opinions we hold. What is lacking here is a third possibility, a party that might unify the people by denying both the existence of the laws *and* belief in the nobility as well. The narration calls this "a sort of paradox," because to deny the nobility is unthinkable. Nietzsche could not do it and, presumably, none of "us" could face the anarchy and despair of being without both the promise of redemption *and* the earthly and traditional, if corrupt, order provided by the nobility. And so we go on, collectively, along the razor edge in our perplexity—a cynical or complicit minority accepting the self-aggrandizing or gratuitous acts of the nobles, a majority cleaving to the faith that a few more centuries of note taking and historiography will somehow end in the moment when "everything will have become clear, the laws will belong to the people, and the nobility will vanish." This is the hope of utopia or of Kingdom Come, the end of history or of time. The story, then, describes our political situation quite as well as our spiritual perplexity. The problem is not that of *my* law nor of *yours*, but—irremediably, and however we vote—of *our* laws.

Before turning back to "Josephine," which, from the standpoint

of pronouns alone is a tour de force, let us consider a few further
aspects of Kafka's *we*. In his fascinating book on Kafka, Paul Goodman describes a tension between the author's profound desire for
humility and the arrogance of asserting himself as an artist:

> To put it schematically, the conflict . . . is between (a) writing as
> art: self-projection, escape from father, and (b) writing as prayer:
> humility, imploring father.[6]

Goodman goes on to argue that Kafka's finished works (including
"Josephine") were those which "by their plot, avoided the conflict."
For example, in "The Judgment" and "The Metamorphosis" the
plots end with the destruction and sacrifice of the surrogates for
Kafka-the-artist (Georg, Gregor), while the existence of the work itself "affirms," Goodman says, Kafka-as-an-artist. I am not sure why
Goodman called this operation an avoidance of the conflict; nevertheless, I believe the conflict itself is genuine. However, in the case of
this last story, of "Josephine," there is actually no plot at all; the
work is static, an extended account of the relation between Josephine
the Singer and the Mouse Folk. And yet there is in it a resolution of
the conflict, as Goodman says there must have been, since it is finished. This resolution is not achieved by the story's plot, but by its
point of view, by the *we*, by Kafka's device of describing this distinctly unhumble artist from the viewpoint of all those humble Mouse
Folk who are not the artist. The father is neither defied nor propiti-
ated. He is still there on the scene, but only in the form of the whole
of the Mouse Folk.

   If, in the earlier examples, the narrative *we* entailed an expansion
of applicability or scope, this same *we* may also imply a degree of
presumption or a deflection of responsibility. The *we* is also a mask.
The acutely solitary and inward writer can become a people, a nation,
a species. Is this presumptuous? Is it dissimulation or vision? One of
Kafka's late aphorisms provides, if not an answer to this question,
at least a justification for the *we*. Moreover, the aphorism itself is very
close in spirit to the lyrical swelling of "Josephine":

> The indestructible is one: it is every human being individually and

at the same time all human beings collectively; hence the marvellous indissoluble alliance of mankind.[7]

Like mankind itself, the pronouns of "Josephine" are amazingly varied, but the overall effect is decidedly collective. The story actually begins with a pronoun, which is not likely to have been an accident. Kafka's opening sentences are always critical, like the first terms in algebra problems: "Given that X equals O. . . ." As "The New Advocate" had begun with such a donnée, a short declarative sentence starting a collective relation to an individual ("We have a new advocate, Dr. Bucephalus"), so does "Josephine" ("Our singer is called Josephine"). The point of view is more firmly established by the rest of the initial paragraph, which is positively crammed with collectives: "a music-loving race . . . what we love best . . . our life . . . we are no longer able . . . we do not much lament . . . we hold to be . . . we stand greatly in need . . . will vanish from our lives . . ."

The second paragraph, however, begins with a little surprise: "I have often thought about what this music of hers really means." So, there is an *I* after all, but an *I* without real distinction, an *I* who cannot or will not assert himself apart from his people. Indeed, he seems to give up at once; for the next sentence offers up the pronoun *we* no less than three times. Still, for a while, there is a hovering, a balance ("in my opinion . . . I do not feel . . ."). By the end of the paragraph, though, we are once more back to *we* ("we admit freely . . .") and stay with it throughout the long third paragraph.

There is a quite virtuosic effect in the fourth paragraph when the pronoun *you* is trotted out. We readers are not Josephines, after all, but, so to speak, mice. To make this politely clear to us, that we are also part of the *we*, Kafka places us literally among the audience of Josephine by means of this involving pronoun *you:*

If you post yourself quite far away from her and listen, or, still better, put your judgment to the test, whenever she happens to be singing along with others, by trying to identify her voice, you will undoubtedly distinguish nothing . . . yet if you sit down before her, it is not merely piping . . .

To round things out, the fifth paragraph employs all three pronouns: *we, I, you* . . . over against, of course, *Josephine, her,* and *she.*
Is the story, then, exclusively about Josephine, as "A Hunger Artist" is pretty exclusively about the Hunger Artist? No, the story belongs at least as much to the Mouse Folk. Not only is this clearly
signified by the story's title, but by an account we have of it. In his
biography, Max Brod quotes one of the little conversation slips Kafka
was reduced to writing after the failure of his larynx in his last illness.
The note implies that the story was once called simply "Josephine"
or perhaps "Josephine the Songstress," but that, on further reflection, Kafka changed his mind:

> The story is going to have a new title, "Josephine the Songstress—
> or the Mice-Nation." Sub-titles like this are not very pretty, it is
> true, but in this case it has perhaps a special meaning. It has a kind
> of balance.[8]

That Kafka is equivocal about just what has a kind of balance seems
appropriate: the title is balanced because the story is, and this balance
may have a special meaning. The story is balanced between *we* and
she, between group and individual; but also—and here one should
recall Goodman—the story is balanced in a quite new way between
father and child. What else are we to make of such a touchingly
charged and lingering paragraph as the following:

> the people look after Josephine much as a father takes into his care
> a child whose little hand—and one cannot tell whether in appeal or
> command—is stretched out to him. One might think that our people
> are not fitted to exercise such paternal duties, but in reality they
> discharge them, at least in this case, admirably; no single individual
> could do what in this respect the people as a whole are capable of
> doing. To be sure, the difference in strength between the people
> and the individual is so enormous that it is enough for the nursling
> to be drawn into the warmth of their nearness and he is sufficiently
> protected.

An artist like Josephine—Goodman's egoistic "self-projector" par ex-
cellence—will not, of course, see it this way. Such paternalism on the

part of her people would be humiliating, although it is humility that
is most needed on her part. All the same, though, the artist is a
child, clamoring and assertive, and so the paragraph concludes in this
beautiful fashion:

> To Josephine, certainly, one does not dare mention such ideas.
> "Your protection isn't worth an old song," she says then. Sure,
> sure, old song, we think. And besides her protest is no real contra-
> diction, it is rather a thoroughly childish way of doing, and childish
> gratitude, while a father's way of doing is to pay no attention to it.

It is as if Kafka, through the collective device of the Mouse Folk, were
able for once to play father to himself, to gain literally a new angle
of vision on his dilemma, an infinitely more understanding and even
indulgent viewpoint than that of, say, the prototypical Bendemann
and Samsa fathers. The reason for this is given in the above passage
itself: ". . . no single individual could do what in this respect the
people as a whole are capable of doing."
   This point is confirmed a good deal later in the story, where Kafka
rings yet another change on his collective narration, describing, more
or less precisely, the earlier "finished" plots, the cruel alternative of
the condemnation by the resuscitated Bendemann and Samsa fathers:

> Suppose that instead of the people one had an individual to deal
> with. One might imagine that this man had been giving in to Jose-
> phine all the time while nursing a wild desire to put an end to his
> submissiveness one fine day . . .

This is just what the Mouse Folk refrain from doing; but in this
passage Kafka's last finished story recalls—as if to indicate the distance travelled—his first, the "breakthrough" story, "The Judgment," in which the father rises up nightmarishly with a "wild
desire" on just such a "fine day." That story begins:

> It was a Sunday morning in the very height of spring.[9]

200 PROFESSORS AT PLAY

Josephine's battle is for recognition, for acknowledgement of her status as an artist. This is the recognition Kafka could not win from his own father, of course. Josephine does not do all that much better, actually. She tries protests, strikes, and threats, especially the comical one about leaving out her grace notes until her petition should be acted upon:

> Well, the people let all these announcements, decisions and counterdecisions go in at one ear and out at the other, like a grown-up person deep in thought turning a deaf ear to a child's babble, fundamentally well disposed but not accessible.

The Mouse Folk are, perhaps, ultimately no more "accessible" than Hermann Kafka, the origin of the laws, or the Gates of India; however, they speak of Josephine with sympathy, they are "well disposed." Josephine may be only "a small episode in the eternal history" of her people (who is more?); and , no doubt, "the people will get over the loss of her." However, the narrator says frankly that this loss will not "be easy for us. . . ." The story ends lyrically, with the last of Kafka's sentences. The tone is one of reconciliation, of a final ascent to the "heights of redemption," with a mingling of Josephine and the Mouse Folk in which oblivion and redemption are truly indistinguishable:

> So perhaps we shall not miss so very much after all, while Josephine, redeemed from the earthly sorrows which to her thinking lay in wait for all chosen spirits, will happily lose herself in the numberless throng of the heroes of our people, and soon, since we are no historians, will rise to the heights of redemption and be forgotten like all her brothers.

• • •

It is almost seventy years since Kafka's death. Since then many readers, critics, clever interpreters, and learned exegetes have become absorbed, poring over Kafka's stories—and not only his stories, but his diaries, letters, and his postcards as well. That is, for such devoted readers Kafka would seem to be very much an individual; it seems the more they know of him the more original and distinct a personality Kafka becomes. This writer does not "interest," he obsesses; he does not "entertain," he imprisons. After all, a prisoner comes to distinguish the bricks of his cell's wall very precisely, while to anyone else they would appear interchangeable. So Kafka's works have come to have, for some, almost the authority of holy books. In view of this, it is neither surprising nor indecorous for the marvelous body of Kafka-criticism to resemble Talmudic commentary. Is it really so unreasonable to say, then, that the work of Kafka—an *I* who says *we*—itself constitutes something like "a message from the whole people to each individual"? Indeed, we can go yet further: such messages are to be found not just in Kafka's work either, since all of literature, all of culture, comes to us (in our childhood, our adolescence) as the embodiment of the images and values of teachers, parents, grownups, and only vaguely imagined forebears whose generations, like those of the teeming Mouse Folk, appear to us countless, because for the young there is no reason why the past should seem less infinite than the future.

Notes

1 Franz Kafka, *The Penal Colony*, trans. Willa and Edwin Muir (New York: Schocken, 1961), 266.
2 Paul Goodman, *Kafka's Prayer* (New York: Hillstone, 1976), 257–258.
3 Hannah Arendt, "Franz Kafka: A Revaluation," *Partisan Review*, Fall 1944 (reprinted in *Story and Critic*, ed. Matlaw and Lief, New York: Harper and Row, 1963, 143).
4 Franz Kafka, Letter to Kurt Wolff Verlag, in *Letters to Friends, Family, and Editors*, trans. Richard and Clara Winston (New York: Schocken, 1977), 193. The four following quotations from "The New Advocate" are from *The Penal Colony*, 135–136.
5 Franz Kafka, *The Great Wall of China*, trans. Willa and Edwin Muir (New York: Schocken, 1946), 254. The three following quotations are from pages 254 and 257.
6 Goodman, *Kafka's Prayer*, 256.

7 Kafka, *Great Wall of China*, 295.

8 Max Brod, *Franz Kafka: A Biography*, trans. G. H. Roberts and Richard Winston (New York: Schocken, 1963), 205–206. The three following quotations are from *The Penal Colony*, 263, 272.

9 *Penal Colony*, 49.

The Mad Scientist

Let's get something straight right away. There is a difference between a mad scientist and a scientist gone mad. One is a bomb that's still ticking; the other is a dud that was left in the wrong place. A scientist who has gone mad would no longer be doing science; he would be doing lunacy. It hardly matters that he used to be a scientist for he is mad in the same way that an accountant or an essayist might be—indeed, they could all share a single ward. But the mad scientist, this dark yet white-clad figure from the underside of modern theology and pop culture, this bent creature scuttling out of dreams and onto our screens, not only functions scientifically just fine, thank you, but does so to all sorts of amazing effects. Somewhere it is written that all mad scientists are also geniuses. Their plans, no matter how crackpot, all work, up to a point. Presumably, the slow-witted scientists are unshakably sane and therefore safe, or vice versa.

Now it is rather odd that in our imaginings about scientists we should associate incompetence with safety and even benevolence, as if Mr. Wizard were not smart enough to transgress, while associating genius with catastrophe, as if this were the secret revenge of the hopeless math students on the brilliant ones. After all, in real life, as they say, it is probably the other way around, isn't it? Or maybe it is only the other way around where the lethally trivial things are concerned: things like nuclear power plants that might inadvertently melt down or an airplane with a penchant for falling apart like a bad argument. With the really big things that worry us, in those anxious moments when we ponder Faust's story and wonder if giving up plagues and famine and hand-to-hand combat has been a sordid boon—at such times it is of course the geniuses we tend to blame and not the mere technicians, for the geniuses do make the biggest changes. That is how we know they are geniuses.

I wonder how it must seem to little boys and girls gifted and ambitious enough to wish to become scientists—*pure* scientists, as the metaphor goes. Fed on the same movies and comic books as the rest of us, do they dream of becoming good enough to qualify as mad? Probably not. As I remember my own scientifically bent colleagues from high school and college, they seem early on to have dismissed the image of the mad scientist from those wonderfully clear minds of theirs, minds they were diligently making pure for the sake of all the terrific science they were going to do. By and large, they were a practical and unromantic lot, those whiz kids, not drawn to science by any visions of heroism in the laboratory, not even inspired by the shower of scientific hagiographies that were being poured over us in those nervous post-Sputnik, post-polio-vaccine days. In short, they really were "pure," drawn much more to science by the joys of the work they wished to do than by what it might do for them. This fact accounts for some of their contempt for mere premeds and engineers, whom they rightly or wrongly regarded as folks who were mostly in it for the money and thus of a decidedly lower sect, though of the same faith. No, the mad scientist may be many things, but he is not a creature the scientists themselves believe in—certainly not the pure ones, who are most in the way of resembling him.

And, since the word seems to be coming up so often, what can we say about the purity of pure science, the unapplied kind, and the purity of those who do it? How can we relate this purity to the madness of the mad scientist who must also be a pure one? Might purity and madness have something in common? What an excellent essay question this would make in any number of college courses: abnormal psychology, comparative religion, Russian literature in translation, subatomic physics, financial management. Well, we can begin here: in our sublunary realm the pure seems always to be also the partial. Whether that of a metal or a moral, purity has to be achieved by refinement, distillation, exclusion. Madness, at least that of our conventionally mad scientist, is likewise characterized by exclusivity. The laboratory door shuts out the world. Frankenstein has little time to spare for his exquisitely patient and boring fiancée. Mad scientists are scarcely ever to be found at rock concerts, cocktail parties, political rallies. Moreover, we feel the mad scientist succeeds in large measure because of his singleness of purpose, his fanatically exclusive concentration. He's a grind. His absentmindedness, should he display some, will not be the endearing abstraction of an aging and harmless professor of, say, philosophy, but rather the sinister and calculated indifference of one who is perpetually thinking of the same thing. Obsession (a word derived from the Latin *obsidere*, to sit before, besiege, occupy, invest) is a thing that the mad scientist is generally agreed to have one of. The psychological meaning of ''obsession'' is a late one, though it probably goes back to old notions of demonic possession. In the purity of the mad scientist's obsession lies both his science and his madness. He can even be said to become mad at the crucial moment when his professional obsession becomes demonic possession: not when he has it, but when it has him.

The pure tend to be ruthless, first with themselves—for how else could they have become pure?—and then with others. Is ruthlessness a kind of madness? The easy-going will say so. Not always seems a more prudent answer, but one can certainly imagine (if one had read no history and had to) the ruthless pursuit of something, anything, assuming the shape of insanity. Much of what passes for the sane pursuit of national interest in the great world comes in time to look mad if the pursuit is ruthless enough. After all, if mad scientists do such effective science, why not mad politicians doing effective politics? Is not ruthless politics often the pursuit of war by other means?

So the pure are without pity, but can they make jokes? Not as rule, I think, or not unless the purity doesn't come by exclusion but by inclusion, as in the wonderful humor of the Zen masters whom I am willing to think of as pure and funny at the same time. But here in the good old dualist West, the pure generally look dour and, like the rest of us exalters of the ego, rather puffed up. What the pure put in place of humor is sarcasm. The mad scientist is like that. He has no genteel irony because he lacks humane skepticism. ''So you think *you* know something, eh?'' he might sneer at a colleague or a reporter. As a positivist he is inflexibly positive; as a perfectionist he is rigidly perfect. If he should make a joke it will only be to get the better of the rest of the world that doesn't know what he knows, which is the only thing worth knowing. In its ignorance, of course, the world fails to understand him. The pure can only condescend to make a joke, and since jokes are basically about limitations, they joke about the limitations of others. Humor is social, and the mad scientist isn't.

So unsympathetic do we feel toward the mad scientist, that being one of the purposes for which we invented him, that it may seem perverse to see him as pitiful or commonplace, even as a bit like ourselves at one stage in our life's adventures. Nevertheless, I am

thinking for the moment of the mad scientist as an adolescent, as a
fantasy of what might come of not outgrowing what is usually a stage
not mercifully brief enough. Here are the similarities: both the mad
scientist and the pubescent are extraordinarily fond of going off to
their rooms alone and refusing to tell anybody what they are up to
in there; both regard themselves as too superior to be understood,
at least by mom and dad; both dream of omnipotence, fail to grasp
what is motivating them most of the time, and, in all the senses,
masturbate. That cautionary saying of the old wives that masturbation leads to madness (pooh-poohed these days by the sex experts)
may even have something to it. Though I must apologize for connect-
ing so unseemly a thing as masturbation with so dignified a thing as
science—even "mad science"—still, if the shoe fits. . . . Consider:
the apparent contradiction between the mad scientist as "pure" and
at the same time "masturbatory" vanishes when the idea of purity
as exclusion is recalled.

The mad scientist, like the onanistic teenager, is doing a secret
thing that leaves unsatisfied the very craving that needs relieving.
His science is a vicious circle leading to a catastrophic orgasm of
discovery, a sterile "Eureka!" His is self-revelation in terms of self-
destruction. D. H. Lawrence, an expert on these matters, called masturbation "the one thoroughly secret act of the human being." Such
secrecy is imaginary suicide. The more he works, filling his lab with
retorts and electrified brains, the more the mad scientist empties out
the self. Knowledge is won at the cost of the knower. As Lawrence
cagily put it, "The only positive effect of masturbation is that it seems
to release a certain mental energy in some people." Mad scientists
are surely such people.

The mad scientist wishes to control everything, of course. This is
why he got into the business in the first place. The urge toward
omnipotence is entirely consistent with a masturbatory mentality
through which he can couple, so to speak, ideally with his own fantasies—fantasies not of mere playmates, but of utter power and domination. In the last two hundred years such fantasies have come to be
called sadistic, a word one feels altogether comfortable in applying
to the mad scientist. But I wonder if people realize how very apt that
epithet is. It was, after all, the highly dignified Baron of Verulam, Sir

Francis Bacon, initiator of British Empiricism, cofounder of the modern scientific method, who epitomized what he had in mind in a shocking metaphor: "Man must put Nature to the rack and torture her for answers to his questions." Scientist as Torquemada. Friedrich Nietzsche, a perversely sarcastic purist himself, a sort of mad metaphysicist, took up the point a century ago and said cunningly that "even in every desire for knowledge there is a drop of cruelty." The mad scientist has a very simple relation to his material and—I am saying this almost against my will—it may not be decisively different from that of any scientist: it is the relation of Galvani to his frog.

In his play *The Physicists* (1962), Friedrich Dürrenmatt has his three scientists elect to remain in a madhouse to show they are not mad. In the play, the genuine madness belongs to a hunchbacked female psychiatrist who recognizes no limits, who takes "King Solomon's power" upon herself, who is sterile and loveless, who therefore longs to dictate to mankind and even announces, in a little poetical geyser, her program to "ransack the solar system and thrust out beyond the great nebula in Andromeda." The interesting thing here is that the madness of the Fräulein Doktor sounds so much like the humanistic poetry of the Renaissance gone rancid. In four hundred years, there's been only a superficial change. Sane scientists nowadays are marked by humility, it's true, but it may be the modesty of total victory. The arrogance of the mad scientist is, like the adolescent's, a sign of insecurity. The proof is that this vainglory gets displayed most fully toward other scientists, just as the greatest violence in religious controversy seems to occur between sectarians of the same faith.

It is an axiom of mad-scientist stories that the crazy genius must be hoist with his own petard, whether the petard in question is a blast from his own death ray, a ravenous fifty-foot insect, a teeny-tiny microbe, or a random fly in his body transporter. The motif is implicit in the story of Faust's damnable bargain, explicit in the tale of Frankenstein and his vengeful monster, and has been a staple of plots ever after. We immediately recognize the moral of each such story, and a simple one it is too: thou shalt not, or else. So the mad scientist is also a sinner in both the Hebraic and Hellenistic modes. He is above all a transgressor, one who crosses the frontier and enters forbidden precincts, messes around with things better left alone. In the more traditionally religious variants it is things he was not *meant* to mess with.

Is there any further sense to be gotten from this conventional verdict of poetic justice? Well, for one thing, the mad scientist's comeuppance is always an irony of ends and means. If the sane scientist presents us with means appropriate to achieving our ends, the mad scientist is the one whose ends are destroyed by his means. To take only one instance, it is a characteristic end of the mad scientist to control everything. He is like that lunatic in Johnson's *Rasselas* who believes he is in charge of the weather worldwide, something that may indeed become somebody's job someday. But this effort at total control leads inexorably to an utter loss of it, like Mickey Mouse as the sorcerer's apprentice in *Fantasia*. His very concentration keeps him from foreseeing the consequences of what he is up to, and the consequences are suitably dire. To put it another way, the dire consequences are the outward manifestation of his inward derangement. Yet a third way: the hoisting is the work of Nemesis, punishing the mad scientist for trespassing on the sacred ground of Moira, and for his hubris in thinking himself the only really sane scientist around.

I might digress briefly here to mention the equivocal nature of the mad scientist, though it doesn't in the least affect the nature of the moral of his story, only the extent of its application and maybe not even that. What I am thinking is that there are two ways of regarding the mad scientist, which can be put simply as: a) *a* man gone wrong, or b) *man* gone wrong. The funny thing, when you think about it, is how little it matters which way you see it: as anecdote or as portentous cultural myth. The tale of the mad scientist comes to the same thing either way, an interesting instance of that poetic mystery by which the particular can represent the general. The myths of Faust and Frankenstein both started out as diverting anecdotes.

Is the mad scientist happy? Happy in his work perhaps, though probably in nothing else, happy to *lose himself* in his work. But the same, I suspect, is true of many sane scientists, as it is of artists and investment bankers. A student of mine once told me about his old high school math teacher, an elderly woman he found dull except for the day she happened to mention to her class that she worked in Los Alamos during World War II. The class, pacifists of the seventies, was horrified, he said. "You helped make the bomb!" they cried, but she just smiled at the memory of joy in the desert. "I couldn't wait to get up in the morning," she confessed. "They had to force me to go to bed at night. It was the same for all of us—the best time of our lives." Sane? Mad? Who cared?

How *do* you tell a mad scientist from a sane one? It is a very curious thing that while, as we began by saying, the madness of the mad scientist has to do with his science, there is no way to tell a mad scientist from a sane one just by looking at the science they are doing. In fact, there is no way of telling them apart except by looking at everything other than their science, and even that might not be of much use. To be sure, it is tempting to say that all you have to do is look at how they treat their children or dogs, what sort of emotions they entertain while watching *E.T.*, whether they profess any sort of morality, or skip lunch, but I don't think even knowing all this can be conclusive. I don't see why a sane scientist cannot be every bit as amoral and preoccupied with what his rats are doing as a mad one. And when we look to their science itself, the problem is much worse. Two things make this problematic: first, that science and sorcery, or technology and magic, are still not completely distinct in our minds; and second, that science is, like music, a universal language. A sane scientist can reproduce the work of an insane one simply by following his directions.

We run into similar problems everywhere. Take, for instance, the sort of insanity Camus recorded in the anecdote of the lunatic who fished in his bathtub. On his first visit, a new doctor, thinking he ought to humor his patient, asked the man if he had caught any fish that morning only to be met with the indignant reply: "Are you mad, Doctor? Don't you know you can't catch fish in a bathtub!" And so we might think that the madness of the mad scientist also would lie in an obsessive inability to see the whole, in an unhealthy concentration on the part. And yet this is just the sort of thing quite sane scientists have been doing for generations: they see deeper and deeper by looking at less and less more and more closely.

We might try to circumvent this irritating diagnostic difficulty by going in for a grander view and asking about the origin of all these cautionary tales about science, not to mention what caused us to divide science from the so-called humanities (as if we wished to suggest science were done by somebody other than human beings). Is it that what looks historically like a fear of reason, arising about two centuries ago, is actually a fear of reason leading to its opposite? That is no rhetorical question, and neither is this one: is the mad scientist mad because he has stuck to sanity too long? But if this is so, then how can we discriminate between a scientist who has been sane too long and one who hasn't?

Nor will it do to say that we shall know the tree by its fruit. If you can only tell whether a scientist is mad after a few cities have been vaporized (and we all know this is what a bunch of sane ones made possible), then you can't really tell at all, can you—especially if you chance to be living in one of the aforementioned cities.

When Giordano Bruno, science's favorite martyr, was executed in 1600 (not for being a premature Copernican, incidentally, but for professing pantheism), did the reverend Inquisitor who struck the first match think Bruno was a mad scientist? Did he and his confrères go on to shut Galileo up because they believed he had gone bonkers? Clearly not. They were just madly cleaving to the barn door of orthodoxy. Nor is Dr. Faustus ever certified; on the contrary, he is venerated, prayed for, and mourned by all his less gifted, less ambitious colleagues and disciples at Wittenberg. And though Victor Frankenstein does suffer from occasional fits of fainting and a three-month bout of "brain fever," Mary Shelley never comes near calling him a psychopath. Actually, she makes him out to be a nice college sophomore who only wants to stamp out death, Switzerland's number one killer.

So this mad scientist thing seems to be a very recent phenomenon and, what's more, a highly dubious one when you come to look at it closely. And if, as soon as we really try, we cannot tell a mad scientist from a sane one (though I have begun by supposing we can distinguish between a scientist who's gone mad and one who hasn't), well then, where are we? Ought we to conclude that the popular figure of the mad scientist is a way of implying that *all* science is "mad"? That sounds like barbarism, if not demonism. Perhaps the currency of this figure only means that we tend to resent science in direct proportion to how much we depend on it, and lately, as the scientists themselves are quick to remind us, we have come to depend upon it for just about everything. Or perhaps the mad scientist is only the most recent incarnation of extremely ancient fears and an only somewhat less ancient tragic vision.

> The stars move still, time runs, the clock will strike,
> The devil will come, and Faustus must be damned.

Between Recurrence and Invention

If one were to believe the Pythagoreans, with the result that the same individual things will recur, then I shall be talking to you again sitting as you are now, with this pointer in my hand, and everything else will be just as it is now, and it is reasonable to suppose that the time then is the same as now.

—*Eudemus*

I once knew a lady who had particular difficulty in describing ordinary things. This was really a gift in that it lent her speech inadvertent freshness. Attempting to give an account of a pretty striped dress, she said, in her frustration: ''There's a line, you see, then you wait a while and there's another one.'' It was a good way of making one feel how space and time fit into one another, though the point was charmingly unintended. The pattern of stripes in space became a rhythm of lines in time.

Perhaps it is true that the imagination can hardly help rearranging things as it describes them and that an experience of recurrence, like the stripes and lines, especially quickens the imagination because it seems made for the imagination. Let's say the recurrence of things, even of stripes in a fabric, is essentially a musical idea. Without our ability to form associations, among which musical recurrence is only the purest because it is inherent in the disembodied music itself, no concourse of sweet sounds could do more than satisfy our appetite for such sounds. Yet I think we value our musical memories more for what they seem to express than for what they may happen to assuage. I say ''memories'' because it is in large part memory that turns sound into music and it is also through memory that music ''comes to express'' things for us. The memory of music is more personal than that provided by recalling other kinds of art. People who would shudder at the notion of reading, say, *Finnegans Wake* a dozen times think nothing at all of listening to the *Emperor Concerto* fifty or sixty.

There is of course nothing at all new in applying a musical notion of recurrence to the metrical aspects of poetry (''lyric,'' ''cantabile''), or the structural aspects of architecture (Hegel's ''frozen music''), or even the supernal regularities of logic and mathematics (''mental music" for Neoplatonists). The Greeks thought up muses for all the arts, but in this sense too—of reliance on recurrence—all the arts are musical. The aesthetes of the last century advocated this idea because they strove to free themselves from a utilitarian reality they felt to be alien and hostile to art—or at least to them: *"La musique avant toutes choses . . .,"* wrote Paul Verlaine; "All art aspires to the condition of music," averred Walter Pater. But there are also many instances of "musical" recurrence that are not specifically artistic. Pythagoras not only discovered the rudiments of harmony in music, but his famous astronomical notion of a "harmony of the spheres" was clearly based on the idea that the recurrence of the observed and projected movements of heavenly bodies must make a music we could not hear—because we had always heard it. And aren't sound waves themselves, like ocean waves, patterns of recurrence? As the waves are not made of air in the one case, or water in the other, they must be abstract forces—like music. All live through a material medium that is not themselves, but without which they are unknowable and unenjoyable. Here is a stranger example: isn't it possible that experiences of déjà vu move us first because of their musical aspect—i.e., recurrence—and only later by our personal associations with the weirdly familiar scenes? If so, this might help to explain why we should always feel these experiences as out of our control and able to be put under our control only by rationalizing them. In this case, to "rationalize" pretty much means to move the experience *inside* ourselves, to psychologize, saying that the experience was created by our own minds, albeit unconsciously—that is, invented. And even if this explanation isn't quite convincing, and one should rebelliously suspect the unconsciousness of the mind of being a modern fudge factor, it still has the effect of rationalizing anyway. A classic example of the same procedure is Fate, an idea of recurrence that the Greeks felt as out of one's control, but which the last century rationalized by equating it with character. Why is Fate an "idea of recurrence"? Not solely because we still affirm the truths of classic tragedy, but also because of the more primitive fatal idea of predetermination. The pattern is laid out in advance so that tragic *occurrence* is *recurrence too. The Fates are, after all, weavers—makers of stripes and lines. The old Oedipus is outraged by the idea that his fate has anything to do with his character:

> Was I the sinner?
> Repaying wrong for wrong—that was no sin,
> Even were it wittingly done, as it was not.
> I did not know the way I went. *They* knew;
> They, who devised this trap for me, they knew![1]

Nowadays, though, we can do even better than the Victorians, replacing character with chromosomes, economic determinism, and environmental conditioning. But in any case, we see that even places and whole lives can "recur" musically. So indeed can any object, state of feeling, mood, sensibility, idea—really anything whatever. And of course things that fall into a pattern promise a meaning.

All this I think we can accept as a kind of common sense underlying common sense. So long as we locate the experience of recurrence inside ourselves, our general notion of reality is unchallenged and these speculations have an effect on us comparable to that of David Hume's idea of causality as a "habit of the mind." That is, examining the nature and effects of recurrence shows us how more important things go on in our minds—thought, for instance. To look at recurrence in this way is commonsensical because it is in accord with our manner of rationalizing. What is common sense if not the collective record of all successfully rationalized experiences? But what if a pattern of recurrence should, so to speak, form musically *outside* the minds of individual human beings? Can we accept that anymore—or, to put the question more answerably, can we accept it without also accepting a system?

Most of us feel that the historical systems of Giambattista Vico and Oswald Spengler do not really conform to the way things are, or happen; but maybe this is in part because we cannot imagine a systematic reality unless the system should be our own. Erich Heller, for instance, judged Spengler's system of history not to be incorrect but "untrue."[2] When William Blake said he must create a system of his own or be enslaved by another's, he may have been expressing more than just the will to be an original poet. Maybe no other system would have been credible to Blake, and the poet's insistence on this point may be yet another "beginning of the modern world," in which we all have our own systems. For that matter, Heller's objection to Spengler comes down to disregarding human freedom, a concept that is alien to systems in general. Kant had to stick it in the noumenal world.

A very practical version of the problem of a musical system of recurrence beyond ourselves has been placed before us by the late Professor Skinner in his philosophical extension of the behaviorist technique of operant conditioning. Here the "music" of recurrent stimulus and reward or punishment is to summon up, by induced conviction, our participation in a well-regulated behavioral dance. The implications of what Professor Skinner says do move all of us "beyond freedom and dignity," save perhaps for the conditioner, the explicator of the system, the Grand Inquisitor. But this last observation, which no one fails to make, tends to metamorphose even such a scientific system as operant conditioning back into individually created musical patterns. The patterns must be invented; at least this will be so once somebody actually takes up these abstract, neutral techniques and uses them to some end on somebody or other. These patterns may, to be sure, be very complicated ones, supported by research, making extraordinary manipulative references to other portions of reality (such as prison populations, for example), but they are located in the individual as solidly as any experience of déjà vu had by a behaviorist. Like music, the abstract pattern of conditioning must be—performed.

Perhaps a shorter way of saying all this would be to remark that one man's freedom may be another man's determinism. Or maybe we should say that freedom is something we tend to grant only to our contemporaries, our forebears and posterity having in common their thrall to the necessity of recurrence.

• • •

With these inconclusive generalizations left to rotate like nebulae in the mind, I want to adduce a specific text. It is one I happened to read by chance; yet it may in fact be the occasion of all this vagrant thinking about recurrence and invention.

In the eighth chapter of Ezekiel the prophet describes how one day during the Exile, while sitting quietly at his home near Babylon surrounded by "the elders of Judah," he was miraculously lifted up and carried off to the ruins of the Temple in Jerusalem. There Ezekiel is placed before a series of "abominations" going on in and around the sanctuary. The whole chapter is good poetry and drama, taking the form of a succession of very potently narrated dumb shows or *tableaux vivants* with paganism and apostacy for subject. But the passage I am particularly intrigued by occurs in verses 6–12:

> And He said unto me: "Son of man, seest thou what they do? even the great abominations that the house of Israel do commit here, that I should go far off from My sanctuary? . . ." And He brought me to the door of the court; and when I looked, behold a hole in the wall. Then said He unto me: "Son of man, dig now in the wall"; and when I had digged in the wall, behold a door. And He said unto me: "Go in, and see the wicked abominations that they do here." So I went in and saw; and behold every detestable form of creeping things and beasts, and all the idols of the house of Israel, portrayed upon the wall round about. And there stood before them seventy men of the elders of the house of Israel, and in the midst of them stood Jaazaniah the son of Shaphan, every man with his censer in his hand; and a thick cloud of incense went up. Then said He unto me: "Son of man, hast thou seen what the elders of the house of Israel do in the dark, every man in his chambers of imagery? for they say: The Lord seeth us not, the Lord hath forsaken the land."

There are many things here worth thinking about, for it is a fine rich passage to have found, full of suggestions and intriguing problems. For instance, I am struck by the motif of descent, so familiar from epic; the ambiguity of a God who claims to be driven away from His sanctuary but who is believed already (and with some justification) to have "forsaken the land"; the Young Goodman Brown-like horror of Ezekiel at seeing the elder Jaazaniah there; the deliberate repulsiveness of the Egyptian rituals and murals out of *The Book of the Dead*; the sense that these exotic blasphemies, occurring in the very foundations of the dilapidated Temple (only ruins can reveal foundations) are themselves the effects of despair. But our theme is recurrence, and especially a recurrence perceived as outside the individual or individuals who perceive it, or even those who act it out.

Of course such a vivid passage is liable to create lots of associations in a reader's mind. But I don't think a recurrence can be the same thing as a mere association, especially if we wish to go out on a limb and exclude the personal and psychological, so to speak redividing fate from character. For instance, as I read the passage from Ezekiel I had both a clear association and a more mysterious sense of recurrence. And these *felt* like different things. My association will immediately be recognized as merely personal and arbitrary when I say that I thought of a motion-picture theater. The darkness and smokiness; the bright, gross images on the wall; the imperative of descent (flashlighted down the aisles); the gathering of a community among which there is no real communion but where instead each person occupies his own "chambers of imagery"—all this I associated with my moviegoing experience. Another difference is that association, unlike recurrence, tends to go on and on if left alone. Thus, my moviegoing association led me on to some more or less interesting and ironic thoughts about the sociology and aesthetics of film, and then to a peculiar secondary association. I thought of Plato's myth of the cave in *The Republic*. But now I thought of Plato's cave in the strange context of both Ezekiel and of movie theaters. Such a train of thought could have been protracted indefinitely, I suppose. Now, of course, these accidents of psychology and education might be made "significant" in some way. But one would have to will it, to make deliberate sense of what is essentially random and gratuitous. Significance would need to be invented. I could, for example, have found material for an essay on the nature of artistic illusion by halting the train of association and then coupling the three elements to the locomotive of some communicable thesis. I might have compared the old Hebraic view of illusion with that of the ancient Greeks and livened the whole farrago up by using modern movies as the focus of the discussion. All this might have been interesting in a way, but it would not have been at all disturbing. Properly speaking, it would have been fanciful. These associations carried, so to say, no intimations of any music beyond what was of strictly home manufacture, mere desultory whistling in the wind. There was, above all, no humility attached to the pattern of association, only a kind of forced vanity. Nor would I expect a reader of this imaginary essay to be much impressed, just as one is not deeply moved by the occasional associations made in the minds of the fashioners of crossword puzzles and double acrostics.

On the other hand, the sense of recurrence I had from the passage was humbling, disturbing, and quite final. It apparently had nothing to do with me—certainly not in the way that the above associations had, for all the Platos and Bijoux, *only* to do with me. It was the sense of recurrence that moved me in the passage, made me respect it, regard it far more highly than as a curiosity giving rise to further curiosities. The difference may be between the system of a crossword puzzle and that of great music. This recurrence had to do neither with my psychology nor my education, though I don't doubt it involved both. Or perhaps it needed to involve them, but only to the extent that they have become parts of me. In this sense, the recurrence involved also my associations with movie theaters and Plato. It subsumed them, and went beyond them. The proof that this sense of recurrence had little to do with me is that it is not communicable. The same fact shows that the recurrence was not embedded in language.

I have to approach the sense of recurrence, the great and mysterious music, as something I do not understand. A while back, having raised the problem of "musical systems" outside ourselves, I implied that when we know these to be inventions of other human beings they can have no ultimate authority for us. It is just as true but more remarkable that the same reservations may also be felt about the systems of our own devising. I guess philosophers have been feeling that kind of malaise ever since Immanuel Kant; but really (since it's come up) this stumbling block of epistemology was already adumbrated in the myth of the cave itself, and thus has been a part of our culture from the beginning:

And if they [the creatures in the cave] were able to converse with one another, would they not suppose that they were naming what was actually before them? . . . To them, I said, the truth would be literally nothing but the shadows of the images.[3]

Whichever direction a man should walk, he will meet Plato on his way back—so an old Greek proverb has it. And thus, by having read Plato, or simply by living in this century, we may know the curiously umbral nature of most of the truth we glimpse. In his idealist myth, Plato identifies the "sun" not only as the source of light, the thing that creates the shadows; he declares its realm to be entirely intellectual, a high-noon world purified of shadows, static and perfect up there in a clear Greek cerulean dome, like Mathematics. Now, it is in this same dialogue that Plato tells us how much he mistrusts artistic experiences in general: they are shadows on the cave wall, moving-picture shows, lies about and rearrangements of a reality that is itself already derivative. For that matter, this mistrust is the same in Ezekiel. The music of the Israelites' pagan rituals, with the incense and painted chimerae, is blasphemous because it holds out false, unfulfillable promises, as when the priests of Ba'al promised they could bring down lightning and couldn't. The mistrust is practical; that is, the nature of the objection to illusion contains its own proof.

Apropos of this mistrust, which we can see is aesthetic and religious at once, both Hellenic and Hebraic, here is a wonderfully apt sentence from a source presumably more friendly to the illusions of invention. It comes from one of Jorge Luis Borges's essays:

Music, states of happiness, mythology, faces belabored by time, certain twilights and certain places try to tell us something, or have said something we should not have missed, or are about to say something; this imminence of a revelation which does not occur is, perhaps, the aesthetic phenomenon.[4]

"Imminence of a revelation that does not occur" is a phrase made to order for those elders of Israel and the chained creatures in Plato's cave—in short, for audiences. This imminence may make of our most moving experiences a touching kind of music—precisely the music of

"certain twilights and certain places." But if the revelation beyond
the music is finally lacking, maybe this is because, in the words of
the Great Gatsby, the music is "only personal."

Those words spoken by Gatsby are, of course, only possible for
one who is really living out "his Platonic idea of himself"; that is,
for someone who has no personal psychology and consequently sees
no shadows. Perhaps this is possible in actuality; yet there is nothing
to guarantee the taste of such a person. For him the music of a mone-
tary voice, of green lights across a bay, of silk shirts and turquoise
lawns may represent a perpetual revelation formally the equal of
Ezekiel's visions in the sky. It is natural that when the idea of revelation becomes secularized only its form matters. That is why the best
reply to the myth of the cave is *Don Quixote*.

So, recurrence arouses at least the hope of a revelation beyond
ourselves and also beyond "the aesthetic phenomenon." To take one
example from among many that might be useful at this point, in the
ninth chapter of Tolstoy's *The Death of Ivan Ilych* we can see the
recurrence of Ezekiel's experience amidst the elders of Israel. Here
Ivan is no longer being merely fanciful about dying. He is beyond
the doctors and bridge games for which Tolstoy expresses such contempt as they are understood to be only features of Ivan's particular,
bourgeois "chamber of imagery." Moreover, Ivan is on the verge of
a revelation beyond the aesthetic. At this point in the story, Ivan has
drawn very close to his author, who insisted on ultimate standards
too (the final chapter of this novella is written in accord with something other than aesthetic considerations). Ivan begins his crisis by
feeling as forlorn and desperate as Jaazaniah must have:

> He removed his legs from Gerásim's shoulders, turned sideways
> onto his arm, and felt sorry for himself. He only waited till Gerásim
> had gone into the next room and then restrained himself no longer
> but wept like a child. He wept on account of his helplessness, his
> terrible loneliness, the cruelty of man, the cruelty of God, and the
> absence of God.[5]

Unlike his typical and mendacious family—who have gone off to see

Sarah Bernhardt—Ivan is now prepared to deal with his "intimate matter," and it is no mere aesthetic one. He soon stops crying and listens "not to an audible voice but to the voice of his soul." It is then that the intimations, the insights into the pattern of his life, and even a preliminary revelation of another truth all come to him: "Maybe I did not live as I ought to have done?" Tolstoy understands recurrence well; Ivan's response to his wife's first pregnancy is identical to his response to his dying. Birth and death—irreducible realities—both mess up his well-regulated and pleasant life. But now, in his last extremity, Ivan is able to hear the recurrent music of his own existence—childhood, education, marriage, family, career—and quite impersonally for once; and we, with equal impersonality, without aesthetic inducement, can hear the recurrent music of men repeatedly brought to such a pass. Like death itself, none of this is accidental. It is fatal irrespective of our character; in fact, these things happen all the time.

But where do such revelations come from anyway? We can only say that we don't know, and have learned to be good and skeptical about them. Although we are not mystics, the music of recurrence may remind us of revelations freely given, give us their taste, excite and confuse our senses, get us ready even to transcend ourselves, our little inventions. But the full score of this music sounds solely in the ears of the old God, who is the only being whose determinism may possibly have been our freedom. Our merely human memories are too short, or the melodies are too long.

Meanwhile, Ezekiel, Plato, Borges, and Tolstoy have put before us a secular definition of apostacy that describes the way in which we live most of the time. It is the condition of being closed in one's own chamber of imagery, where each hears over and over again his privately invented music; it is a condition not limited to modern poets or Biblical elders. This private music is the only sort with which we can say truly that we are familiar, and it is a fanciful music. To hear it is normal enough. Occasionally though, we hear something else and are disturbed and excited by it. To hear this is abnormal. These are the grand recurrences, memories of melodies for which we do not feel responsible and do not feel that anyone else is responsible. Between recurrence and invention is where we mostly live.

Notes

1 *Oedipus at Colonus*, lines 271–275.
2 Erich Heller, *The Disinherited Mind* (Cleveland: Meridian Books, 1959), 193.
3 *Dialogues of Plato*, transl. Benjamin Jowett (New York: Pocket Library, 1955), 358.
4 Jorge Luis Borges, "The Wall and the Books," in *Labyrinths* (New York: New Directions, 1962), 188.
5 Leo Tolstoy, "The Death of Ivan Ilych," transl. Louise and Aylmer Maude, in *Tolstoy's Short Fiction* (New York: W. W. Norton, 1991), 160.

The Proverbs of
Klaren Verheim

1. The man who leaps from the bridge is not the same as the one who drops into the river.
2. All the visions of summer are futile.
3. The rich man steals; the poor man dreams of theft.
4. A mirror shows you half the truth backwards.
5. There are only two ways to escape the horizon: to leave the earth or to shut your eyes.
6. All virtues vanish when your hair is dirty.
7. Ever since man lost his tail, the future of toenails has looked bleak.
8. Women change size when they lie down, men when they stand up.
9. Nobody is ever a man-of-the-people.
10. Eat the best lambchop first; better to choke on it than the bad one.
11. Some roads are nothing but middle.
12. A man with two shirts sweats less than he who has but one.
13. Forwards or back; it is the same with ships—to go sideways is to sink.
14. A dead man forgives no one, reproaches everyone.
15. Gossip is either a punishment or a reward for the division of labor.
16. An uprooted tree is not a lesson in tolerance, but in survival.
17. Without water, no soup; without roses, no thorns.
18. Music is the best way of telling off an infinity of time.
19. To Eden there are only back doors.
20. A potato has less potential than a farmer.
21. Gluttons invariably devour the things they love.
22. Power without conflict is an amnesiac orphan, having lost its past, present, and future.
23. To build a wall is to turn your hands into stones.
24. Logic: a form of interior decoration.
25. Three men can share what two will murder each other to possess.
25. The truth can't be revised, only our understanding.
27. The world likes imagination more than imagination likes the world.
28. All life depends on the radius of a single orbit.

29. A man sitting still may also be going in every direction at once.
30. If others laugh, the jester eats. When the jester eats, no one laughs.
31. Heraclitus said all things are fire; perhaps he was only prophesying.
32. Of any assembly of drunkards, half are trying to forget, half to remember.
33. It is nature that allows an airplane to stay aloft, rain to come down.
34. In order to lose oneself one must first have the wish to gamble.
35. Light lets you see; darkness makes you feel.
36. When people speak of "getting along" it is usually a plea for indifference.
37. The trick is not to sell your soul either to the Devil or to God.
38. Most people have contempt for their own desires.
39. Children could be innocent, but they lack persistence.
40. Not the art of conversation, but the art of belonging is lost.
41. All names are values; all numbers are prices.
42. A skeptic is the most patient of men—he reserves judgment.
43. Where is the man who fails to claim that the common good is his own and does not secretly contrive that it should be otherwise?
44. If you look closely enough, every deception is self-deception.
45. A dog never depends on his vision; that's why he makes the best detective.
46. Butchers and priests must change clothes before leaving work.
47. There is no such thing as a well-earned vacation.
48. The honest man admits the constancy of change; the dishonest man changes constancies.
49. Poetry has always been a mnemonic device.
50. A really good rainbow can make the earth look like an optical illusion.
51. Naturally, an indirect man finds a direct one vulgar; it is for the same reason that embezzlers rank themselves above robbers.
52. The most significant events occur morning, afternoon, and night.
53. Nature's open secret is randomness: that is why a premeditated birth is curiously upsetting to all of us accidental children.

54. The only perpetual war would be one with an infinite number of truces.
55. When the law-abiding man chooses lawlessness, heaven and hell both open.
56. One laments over the ruins; another takes careful note of the properties of the buildings left standing.
57. There is infinite variety in ignorance, but stupidity is one.
58. Before all stories pose the enchanting once-upon-a-time.
59. As there is no beauty in waste, so there is no waste in beauty.
60. Two theories of art: order and chaos. These depend on the traffic jam and when you do the dishes.
61. In the end even honest men will prefer that you don't trust them.
62. A battle between those who want to say "we" and those who want to say "I."
63. The psychiatrist denies that a man can manufacture unhappiness within himself. The politician doesn't care about this; he asserts that happiness can be gained by voting for him. Both agree that nothing comes from nothing.
64. Since, even though they do not really exist, fathers and sons have always insisted on speaking of the differences between generations, it must be a way of avoiding speech with each other.
65. Why do you believe that in the just society only those without ambition will rise?
66. People are entropic, and the proof is that even the largest homes have no empty rooms.
67. A great leader always represents the suffering of his people. It is the only way he can bear their hopes.
68. Professor X. is full of great ideas whose time has passed. It is through knowing this that he is such a tough grader.
69. Even at the beginning of his book Solomon candidly informs his son that wisdom will be a "chain around his neck." Could this be giving up in advance? How many sons believe in the wisdom of chains?
70. All statues of the Buddha are more or less identical. This was absolutely necessary; otherwise people might have deduced a nervous tic.

71. The smaller the animal the further it may be safely dropped; that is, the more liberties it may take with gravity.
72. Isn't the expansion of freezing water a suspension of the laws of nature?
73. How many things are like bicycle-riding? At first it seems impossible to stay up, but then impossible to fall.
74. Many men say that the myth, because it is a myth, is untrue. Others declare the myth to be the truth, and for the same reason. This disagreement can be resolved, but only mythically.
75. At least since Bacon, certain men have searched for some beauty in all strangeness.
76. Whenever we actually look closely at something it is found to be in transition. Thus, a final word must always be pronounced, literally, with aversion.
77. Many people believe they are heading straight toward the mark when, in reality, they are pursuing the vector of two marks and consequently will never arrive at either.
78. As there is no cold, but only degrees of heat, so perhaps there are no pleasures of the mind, but only degrees of pain.
79. If the nature of light is itself so ambiguous, then nothing can be illuminated without preserving a certain vagueness.
80. Among crows scavenging is the most respectable profession.
81. If perfect happiness had not been found boring, would we then still be in paradise?
82. It is always easier to believe in the nobility of the past (even one's own) than in the free will of those who inhabited it (even one's own).
83. A river without fish, a field without trees, a school without questions.
84. Imagine a man who could feel the weight of the air on his head. That is truly oppressive sensitivity.
85. Europe is always fled, America always discovered. Therefore Americans who flee to Europe are merely taking the long way around.
86. Levitation is the mystic goal after which all the lazy strive. That is why it has never been attained.

87. Wood cracks with the grain, and so do we. Whatever is against the grain is what we were constructed to resist.

88. Too much refinement always celebrates its victims.

89. Those who are truly weak are indistinguishable from those whose strength has only been temporarily lost inside them.

90. In his youth X. saw a difference between happiness and the good which he now is forced to deny under the stress of the difference and the ease with which he attained only the former.

91. Pity those who make security their only purpose; the campsite at the end of their trail rests on quicksand.

92. The sky is a father's face; the sea a mother's breast; but all the earth is one's own.

93. Few jobs are more difficult than simply and honestly to bear witness.

94. The most beautiful women are those who have seldom been told they are beautiful. Nevertheless, it sometimes helps to tell a man that he is honest.

95. Whatever can be explained can be explained away.

96. Mr. A. says proudly that when he moves in the world of ideas he moves in his own element. Poor A! He misunderstands the vital difference between swimming and drowning.

97. The marvelous thing is not the infinite extent of the universe, but the fact of its having an infinite number of centers.

98. Those without a sense of humor generally wish they did not have bodies either.

99. Everyone is interested in his own destiny; only a very few consider that of the man who is piloting their plane.

100. When Adam and Eve were cast out of paradise so were the animals. Since then the animals have been too busy to wonder why.

101. It was old people who began the habit of idolizing youth. The young have never quite gotten over this lack of self-regard on the part of the elderly and take it as the due of nature.

102. What a wonder is Art! When we become too placid, it braces our sleepiness with the tonic of chaos; when too disoriented, it alone can slake our thirst for order.

103. The first duty of a nightwatchman is not to watch but to stay awake in order to watch.
104. A proverb contains about as much wisdom as an heirloom does one's grandmother.
105. The wish to destroy oneself may be sheer vanity. The humble man holds on to what limits him.
106. Those at a loss for a helping word will sometimes substitute a kick.
107. Virtue often consists only in a willingness to commit the smaller vice.
108. Place is time and vice versa. When we can find ourselves nowhere we cannot really exist. This not-existing will seem to some transcendence.
109. What everyone agrees on as real is not all of reality to anyone.
110. The best things we do, we do to think well of ourselves; the worst, so others will think well of us.
111. The telephone is the modern rack and wheel.
112. When you come to weigh what you have learned from experience, consider also what it has made you forget.
113. Education is rapidly becoming another of the mass media. Already a good deal of it is made up of extended commercials.
114. When sports become professional they cease being a preparation for life and are instead a substitute for it.
115. The present war: the wish to control what is so distant most resembles the fantasies bred by self-abuse.
116. Remember the alert indifference of green things.
117. Even insignificance has its romance.
118. The religious is like a planet around which the ethical, its moon, revolves.
119. The world is full of half-hearted recluses who lack even the conviction to slam the door.
120. Each of us is given the same choice: either use the world or use yourself up.
121. The family is the wall against which the young person throws himself, seeking independence. However, this longed-for independence usually consists in nothing more than the choice of whether to lean or to push.

122. The essence of secrecy is not the idea of concealing something, but of concealing it from someone else. Hermits can have no secrets, being secrets themselves.
123. Modern painting: still life and abstraction tell us that at a certain moment the human became an embarrassment. Thus, even in genocide, life imitates art.
124. There is some loss in every gain. Even happiness can spoil loneliness for us.
125. There is some gain in every loss. Even loneliness can teach us the conditions of happiness.
126. In the war of nerves, the analysts are the profiteers.
127. The first modern tragic hero was Galvani's frog.
128. Devoted readers are insatiable. They always want to smoke Sherlock Holmes's pipe with him.
129. In coitus is to be found the greatest potential for loneliness, for there imagination itself is annihilated. Without some immediate redemption, it even dies in bitterness.
130. Most of us live in elevators: going up or down we visit the same places.

The Proverbs of Klaren Verheim
Editor's Note

Klaren Verheim was born in 1935 in the Ober-Dobling district of Vienna. When he was two, his parents emigrated to New York City. His father, formerly a banker, secured employment with a furrier (Shachman and Bloch) while his mother devoted herself to playing an out-of-tune piano and raising Klaren and his younger sister, Hannele, who was born in 1940. Verheim attended New York public schools, then went on to Columbia University, from which he graduated in 1956 with a degree in Musicology. He then joined his father, who had gone into business for himself after the war. From the time of his college graduation Verheim lived alone in a small apartment on West 89th Street. In 1966, while crossing Fifth Avenue not far from his home, Verheim was struck by a school bus and killed instantly.

According to his sister, Klaren Verheim was extremely shy, scrupulous, a great reader and music-lover. His humor tended to be disturbing rather than jolly. She knows nothing of his relations with women, except that he never married and was painfully awkward around her friends. Hannele remembers her brother's kindness to everyone. "He liked to give his money away," she says, "which led to tremendous fights with Father." Apart from that Hannele speaks of the false impression she feels her brother's shyness created. "People tended to think him rather worthless. Father was always so noisy and vital, while Klaren always kept quiet when company was around. My girlfriends used to giggle at him when he was still living at home. He was rather gawky, angular and thin and over six feet tall. You'd never think he'd make a good athlete, but he was. He especially liked running." Of his inward life Hannele claims to know nothing. She reveres his memory.

Verheim's 130 proverbs came to me from Hannele, to whose house for dinner I was invited by a mutual friend. She brought them out after we had eaten. At the table the conversation had turned to the death that day of a well-known poet. "My brother might have been a poet," Hannele said. "Oh God, not the fortune cookies!" exclaimed her husband Ralph. Hannele straightened up indignantly, then left the room and returned with a large accordion envelope. "Ah, the reliquary," sneered Ralph. Hannele glowered at him and handed the envelope to me.

It was stuffed with remarkably variegated bits of paper: there were regular sheets off of notepads, torn envelopes, a couple laundry tickets, cancelled checks, formal invitations, even two pages ripped from cheap novels. Each was scribbled on in a regular, upright, yet hard-to-decipher hand. Hannele explained that she had collected them all at the time of her brother's death when she went through the apartment on 89th Street. "I haven't read them for years," she confessed. "Oh, how I am fallen from myself," murmured Ralph cruelly. It was my friend's suggestion that I edit the proverbs and try to publish them; indeed, I later discovered that this was the reason for the dinner invitation.

The arrangement of the proverbs is pure guesswork on my part. It seems clear that they were written over a period of some years, but there is no way of telling how many years or even in what order. Given the nature of the proverbs, there is nothing one could call internal evidence and, to be candid, I really have no idea which ought to come first and which last.

In the world of the spirit there are neither lotteries nor legacies; all that is gained must be earned. The 130 proverbs of Klaren Verheim, in so far as they contain a spiritual element, must therefore be presumed to conform with the following remark of John Keats:

> Even a Proverb is no proverb to you till your life has illustrated it. . . .

On the other hand, for me it is the inwardness of Verheim's proverbs that is their leading quality, as it seems to have been of his life. There are only the vaguest of clues to the life that might have illustrated them. Many embody a kind of aphoristic speculation that does not appear to be practical or derived from particular occurrences but which still manages to illuminate some corner of human experience. Many are really not proverbs at all, but tiny essays or concise bits of journalism. I find a certain chilliness here, a distance from life that need not have been incompatible with the generosity described by Verheim's sister. The generosity was perhaps the other side of his shyness, a way of dealing with a world in which he was profoundly uncomfortable—quite possibly, a world he thought of as his father's.

As a self-portrait, then, the proverbs are indirect and only sketchily suggest aspects of their author's mind: a concern with art surely, and with the family, ethical sensitivity, a somewhat abstract interest in politics; many have a mordantly humorous character. Yet one cannot avoid the idea that these are the thoughts of a skeptical mind with a strongly religious bent, a restless intelligence expressing itself in the most disembodied of forms: little texts without context. The outward features of Verheim's life are unremarkable; they suggest a frustration of the spirit, a self-imposed constraint, but it is perhaps because of this very frustration and constraint, this impersonality, that some of his proverbs attain universality. At moments it seems to me that they are less a response to living than to life itself.